Elias Nason

The Life and Times of Charles Sumner

His Boyhood, Education and Public Career

Elias Nason

The Life and Times of Charles Sumner
His Boyhood, Education and Public Career

ISBN/EAN: 9783337366438

Printed in Europe, USA, Canada, Australia, Japan

Cover: Foto ©Raphael Reischuk / pixelio.de

More available books at **www.hansebooks.com**

THE

LIFE AND TIMES

OF

CHARLES SUMNER.

HIS BOYHOOD, EDUCATION, AND PUBLIC CAREER.

BY ELIAS NASON.

AUTHOR OF "THE LIFE OF THE HON. HENRY WILSON," "THE GAZETTEER
OF MASSACHUSETTS," AND OTHER WORKS.

"Justum et tenacem propositi virum,
Non civium ardor prava jubentium,
Non vultus instantis tyranni,
Mente quatit solida."
HOR. CAR., Lib. iii. 3.

———•———

BOSTON:

B. B. RUSSELL, 55 CORNHILL.

PHILADELPHIA: QUAKER-CITY PUBLISHING-HOUSE.

DETROIT: R. D. S. TYLER.

1874.

TO THE

FRIENDS OF FREEDOM

THIS BIOGRAPHY OF A CHAMPION OF HUMAN RIGHTS

IS

Most Respectfully Inscribed.

PREFACE.

THE design of this work is to set forth in distinct relief the life, character, and public career of an accomplished scholar, an incorruptible statesman, and an eminent and eloquent defender of human freedom. In every age men have arisen, and, by the force of an original genius and a lofty aspiration, have come to stand as heralds in the fore-front of national progress. Their high mission has been to point with a prophetic finger to the coming issues; to sway and elevate with a commanding eloquence the public mind; to meet the exigencies of the times; and to pursue, unterrified by power and above the reach of bribery, their own elected course with an unfaltering steadiness to the end. Such was the dauntless John Hampden of the Long Parliament in the days of Charles the First; such was the patriot Samuel Adams in our Revolutionary crisis; such was the golden-voiced Charles Sumner in the ordeal from which we now are slowly rising. In the late tremendous struggle for human freedom he stood forth pre-eminent as a prophet, as a leader, as a counsellor, as an unflinching friend of the oppressed; and to his brave outlook over the whole field of contest, to his extensive knowledge of political history, to his grand ideal of a perfect commonwealth, and to his impassioned eloquence, must be in part ascribed the ardor which inspired our Union army, and the success which crowned the contest. Others grandly spoke and fought for freedom : but none more eloquently, more learnedly, more effectively, enunciated its eternal principles than he ; nor more profoundly and persistently instilled into the public mind its justice, grandeur, and necessity. The life of such a man is therefore a lesson and an inspiration. It will ever be held as a kind of beacon-light by the *avant-couriers* of freedom, not only in America, but throughout the world. In attempting to portray it, I shall endeavor to be guided by the words of his own favorite Shakspeare : —

> "Speak of me as I am: nothing extenuate,
> Nor set down aught in malice."

As often as practicable, he will be permitted to speak in his own language ; and many of the most eloquent passages from his ablest orations will be introduced. It is hoped that this record, the materials for which have been drawn from the most reliable sources, may prove acceptable to the patriot, the scholar, the orator, and the friend of freedom ; that it may serve in some degree to promote the principles of liberty, fraternity, and equality among men, and to awaken some fresh aspirations for a still nobler national life and destiny. The author would here express his sincere thanks to those personal friends of Mr. Sumner, and also to other gentlemen, who have kindly assisted in this undertaking.

Boston, March 24, 1874.

CONTENTS.

CHAPTER I.

CHAPTER II.

CHAPTER III.

CHAPTER IV.

CHAPTER V.

CHAPTER XI.

CHAPTER XII.

CHAPTER XIII.

CHAPTER XIV.

CHAPTER XV.

CHAPTER XVI.

CHAPTER XVII.

CHAPTER XVIII.

CHAPTER XIX.

APPENDIX.

THE LIFE AND TIMES

OF

CHARLES SUMNER.

CHAPTER I.

The Sumner Family. — Name and Origin. — Physical Strength and
Intellectual Energy. — Settlement in America. — William and
Mary Sumner. — Gov. Increase Sumner. — Ancestral Line of
Charles Sumner. — Major Job Sumner. — Charles Pinckney Sum-
ner.—The Birth of Charles Sumner. — His Brothers and Sisters.

"Nothing is more shameful for a man than to found his title to esteem, not
on his own merits, but on the fame of his ancestors. The glory of the fathers is
doubtless to their children a most precious treasure; but to enjoy it without
transmitting it to the next generation, and without adding to it yourselves, —
this is the height of imbecility." — *The True Grandeur of Nations*, by CHARLES
SUMNER.

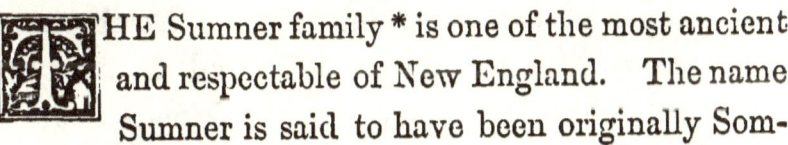HE Sumner family * is one of the most ancient
and respectable of New England. The name
Sumner is said to have been originally Som-

* See Genealogy of the Sumner Family, by William B. Trask.
Boston : 1854.

moner, or Somner, given to one whose office was to summon parties into court. The family has long been noted for its physical strength and intellectual energy; and from it have sprung many men of mark and influence. The name is frequently met with in the college catalogues, and in the early archives of the Commonwealth. The American head of the family was WILLIAM SUMNER, who, with his wife Mary and three sons, — William, Roger, and George, — came from Bicester, Oxfordshire, Eng., and settled in Dorchester, Mass., anterior to 1637. The country now covered with highly-cultivated farms and gardens, and decorated with handsome villas and imposing mansions, was at that period a wilderness, the dreary abode of prowling beasts and savages. With the other colonists, William Sumner bravely met the dangers and endured the hardships of the new settlement, and bore a prominent part in laying the foundation of the important town of Dorchester. He was made a freeman in 1637, and for twelve years was elected as a deputy to the General Court. In 1663 he was chosen " clerk of ye training band; " and in September, 1675, was on a jury for a trial " of ye Indians in Boston." The old portraits of William and Mary Sumner, surmounted with the family coat of arms and insignia, and bearing date of 1623, were kept until within a few years by one branch of the family, when they fell "to shreds under the hand of Time."

From William, the original settler, through his son William, grandson George, great-grandson Edward, and great-great-grandson Increase (noted for his colossal size and herculean strength), was descended Gov. Increase Sumner, a man of commanding presence and of vigorous intellect, who was born in Roxbury, Nov. 27, 1746; graduated at Harvard College in 1767; and succeeded Samuel Adams as governor of the State in 1797. In reference to his stately bearing, as contrasted with the decrepitude of his predecessor, an old apple-woman said, on seeing him pass at the head of the legislature from the Old South Church, " Thank God! we have got a governor that *can walk*, at last." Among the many honest and characteristic declarations which he made, the following seems to have been a guide, not only to his own, but to the political course of other members of the Sumner family: —

" The man who, regardless of public happiness, is ready to fall in with base measures, and sacrifices conscience, honor, and his country, merely for his own advancement, must (if not wretchedly hardened) feel a torture, the intenseness of which nothing in this world can equal."

Roger Sumner, second son of the original settlers

William and Mary Sumner, early removed to Lancaster with other Christians for "the gathering of a church." Remaining there until the town was destroyed by the Indians, he returned to Milton, where he died May 26, 1698. His son William, it is supposed, married Esther Puffer of Dorchester, Jan. 2, 1697, and had, *inter alios*, Seth, born Dec. 15, 1710; and married for his second wife Lydia Badcock in 1742. He was the father of thirteen children; among whom Job, the fifth son, born April 23, 1754, graduated at Harvard College in 1778, and became a major in the Massachusetts line of the army of the Revolution. He was a man of ability, "sustained the reputation of an attentive and intelligent officer," and died from being poisoned "by eating of a dolphin," Sept. 16, 1789; leaving a son Job, who was born at Milton Jan. 20, and baptized March 17, 1776. His name was subsequently changed to Charles Pinckney. He was educated at Harvard, and possessed considerable poetic ability. At his graduation he delivered a commencement-poem on "Time," together with a valedictory class-poem, both of which possess some degree of merit, and are still preserved. In the last year of his collegiate course he published a poem entitled "The Compass," in which occurs a quatrain that seems to indicate, to some extent, the leading idea, the aspiration, and the effective life-work, of his illustrious son.

> " More true inspired, we antedate the time
>   When futile war shall cease through every clime ;
>   No sanctioned slavery Afric's sons degrade,
>   But equal rights shall equal earth pervade."

Mr. Sumner studied law, was admitted to the bar, was several years elected clerk of the General Court, and in 1825 was appointed to the office of sheriff of Suffolk County. In this position he remained until his decease, which occurred on the twenty-fourth day of April, 1839. " He was the last high sheriff who retained the antique dress derived from English usage." He was a gentleman of the old school, — tall, well-bred, and dignified in demeanor, fond of reading, and of considerable oratorical ability. He delivered an appropriate eulogy on Washington at Milton, Feb. 22, 1800 ; and a Fourth-of-July oration in Boston in 1808. He was highly esteemed for the integrity and independence of his character. Mr. Sumner married Miss Relief, daughter of David * and Hannah (Hersey) Jacobs of Hanover, April 25, 1810, --- a lady of strong mind, of an amiable disposition,

---

* He was the son of David and Hannah (Richmond) Jacobs of Hanover. He served as one of the committee of safety during the Revolution ; and died in 1808, aged 79 years. He was the son of Joshua Jacobs of Scituate, who married Mary James in 1726. His father was David Jacobs, who settled in Scituate as early as 1688, and was a schoolmaster, and a deacon in the church.

and of graceful bearing. They resided in Hancock Street, and were attendants of King's Chapel, of which Mr. Sumner was for some time the clerk, and of which the Rev. James Freeman, D.D., the Rev. F. W. P. Greenwood, D.D., and afterwards the Rev. Ephraim Peabody, D.D., were the eloquent pastors.

CHARLES SUMNER, whose name is intimately associated with the stirring political events as well as with the literature of the country for the last thirty years, and whose life and public services this work is intended to commemorate, was the oldest son of Charles Pinckney and Relief (Jacobs) Sumner, and was born in May (now Revere) Street, Boston, on the sixth day of January, 1811. The site of his birth-place is now occupied by the Bowdoin Schoolhouse. His father subsequently removed to the plain, unostentatious, four-story brick building, No. 20, Hancock Street, which was for a long period the home of the family. The house, of which a good view is here given, fronts toward the west, and stands on an eligible site about half way down the declivity of the street. It is now occupied by the Hon. Thomas Russell, late Collector of the port of Boston, and contains many interesting mementoes of the Sumner family, among which may be mentioned the old mahogany writing-desk on whose tablet the eloquent senator penned many of those pregnant sentences

THE EARLY HOME OF CHARLES SUMNER,
No. 20 Hancock St., Boston.
Now the Residence of the Hon. Thomas Russell.

which moved to its profoundest chambers the free spirit of the nation.

The other children of Charles Pinckney and Relief Sumner were, — MATILDA, twin-sister of Charles: she was slender and fragile in person, and modest and retiring in manner. She died of consumption, March 6, 1832, and is buried at Mount Auburn. ALBERT, born Aug. 31, 1812: he became a sea-captain, married Mrs. Barclay of New York, and was drowned, together with his wife and only daughter KATE, an interesting girl about fourteen years old, on their way to France, whither the parents were going for the sake of their daughter's health. HENRY, born Nov. 22, 1814, married and died in Orange, N.J. GEORGE, born Feb. 5, 1817, who became a traveller, scholar, and author, and died in Boston Oct. 6, 1863. JANE, born April 28, 1820, a very lovely girl: she died of spinal disease, Oct. 7, 1837. MARY, born April 28, 1822, and died unmarried. HORACE, born Dec. 25, 1824, and was lost by the wreck of the ship "Elizabeth" on Fire Island, July 16, 1850. And JULIA, born May 5, 1827, and now the wife of John Hastings, M.D., of San Francisco. They have three children, — ALICE, EDITH, and JULIA. Mrs. Relief, widow of Charles Pinckney Sumner, was born Feb. 29, 1785, died of consumption, in Boston, June, 1866, and is buried beside her husband in the family enclosure in Mount Auburn.

Charles Sumner came into life under favorable auspices. He was of the vigorous and healthful Puritan stock : his father was a gentleman of education and of courtly manners, his mother a lady of remarkable good sense and benevolence. They were both emulous, and they had the means, to give a sound and accomplished education to their children. The tuition of Charles was at first confided to his aunt, Miss Hannah Richmond Jacobs,* who long taught a private school on Beacon Hill, Boston, and who is still living in Hanover at the advanced age of ninety-one years.

He was a bright-eyed, obedient, and well-behaved boy, of tall and slender form, and quick of apprehension. He began to ascend the ladder of learning

* This lady, whom I visited in March, 1874, still retains her faculties, and writes a fair and handsome hand. She has knit four pairs of worsted stockings since Christmas last. She is tall and slender in form, correct and animated in speech, and very bright for a person of her age. She early went to live in Boston with her sister Relief, who boarded in the same family with Mr. Charles Pinckney Sumner, where an acquaintance was formed which eventuated in marriage. Her sister Matilda was the second wife of Deacon Galen James of Medford. Miss Hannah Richmond Jacobs speaks of Charles Sumner as an obedient, studious, and promising pupil, very fond of reading and of repeating speeches, and as having been uniformly kind to her through life. In his will he remembered her by a life-annuity of $500.

by the study of Perry's Spelling-book and "The Child's Assistant;" and, with his twin-sister Matilda, was soon initiated into the elements of arithmetic, grammar, and geography. "The Columbian Orator" of Mr. Caleb Bingham, then a popular school-book in Boston and vicinity, gave him great delight. He early became an excellent reader; and his speech, as might be well inferred from the influences of a home of culture, was naturally correct and easy. The eloquent Dr. James Freeman was his early pastor, and, with other learned gentlemen, a frequent visitor at the Sumner house, which was then, as afterwards, the centre of an intellectual and refined society. In accordance with Juvenal's idea,* the courteous father of Charles Sumner entertained great reverence for boys, and most assiduously instructed his children, not only in respect to a polite behavior and the laws of health, but also in regard to the use of the most appropriate forms of speech; so that the training of his first-born son to the art of oratory might almost be said to have commenced with infancy.

It is felicitous that the earliest words which greet the ears of children are correctly spoken. The mother's tongue is the child's first grammar. To the care which his parents, his pastor, and his teacher

---

* "Maxima debetur puero reverentia." — Lib. 5, Sat. 14.

bestowed upon his speech in his young life, something of that elegance of diction and that *copia verborum* for which Charles Sumner subsequently became distinguished is no doubt attributable.

In his boyhood he was agile, healthful, hopeful, and obliging; yet ever more intent on reading and improvement than on boisterous sport and pastime. He was sent to the dancing-school; yet for this amusement he had but little inclination. Occasionally he attended his father in his visits to the court-room, and listened with juvenile curiosity to the arguments of the bar: now and then he sent his mimic boat across Frog Pond, his paper kite over the Capitol, coasted down the slopes of Beacon Hill, or spent a few days on a visit to his mother's early home in Hanover, where, instead of working with the boys upon the farm, he preferred to "speak his pieces' in the barn or the old pine grove.* Yet his time was mostly passed in his father's family, or in his aunt Hannah's school-room, steadily pursuing the elements of learning under the severe and rigid discipline of that period. It was, however, noted even

* The old homestead of his grandfather David Jacobs, and the birth-place of his mother, is in that part of Hanover called Assinippi, and is now the residence of the Hon. Perez Simmons. An air of quiet and comfort pervades the place.

at this time that he had an aspiration; and a boy with an aspiration is sent into the world for some high purpose. He had also a decided will; and where there is a will there is a way.

CHAPTER II.

> " What manner of child shall this be ? "
>
> St. Luke.

> " And like a silver clarion rung
> The accents of that unknown tongue, —
> ' Excelsior ! ' "
>
> H. W. Longfellow.

AT the age of ten years, Charles Sumner
was found qualified to enter the Boston
Latin School, then under the charge of the
accomplished classical scholar Benjamin A. Gould,
and noted, as at present, for its thorough and persistent drill in the inceptive classical studies. Here
the tall and slender lad applied himself closely to his
lessons; studying Adam's Latin Grammar (which
Mr. Gould edited with ability), the Gloucester Greek

22

Grammar, Euler's Algebra, Horne Tooke's Pantheon, Irving's Catechism, and reading Cornelius Nepos, Sallust, Cæsar, Cicero, and Virgil; together with Jacobs's Greek Reader, Mattaire's Homer, and other books preparatory to admission to Harvard College. The late Joseph Palmer, M.D., was an assistant instructor in the school, but was not then conscious that he was moulding the spirit of one whom he was afterwards to greet as the leading speaker on behalf of freedom in America. Among his school companions at this period were George T. Bigelow, Robert C. Winthrop, George S. Hillard, James Freeman Clarke, Thomas B. Fox, William H. Channing, Samuel F. Smith the poet, and others who have since attained celebrity. Although Charles Sumner did not hold the highest rank in scholarship on the appointed lessons of his class, he was distinguished for the accuracy of his translations from the Latin classics, and for the brilliancy of his own original compositions. He received in 1824 the third prize for a translation from Sallust; when one of the examiners remarked, " If he does this when a boy, what may we not expect of him when a man? " Two years later he obtained a prize for a theme in English prose, and also another for a Latin poem. On graduating he was honored with the Franklin Medal. He is remembered by his schoolfellows at this period as being kind-hearted, thoughtful, courteous, though exhibiting some slight consciousness of "being to the manor born." This last trait in his character sometimes drew a smile from the members of his family. On his lying in bed one morning until after the household had breakfasted, his mother rather sharply said to him as he came down, "Why so late this morning, Charles?" "Call me Mr. Sumner, mother, if you please," said he, as if his dignity were offended; and so the point of the rebuke was broken.

Another anecdote exhibits the purity of his spirit at this period. A certain lady nearly of his own age was wont to meet him frequently on his way to school; when he would always greet her cheerfully with the salutation, "Good morning! *Macte Virtute*" (follow virtue), as if this saying were his creed. Whenever in after life she heard his name, this salutation came to her impressively, knowing as she did the strict integrity of his life.

He continued five years at the Latin School; when, at the age of fifteen, he was found well prepared for entering Harvard College, whose terms of admission were somewhat less exacting than at present.

In the year 1826 he commenced his studies in the classic halls of Cambridge. Among his classmates were, Thomas C. Amory, Jonathan W. Bemis, James

Dana, Samuel M. Emery, John B. Kerr, Elisha R. Potter, Jonathan F. Stearns, George W. Warren, and Samuel T. Worcester. The accomplished John T Kirkland was president of the university; and among the instructors were Edward T. Channing in rhetoric, Levi Hedge in logic, George Otis in Latin, John S. Popkin in Greek, George Ticknor in modern languages, and John Farrar in natural science. His room during his first year was No. 17, Stoughton Hall. In person he was at that time unusually tall for a youth of fifteen summers; and, though one of the six youngest of his class of forty-eight, he stood among his fellows in respect to height conspicuous. "When he entered college," one of his classmates writes to me, "he was tall, thin, and somewhat awkward. He had but little inclination for engaging in sports or games, such as kicking football on the Delta, which the other students were in almost the daily habit of enjoying. He rarely went out to take a walk; and almost the only exercise in which he engaged was going on foot to Boston on Saturday afternoon, and then returning in the evening. He had a remarkable fondness for reading the dramas of Shakspeare, the works of Walter Scott, together with reviews and magazines of the higher class. He remembered what he read, and quoted passages afterwards with

2

the greatest fluency. He did not study for college rank, as many do, but took a good position in the classics, and was excellent in composition. In declamations he held rank among the best; but in mathematics there were several superior. He was always amiable and gentlemanly in deportment, and avoided saying any thing to wound the feelings of his classmates."

Another member of the class of 1830 communicates to me the following items: "Though reasonably attentive to his college studies, and rarely absent from the recitations, I do not think that Mr. Sumner, as an undergraduate, was much distinguished for close application. Having been much better fitted for college, especially in Latin and in Greek, than the majority of his class, he continued to sustain a high rank in both the ancient and the modern languages throughout his college course. He stood well also in elocution, English composition, and the rest of his rhetorical pursuits. In the last years of his college course, he failed in all the more abstruse and difficult mathematics. His memory was retentive; and it was sometimes said of him that he learned by heart the most difficult mathematical problems, without having a very clear understanding of their import. Morally, so far as I have ever heard, his character was without reproach."

The following incident, which occurred during young Sumner's freshman year, illustrates well that firmness of purpose, and persistent adherence to preconceived opinions, by which his whole course was signalized. " At the time our class entered," writes to me the Rev. S. M. Emery, D.D., one of his classmates, " undergraduates were required by the college laws to wear a uniform, consisting of an Oxford cap, coat, pantaloons, and vest of the color known as ' Oxford mixed;' but in the summer a white vest was permitted, no fancy colors being allowed. Sumner, probably having in his mind Edmund Burke, who on state occasions wore a buff-colored waistcoat, as Daniel Webster did when he was to speak in the Senate, procured a vest so near to buff color as not likely to be mistaken for white by the observer of the legal color. Now the tutor, proctors, and other teachers, one of whom had his room in each hall, as a sort of police, constituted what was called the ' parietal board.' They held their meetings once or twice a week to consider delinquencies of the students, to report to the faculty at their weekly meetings, and to summon the delinquents before them. Sumner's vest did not escape the keen eyes of this police. He was summoned before the assembled board, to answer to the charge of disobeying the laws by wearing a vest which was not of the lawful color. He protested, in the best-natured way possible, that nothing was farther from his mind than to disobey the college rules in all respects; but that the article of apparel in question was white: it might need the manipulations of a laundress; but it was certainly white. The board dismissed him with the injunction not to appear again in public without a regulation-vest. Conscious that his vest was white, he took no notice of the gentle admonition of the board, but continued to wear the same objectionable garment. Two or three weeks elapsed; and he was again called before the board on the same charge. He maintained with much eloquence that his vest was white. He was told that the board would be obliged to report him to the faculty if he persisted longer in his course, and he was then dismissed with the same advice as before. Disregarding the parietal board, he appeared the next day wearing the same colored vest. This he continued to do for several weeks, when he was again called before the same tribunal, on the double charge of disregarding its admonitions and of disobeying the college laws. The board threatened more earnestly than ever to report him to the faculty, and also to recommend to it a public admonition. He was undismayed, and argued his cause with as much earnestness as he since has many questions in Congress. He left the board this time feeling confident there was no escape from a public admonition. What was his surprise, however, to learn a day or two afterwards, that, as the easiest way of settling the case, the board had voted, ' *That in future Sumner's vest be regarded by this board as white.*' "

"He was," continues Dr. Emery, "so well prepared for college at the Boston Latin School, that the lessons in the classical department were mere boy's play to him. His declamations were an outburst of subdued eloquence, showing as much earnestness as he would in addressing the Senate. He had been accustomed to literary society from his youth, and was brought up among books, so that study was with him a kind of second nature. He never studied, as many students do, for college honors, but for the love of study, and for cultivating his mind, already well-disciplined and refined. His good taste, if nothing else, kept him from the company of ' fast young men ' and from any bad habits. His greatest pleasure was found in his room, attending to his favorite studies, which were something relating to the humanities.

" Many a time has he rushed down to my room and begun a speech, as if in a legislative body : 'I rise, Mr. President, to present a petition ' (stating what object), when he would go on with a speech,

3*

in which he would introduce quotations from Virgil, Horace, and Juvenal. The quotations were the very same which, thirty years afterwards, I read in some of his congressional speeches; and they were always accurate. I recollect accompanying him to an ecclesiastical council (*ex parte*) held in the old court-house in Cambridge, to dismiss the Rev. Dr. Holmes. Mr. Hoar of Concord was counsel for the party opposed to Dr. Holmes. We went to hear his argument, in the course of which he quoted the familiar line, ' *Tempora mutantur et nos mutamur in illis.*' But instead of saying ' *in illis,*' he said ' *cum illis.*' Sumner was greatly shocked at the mistake, and turning to me said, ' A man ought to be ashamed of himself who attempts to quote an author, and does not quote correctly.' This slight misquotation condemned the scholarship of Mr. Hoar in his estimation; and he had no confidence in his learning afterwards. He was a person of great self-possession, a trait which he inherited from his father, who when high-sheriff of Suffolk County was called upon to read the Riot Act on the stage of the Federal-Street Theatre, where a riot was in progress, and went steadily through it in the midst of a shower of brickbats.

" He delighted in the society of distinguished men, of whom Judge Story was then one of the foremost in Cambridge. He was deeply impressed with the beauty of the Prayer Book of our Church; and I have often heard him read in a very solemn manner many portions of it, especially the burial-service, which he would render with great pathos."

Another of his companions, in a carefully-written letter, says to me, " He was more given to study than to companionship. He had the reputation of being a diligent reader out of the course, and was often praised for his themes and forensics. For scholarship he stood among the upper third, but was not remarkable; yet this was true of several of his classmates who have since obtained distinction. As I recall him at the college, in chapel, or in the yard, he was of a height above the average, slender, awkward in his ways and movements, rather shy, and not by any means inclined to merriment."

Those who enter college at a very early age often excel in the classical and rhetorical studies, but, for the want of that maturity of mind which years alone can bring, find themselves unable to grapple successfully with the higher branches of mathematical science and of ethical philosophy. The failure comes not so much from any deficiency in aspiration or of original mental power, as from the need of time for due development. The strength of the contestant is not equal to the armor. This was the condition of Charles Sumner. His tastes and inclinations also led him to the belles-lettres and humanities. He practically took, as every one who means to make the most of his abilities will do, a kind of elective course. He gave himself to the study of history, of rhetoric, eloquence, and poetry. He read with zest and keen avidity the works of the great masters. He was fascinated by the splendid diction of Hume and Gibbon, the charming style of Addison and Goldsmith, the glowing eloquence of William Pitt, of Richard Brinsley Sheridan, and of Edmund Burke. His imagination was enkindled by the golden thoughts of Dante, Milton (always with him a favorite), Dryden, Pope, and Shakspeare. With these immortal geniuses he lived, and from them drew his inspiration. He strolled, moreover, into distant and untrodden fields of literature, and, as the bee, selected honey from unnoticed flowers. Here he gathered sweets from some French poet of the mediæval ages; here from some neglected Latin or Italian author; here from some Saxon legend, some Highland bard, or some Provençal troubadour. This material afterwards came in to beautify his grand pleas for peace, humanity, and freedom.

"It was my fortune," says the Hon. G. W. Warren, "to be one of nine classmates who formed a private society in our senior year, meeting once a

week for literary exercises. Of that little circle
were Browne, Hopkinson, and Sumner, now departed; and among the surviving are Worcester (formerly representative in Congress from Ohio, having succeeded Senator Sherman) now of Nashua,
N. H., and the Rev. Dr. Stearns of Newark, N. J.
Those hours spent together (for no one missed a
meeting) were indeed literary recreations.

"Sumner was also a member of the Hasty-Pudding
Club. The records show at least one made by him
when temporary secretary, which is characteristic
of the style of his later days. The moot court
was then the literary exercise of the club; and in his
turn he filled the judge's chair, and displayed his
legal learning in advance. On his motion the first
catalogue of the past and present members was
printed, as I well remember; for the principal labor
fell upon me as secretary."

Of his appearance and studies in college, the same
surviving classmate says, "Youngest of his class,
he had in college that same manly form, and open,
expressive countenance. He was the tallest of his
class. His genial companionship was much sought.
He was noted also for his retentive memory. A
diligent reader of history, and a thorough belles-
lettres scholar, he never forgot a date of any event,
nor made a misquotation. He was, as might be sup-

posed, a splendid linguist, a good writer, and a forcible speaker; for in those days declamation before the whole class was an established exercise, coming round to each in turn some dozen times a year, for which special preparation was made. He had little taste for mathematics and metaphysics; and his rank was consequently not of the highest. But he spent the first year after his graduation mainly in reviewing those studies; and he amply made up this deficiency."

He occasionally attended the theatre, and greatly enjoyed the representation of dramas of the higher class. For music he had but little taste; and dancing, after leaving school, he never practised. Mr. Sumner's chum in college was, for a part of the time at least, the late John White Browne of Salem, an excellent scholar, and in later years a strenuous advocate of freedom; who died May 1, 1860, and to whose memory Mr. Sumner subsequently paid an eloquent tribute.

He occupied during his sophomore and junior years No. 12, Stoughton Hall, and during his senior year No. 23, Holworthy Hall.

The following pleasant story is told of him and a classmate who were strolling, one day in their freshman year, along the road to Brighton to a cattle-show. Their hopes of being unobserved were suddenly dispelled by meeting their fathers on the way. " Why, Charles ! " said Sheriff Sumner with surprise: " how came you here ? "   " I thought," replied the son, "that we could leave without detriment to our studies, and could see how things were going on." The fathers concluded to make the best of it, and wished their boys a quick return without incurring a college censure. Before separating, however, the sheriff took the classmate aside, and asked him: " How is Charles in mathematics? "   " Very good indeed, sir," was the kind reply. " I'm glad of it," said the sheriff. " He, then, is doing better than I did ; for I let drop the links, and lost the chain, and have never been able to take it up again."

Mr. Sumner graduated in 1830, with a medium standing, to be sure, but with the good-will and friendship both of his instructors and his classmates, and with, perhaps, a better knowledge of the standard authors in prose and poetry, particularly of Shakspeare,— a copy of whose works, inscribed THE BOOK, was ever on his study-table, — than any other member of his class. He ever retained a filial regard for his *alma mater*, and heartily rejoiced in its prosperity. Several of its professors, as Chief Justice Story, H. W. Longfellow, and Louis Agassiz,

were his most intimate companions; and associated
with its classic halls were many of his dearest memories. The university now points to him as one of
the most brilliant stars in its broad constellation.

CHAPTER III.

"It is by dint of steady labor; it is by giving enough of application to the
work, and having enough of time for the doing of it; it is by regular pains-
taking and the plying of constant assiduties, — it is by these, and not by any
process of legerdemain, that we secure the strength and the stability of real
excellence. It was thus that Demosthenes, clause after clause, and sentence
after sentence, elaborated, and that to the uttermost, his immortal orations."
— THOMAS CHALMERS.

ON leaving college, at the age of nineteen years,
Charles Sumner had a well-developed, manly
form, a clear and resonant voice, and a character of unimpeachable integrity. His health was
excellent, his aspiration lofty. He at once commenced upon a course of private study, reviewing

carefully his college text-books, extending his knowledge of the modern languages, and his course of
English reading. He listened on the sabbath to the
eloquent discourses of the Rev. Dr. Greenwood at
King's Chapel, and occasionally heard the polished
sentences of Edward Everett on the platform, and
the solid arguments of Rufus Choate and Daniel
Webster at the bar. His father's position as high
sheriff of the county gave him ready access to the
society of the leading lawyers of the day, and naturally inclined him to adopt the law as his profession.
Whether at this period he read Mr. Garrison's uncompromising " Liberator," established on the 1st of
January, 1831, or sympathized with the rising pulse-
beat of that tremendous power of which he was to
become a prominent director, and which was to
change the destiny of this nation, is not now clearly
known : but the immortal works of genius whose
spirit he had fondly breathed are instinct with the
love of human liberty ; and his mind had thus been
nurtured for the acceptance and performance of his
mission, whenever his day should come. Daniel
Webster, even then, in his reply to Col. Robert Y.
Hayne (Jan. 26 and 27, 1830) had brought the
North up somewhat towards its true position ; and as
a Whig and genuine admirer of the principles and
eloquence of the great senatorial leader, Mr. Sum-

ner must have caught, even at that early day, some glimpses of a grand impending crisis.

Entering the Cambridge Law School in 1831, he came immediately under the instruction of that eminent jurist and accomplished scholar, Joseph Story, LL.D., who very soon began to appreciate the ability and to gain the affection of his pupil. Mr. Sumner now bestowed his undivided attention upon his legal studies, guided by the eloquent tongue of his distinguished master. He set himself to search from every source available original facts and principles. Not content with the decisions of the courts, he ransacked every nook and corner of historic lore, that he might settle legal questions on the solid grounds of equity and justice. He made himself acquainted with the contents of every volume that the Law-School library, of which he had the charge, contained; and it is said that there was not a book in that valuable collection which he could not lay his hand upon immediately in the dark.

"When he entered the Law School," says Judge James Dana, "he buckled on his armor and went to his studies with a will, and soon became the leading man in the school, for which he always manifested a strong interest." Mr. Justice Story was a fine belles-lettres scholar, an earnest lover of the beautiful, the good, and true; and remarkable for his conversational powers, as well as for his genial urbanity, his radiant smile, and graceful manner. Between him and Mr. Sumner, whose eager mind was open to the charming influences of such a sweet-tempered and learned jurist, a mutual sympathy at once arose, which gradually deepened into the sincerest friendship. How strong the tie between these two kindred spirits came to be, the reader may infer from the tribute paid to Mr. Justice Story in Mr. Sumner's elegant oration on "The Scholar, the Jurist, the Artist, the Philanthropist," delivered before the Phi Beta Kappa Society of Harvard University on the twenty-seventh day of August, 1846.

"By the attraction of his name," says Mr. Sumner, "students were drawn from remote parts of the Union; and the Law School, which had been a sickly branch, became the golden mistletoe of our ancient oak. Besides learning unsurpassed in his profession, which he brought to these added duties, he displayed other qualities not less important in the character of a teacher, — goodness, benevolence, and a willingness to teach. Only a good man can be a teacher, — only a benevolent man, only a man willing to teach. He was filled with a desire to teach. He sought to mingle his mind with that of his pupil. He held it a blessed office to pour into the souls of the young, as into celestial urns, the fruitful waters of knowledge. The kindly enthusiasm of his nature found its response. The law, which is sometimes supposed to be harsh and crabbed, became inviting under his instructions. Its great principles, drawn from the wells of experience and reflection, from the sacred rules of right and wrong, from the unsounded depths of Christian truth, illustrated by the learning of sages and the judgments of courts, he unfolded so as best to inspire a love for their study; well knowing that the knowledge we may impart is trivial, compared with that awakening of the soul under the influence of which the pupil himself becomes a teacher. All of knowledge we can communicate is finite: a few pages, a few chapters, a few volumes, will embrace it. But such an influence is of incalculable power: it is the breath of a new life; it is another soul. Story taught as a priest of the law, seeking to consecrate other priests. In him the spirit spake, not with the voice of an earthly calling, but with the gentleness and self-forgetful earnestness of one pleading in behalf of justice, of knowledge, of human happiness. His well-loved pupils hung upon his lips, and, as they left his presence, confessed a more exalted reverence for virtue, and a warmer love of knowledge for its own sake."

To his association and communion with this distinguished jurist, whose juridical acquirements and decisions commanded the respect even of the English bench, Mr. Sumner was to no small extent indebted for his profound views of equity and of human rights, as well as for those aspirations for the attainment of eminence in legal science, which formed the basis of that solid and enlightened statesmanship for which he subsequently became so signally distinguished. It was under the genial and erudite tuition of Judge Story, and in the moot courts and discussions of the Law School, that Mr. Sumner first began to command the admiration of his fellow-students, as a man of marked ability and rhetorical power.

During his connection with this institution, he wrote several articles, evincing varied learning and profound research, for " The American Jurist; " and on receiving his degree of LL.B., in 1834, he was considered, both in point of legal science and of oratory, one of the most accomplished of his class. How well Mr. Sumner loved the Law School may be seen from this extract from a report on the condition of that institution, drawn up by him in 1850 : —

" This library is one of the largest and most valuable, relating to law, to be found in the country. As an aid to study, it cannot be estimated too highly. Here the student may range at will through all the demesnes of jurisprudence. Here he may acquire a knowledge of the books of his profession — learning their true character and value — which will be of incalculable service to him in his future labors. Whoso knows how to use a library possesses the very keys of knowledge. Next to knowing the law, is knowing where the law is to be found.

"There is another advantage, of a peculiar character, afforded by the Law School, in the opportunity of kindly and instructive social relations among the students, and also between the students and their instructors. Young men engaged in similar pursuits are professors to each other. The daily conversation concerns their common studies, and contributes some new impulse. Mind meets mind; and each derives strength from the contact. But the instructor is also at hand. In the lecture-room, and also in private, he is ready to afford counsel and help. The students are not alone in their labors. They find an assistant at every step of their journey, ready to conduct them through its devious and toilsome passes, and to remove the difficulties which throng the way. This twofold companionship — of the students with each other, and of the students with their instructors — is full of beneficent influences, not only in the cordial intercourse which it begets, but in the positive knowledge which it diffuses, and in its stimulating effect upon the minds of all who enjoy it.

"In dwelling on the advantages of the Law School as a seat of legal education, the committee place side by side with the lectures and exercises of the professors the profitable opportunities afforded by the library, and by the fellowship of persons engaged in the same pursuits; all echoing to the heart of the pupil, as from the genius of the place, constant words of succor, encouragement, and hope."

Mr. Sumner read law for some time in the office of Benjamin Rand, Esq., a counsellor distinguished alike for his conversational powers, his love of books, and his knowledge of the law. Every sailing packet which arrived from England brought him the latest legal publications, which he devoured with singular voracity, and then discussed their contents with his brilliant pupil. G. W. Warren and Francis J. Humphrey were his classmates in this office.

"He is remembered there," writes the latter gentleman to me, "chiefly as a most indefatigable student and lover of books. His personal demeanor was that of a shy and modest maiden. He always greeted me with a cheerful word and a most radiant smile. The notion of 'arrogance,' as a quality in the character of Charles Sumner, can excite in me only the emotion of ridicule."

Mr. Sumner was admitted to the bar at Worcester in 1834, and commenced the practice of law in Boston. Thoroughly prepared as he was for meeting the demands of his vocation, he soon came to enjoy extensive patronage. He was shortly afterwards appointed Reporter to the circuit court of the United States; and while serving in this capacity published the three volumes now known as "Sumner's Reports," embodying the important legal decisions * of Mr. Justice Story. He also edited with signal ability "The American Jurist," a standard quarterly journal of jurisprudence. During three successive winters subsequent to his admission to the bar, he delivered lectures to the students of the Dane Law School at Cambridge, and for a brief period had the sole charge of that institution. Such fidelity to his trust, such an affluence of learning, and such legal acumen were exhibited in these lectures, that in 1836 a professorship in the school was

---

* The following compliment was paid by Baron Parke to Mr. Sumner, and his Reports of the Decisions of Mr. Justice Story:—

On an insurance question, before the Court of Exchequer, one of the counsel having cited an American case, Baron Parke, the ablest of the English judges, asked him what book he quoted. He replied, "Sumner's Reports." Baron Rolfe said, "Is that the Mr. Sumner who was once in England?" On receiving a reply in the affirmative, Baron Parke observed, "We shall not consider it entitled to the less attention because reported by a gentleman whom we all knew and respected."

tendered to him. This he declined. "Mr. Sumner's position in the legal world," says Mr. D. A. Harsha, " was an enviable one: he was universally regarded as a young lawyer of exalted talent, brilliant genius, and commanding eloquence." His legal acquirements attracted the attention, and received the compliments, of Chancellor James Kent and other eminent civilians. His reputation as a lawyer was extended by the able editorship of Andrew Dunlap's standard work on " Admiralty Practice," to which he added valuable notes and comments, and which was published in Philadelphia in 1836. On his death-bed Mr. Dunlap stated that Mr. Sumner had worked over it " with the zeal of a sincere friend, and the accuracy of an excellent lawyer." By the labors of Mr. Sumner thus far, it appeared that his future career was to be only that of a distinguished lawyer; but, as remarked above, the study of juridical science is essential to the exercise of broad and enlightened statesmanship, for which, though it might have been unconsciously, he was then making preparation. "I knew Mr. Sumner," says R. B. Caverly, Esq., in a letter to me dated Lowell, April 1, 1874, " in his early manhood. I was with him quite constantly in 1835–36 and '37 in the Cambridge Law School, where he occasionally appeared as a professor in place of Judge Story. He was then in manner reserved, yet courteous; in form tall, and comparatively slender. He was prompt in his attendance, and ready in the law. I remember that on his return from Europe he seemed proud to relate that Lord Brougham had expressed to him the opinion that Mr. Justice Story was the greatest judge in the world."

Mr. Sumner's acquaintance with Dr. S. G. Howe — a true and intimate friend — commenced, it is said, at the great Broad-street riot in 1837. " The rioters had got possession of some barrels of whiskey; when Dr. Howe, seeing a stalwart young man endeavoring with an axe to knock in the head of one of the barrels, hastened to his aid." This young man proved to be Charles Sumner, with whom he then commenced a friendship, which, cemented by kindred views on the leading questions of human progress, continued until broken by death.

CHAPTER IV.

"He (Charles Sumner) presents in his own person a decisive proof that an
American gentleman, without official rank or wide-spread reputation, by mere
dint of courtesy, candor, an entire absence of pretension, an appreciating
spirit, and a cultivated mind, may be received on a perfect footing of equality
in the best circles, — social, political, and intellectual; which, be it observed,
are hopelessly inaccessible to the itinerant note-taker, who never gets beyond
the outskirts of the show-houses." — *Quarterly Review.*

IN the autumn of 1837 Mr. Sumner sailed for
Europe, taking with him letters of introduc-
tion to distinguished gentlemen abroad, from
Mr. Justice Story and other eminent civilians.

"Mr. Sumner," says Judge Story in his letter, "is
a practising lawyer at the Boston bar, of very high
reputation for his years, and already giving the prom-

ise of the most eminent distinction in his profession: his literary and judicial attainments are truly extraordinary. He is one of the editors, indeed the principal editor, of ' The American Jurist,' a quarterly journal of extensive circulation and celebrity among us, and without a rival in America. He is also the reporter of the court in which I preside, and has already published two volumes of reports. His private character, also, is of the best kind for purity and propriety. But, to accomplish himself more thoroughly in the great objects of his profession, — not merely to practise, but to extend the boundaries in the science of law, — I am very anxious that he should possess the means of visiting the courts of Westminster Hall under favorable auspices; and I shall esteem it a personal favor if you can give him any facilities in this particular." Mr. Sumner was received with enviable distinction into many of the best circles of English society, and was honored with marked attention by the leading members of the bench and bar. He was once invited to sit with the lord chief-justice of the king's bench. A novel point arising during the trial, his lordship, turning to Mr. Sumner, inquired if any American decision touched that point. " No, your lordship," Mr. Sumner instantly replied; "but the point has been decided in your lordship's court in such a case,"

which he then cited. This singular promptitude gave
him much celebrity with the English bar. During
his residence in England, which embraced a period
of almost a year, he frequently attended the debates
in parliament, and made the acquaintance of the
leading speakers and the eminent statesmen of the
day. In a letter to him, dated Aug. 11, 1838, Mr.
Justice Story says, —

" I have received all your letters, and have devoured them with unspeakable delight. All the
family have read them aloud; and all join in their
expressions of pleasure. You are now exactly where
I wish you to be, — among the educated, the literary,
the noble, and (though last not least) the learned, of
England, of good old England, our mother-land : God
bless her ! Your sketches of the bar and bench are
deeply interesting to me, and so full that I think I
can see them in my mind's eye. I must return my
thanks to Mr. Justice Vaughan for his kindness to
you : it has gratified me beyond measure, not merely
as a proof of his liberal friendship, but of his acute-
ness and tact in his discovery of character. It is a
just homage to your own merits. Your Old-Bailey
speech was capital, and hit by stating sound truths
in the right way." During his residence in London,
Mr. Sumner formed the acquaintance of Thomas B.
Macaulay, whose " wonderful conversation," said he,

"left on the mind an ineffaceable impression of eloquence and fulness, perhaps without a parallel." Of the manner of his introduction to Richard Monckton Milnes, he gave the following account to his friend James Redpath: —

"I was at Sydney Smith's breakfast-table one morning, with perhaps a dozen others, when he suddenly asked me how English literary reputations stood in America." "We sometimes presume," said Mr. Sumner, "to rejudge your judgments; to refuse a reputation where you give one, and to bestow a name where you withhold it.' 'An example! an example!' exclaimed Mr. Smith in his caressing style. Here I was, a young Yankee Doodle, to use a phrase of Mr. Carlyle, at the table of the greatest wit, probably, that England ever saw, singled out by him to maintain a position which I had advanced. But I did not feel inclined to let the matter go by default, so I said at once: —

"'Carlyle!' 'Carlyle!' said Smith, 'we don't know him here: what have you got to say of Carlyle?' I said, 'I am not an indiscriminate admirer of Carlyle; I find much in him to criticise: but I have always been impressed by his genius; he seems to me to write as if by flashes of lightning.' This declaration seemed to surprise the company, with the exception of one gentleman, whom I observed to listen very attentively. When the conversation was resumed, he rose and placed his card in my hand, saying, 'Mr. Sumner, I thank you for what you have said of Carlyle. I am the only man here who appreciates him. This is my card; I shall be obliged for yours, and desire to visit you.'

"It was Richard Monckton Milnes, the poet and member of Parliament. The conversation of Mr. Carlyle resembled in style his published writings. It was racy, suggestive, thoughtful, matterful."

From England Mr. Sumner went to Paris, where he found ready access to the highest literary circles. His knowledge of the French language and literature enabled him to appreciate the brilliant intellectual society of the French capital. He made the acquaintance and secured the friendship of the gifted poet Alphonse de Lamartine, then becoming liberal in his political views; of Victor Hugo, then struggling into fame; of M. Alexis de Tocqueville, who had recently published the first part of his great work on " Democracy in America; " and of other well-known authors. Not a moment of his time was wasted. " He attended the debates of the Chamber of Deputies, and the lectures of all the eminent professors in different departments, — at the Sorbonne, at the College of France, and particularly in the Law

School.* He became personally acquainted with several of the most eminent jurists, — with Baron Degerando, renowned for his works on charity; with Pardessus, at the head of commercial law; with Fœlix, editor of the ' Review of Foreign Jurisprudence;' and other famous men. He attended a whole term of the Royal Court at Paris, observing the forms of procedure, received kindness from the judges, and was allowed to peruse the papers in the cases. His presence at some of these trials was noticed in the reports in the law journals."

While in France, his thoughts were turned especially to the leading social questions of the day; and, from his intercourse with the liberal philosophers of that period, his views of prison-discipline, of universal peace and brotherhood, which came so grandly forth in his first remarkable orations, received fresh coloring and confirmation. Through Mr. Sumner many of the advanced ideas of France in respect to legal and social science were introduced into

* "In Paris," says Mr. Sumner, in his argument against separate colored schools, Dec. 4, 1849, "I have sat for weeks at the Law School on the same benches with colored persons listening, like myself, to the learned lectures of Degerando and of Rossi (the last is the eminent minister who has unhappily fallen beneath the dagger of a Roman assassin); nor do I remember observing, in the throng of sensitive young men by whom they were surrounded, any feeling towards them except of companionship and respect."

America. Lewis Cass was then our minister at Paris; and at his solicitation Mr. Sumner wrote a strong defence of our claim in respect to the north-western boundary, which was published in "Galignani's Messenger," and extensively copied by American journals, and which evinced the liberal policy of the writer, and materially aided in the settlement of that vexed question. In the art-galleries of this city he began to make that collection of engravings which subsequently came to be one of the finest in America.

From Paris Mr. Sumner repaired to Italy, the land of art, of poetry, and song. Here he gave himself up to the study of the works of the grand masters, and to the ruins of ancient Rome. He himself glowingly describes the country as the "enchanted ground of literature, of history, and of art, strown with richest memorials of the past, filled with scenes memorable in the story of the progress of man, teaching by the pages of philosophers and historians, vocal with the melody of poets, ringing with the music which St. Cecilia protects, glowing with the living marble and canvas, beneath a sky of heavenly purity and brightness, with the sunsets which Claude has painted, parted by the Apennines (early witnesses of the unrecorded Etruscan civilization), surrounded by the snow-capped Alps and the blue, classic waters of

the Mediterranean Sea. . . . Rome, sole surviving
city of Antiquity, who once disdained all that could
be wrought by the cunning hand of sculpture,

"Excudent alii spirantia mollius aera,
    Credo equidem : vivos ducent de marmore vultus,"

who has commanded the world by her arms, by her
jurisprudence, by her church, now sways it further
by her arts. Pilgrims from afar, where neither her
eagles, her prætors, nor her interdicts ever reached,
become the willing subjects of this new empire ; and
the Vatican stored with the precious remains of
antiquity, and the touching creations of a Christian
pencil, has succeeded to the Vatican whose thunders
intermingled with the strifes of modern Europe."

During his residence in Italy he often studied
twelve hours a day: he mastered the Italian language, and read many of the Italian poets and historians. His art-studies at Rome he pursued under
the guidance of Thomas Crawford, one of our most
eminent American sculptors, then a resident of the
Eternal City. In the galleries of the Vatican, of the
Capitol, and of the palaces, he spent many days with
this distinguished artist, admiring and criticising the
resplendent works of the great masters.

"He once told me," says a personal friend, "that
a Catholic bishop, after endeavoring in vain to con-

vert him to the Roman faith, had finally assured him, that, if he would but read the works of St. Thomas Aquinas, he would certainly be convinced; when he promptly informed him that he had already read every word of that esteemed father in the original Latin; and, though he had not become a Catholic in religion, he was catholic enough to admit that the Angelic Doctor had, in his opinion, one of the first of intellects, if not the very first, that the earth had known." Mr. Sumner added, in narrating this incident, that in speaking further of Aquinas he expressed his wonder that one who died so young should have been able to write so many works as he had left behind; whereupon the bishop had asserted that he lived to a good old age. Assuring him that he was certainly mistaken, the senator turned to a cyclopædia of biography, and showed the bishop that the father died at the early age of forty-eight years."

Returning home by the way of Germany, he there was courteously received by the celebrated Prince Metternich, and formed an acquaintance with the historian Leopold Ranke, the geographer Carl Ritter, the eminent scientist Alexander von Humboldt, and other prominent savans. Mr. Sumner visited Europe for the sole purpose of study and observation. He left no opportunity for acquiring information and a higher culture unimproved. With ready access to the best society, with a mind eager for new truths, with a taste refined by classical pursuits, a memory as retentive as a vice, and an aspiration which no impediment could repress, he treasured up a golden store of intellectual wealth, and on his return to Boston early in 1840 possessed an affluence of learning and a felicity of diction which commanded the admiration of our most accomplished scholars.

"You have indeed," wrote Mr. Prescott the historian to him, "read a page of social life such as few anywhere have access to; for your hours have been passed with the great, — not merely with those born to greatness, but those who have earned it for themselves."

With what delight Mr. Sumner again beheld the domes of Boston, and how well he loved his native city, may be inferred from these remarks he subsequently made concerning it: —

"Boston has always led the generous and magnanimous actions of our history. Boston led the cause of the Revolution. Here was commenced that discussion, pregnant with the independence of the colonies, which, at first occupying a few warm but true spirits only, finally absorbed all the best energies of the continent, — the eloquence of Adams, the patriotism of Jefferson, the wisdom of Washington. Boston is the home of noble charities, the nurse of true learning, the city of churches. By all these tokens she stands conspicuous; and other parts of the country are not unwilling to follow her example. Athens was called the eye of Greece: Boston may be called the eye of America; and the influence which she exerts is to be referred, not to her size, for there are other cities larger far, but to her moral and intellectual character."

On reaching home, he found a widowed mother — who during his absence had followed the remains of her accomplished daughter Jane, and then in 1839 of her beloved husband, to the silent grave — in charge of the bereaved family. His reception was most cordial and affectionate; and, choosing for his study the front chamber above the parlor, he arranged the specimens of art and the books he had secured abroad, and there for many years pursued his literary course. His books were his society, his pen the instrument of his toil. He labored unremittingly; now delving into classical lore, now poring over the tomes of mediæval learning, now studying the works of the French and English statesmen, and now communing with the spirits of the Revolutionary patriots, — Adams, Ames, Jay, Franklin, Jefferson, Hamilton, Washington. To use the language which he loved, it could be truly said of him, —

"Come l'ape succhia i fiori,
Succhia i detti de' migliori."

Thus he treasured up that precious store of facts, principles, and illustrations with which he embellished (sometimes at the risk of being called a pedant) his discourses.

He resumed the practice of the law: but his thoughts were given rather to its principles and its literature than to its prosaic and dry details ; and he therefore found it a relief to steal away from his profession, and present his thoughts concerning intellectual and social questions on the platform of the lyceum, where he soon obtained remarkable success. During the winter of 1843 he again delivered a course of lectures to the students of the Cambridge Law School, and subsequently engaged in the laborious work of editing the twenty volumes of " Vesey's Reports," to which he added sketches of distinguished counsellors mentioned in the text, and also valuable notes.   In speaking of the execution of this task, " The Law Reporter " makes the following discriminating remarks : —

" Wherever occasion offers itself, the editorial note has been expanded till it assumes something of the port and stature of a brief legal dissertation, in which the topics are discussed in the assured manner of one who feels that his foot is planted on familiar ground, and whose mind is .so saturated with legal knowledge that it readily pours it forth at the slightest pressure; reminding us of those first 'sprightly runnings' of the wine-press, extracted by no force but the mere weight of the grapes. Mr. Sumner has also introduced a new element into his notes: we allude to his biographical notes of the eminent men whose names occur in the reports either in a judicial or forensic capacity, and to his occasional historical, political, and biographical illustrations of the text. In what may be called the literature of the law, —the curiosities of legal learning, —he has no rival among us."

CHAPTER V.

The steady Increase and Arrogance of the Slave-Power. — Mr. Garrison's Efforts to resist it. — Opprobrium cast upon the Abolitionists. — The Annexation of Texas. — Mr. Sumner's View of Slavery in "The True Grandeur of Nations." — Compliments of Richard Cobden, Chief-Justice Story, and Theodore Parker. — Extracts from the Speech. — Efforts to Prevent the Final Vote on the Annexation of Texas. — Mr. Sumner takes open Ground against Slavery in his Speech of Nov. 4, 1845. — Extracts from this Speech. — Notice of Mr. Sumner's Stand by Mr. Wilson. — Mr. Sumner's Preparation for his Course. — His Persistency.

" Though all the winds of doctrine were let loose to play upon the earth, so Truth be in the field, we do injuriously, by licensing and prohibiting, to doubt her strength. Let her and Falsehood grapple." — JOHN MILTON.

" Before thy mystic altar, heavenly Truth,
    I kneel in manhood as I knelt in youth:
    Thus let me kneel till this dull form decay,
    And life's last shade be brightened by thy ray:
    Then shall my soul, now lost in clouds below,
    Soar without bound, without consuming glow."
                                        SIR WILLIAM JONES.

URING Mr. Sumner's residence in Europe from 1837 until 1840, and for many subsequent years, the slave-power, which had early struck its roots deeply into the councils of the nation, continued to extend its baleful influence even to the contamination of the entire body politic.

Its steady and persistent aim was the complete dominion of the legislation of the country. To resist the encroachments, or even to discuss the principles, of the servile system was deemed fanatical and revolutionary. William Lloyd Garrison, an invincible champion of freedom, was indeed, through the columns of his " Liberator," boldly denouncing the inhumanity of the peculiar institution, and warning the public of the steady advance of the slave-power; but to accord to him or his compeers any word of sympathy was to forfeit political caste, and to be branded as an agitator and an abolitionist, — reproaches which it then demanded an unflinching heroism to incur. In spite, however, of this general opprobrium, of legislative menace, or the perils of a ruthless mob, the tide of sympathy for our fellow-men in bondage was slowly swelling ; and one friend of freedom after another, as Edmund Quincy, Wendell Phillips, William H. Burleigh, and Henry Wilson, nobly rose to assert that the aggressions of the slave-power could and must be met. Now where will Mr. Sumner take his stand? He is the pride of the aristocratic circles of Boston, a popular alumnus of Harvard University, an intimate friend of Mr. Justice Story, — who said that he should die content, if his young *protégé* could take his empty chair in the Cambridge Law School, — and of whom Chancellor James Kent declared, "He is the only person in the country competent to fill it." He is a gentleman of varied and extensive learning; and his culture is enhanced by foreign travel, and by personal intercourse with the ripest scholars and men of genius of his age. What course will he pursue? On the one hand there is the grand old Whig party, with Daniel Webster, Abbott Lawrence, and Robert C. Winthrop at the head, with fame and fortune in the distance. On the other hand, there are a few radical anti-slavery agitators, who are held by men in power as contemptible disturbers of the public peace, and who may incur the fate of Elijah Parish Lovejoy, murdered by the mob at Alton. Which line of action will this accomplished young civilian take? We shall soon see.

In the summer of 1844 Mr. Sumner had a severe sickness, from which it was feared he would not recover. William Prescott, the historian, thus refers to it in his journal, under the date of Nahant, July 21: "Been to town twice last week, — most uncommon for me, — once to see my friend Calderon, returned as minister from Spain; and once to see my poor friend Sumner, who has had a sentence of death passed on him by the physicians. His sister sat by his side, struck with the same disease. It was an affecting sight to see brother and sister thus, hand in hand, preparing to walk through the dark valley. I shall lose a good friend in Sumner, and one who, though I have known him but a few years, has done me many kind offices." His sister Mary, a very amiable and accomplished lady, succumbed to the disease, from which her brother Charles, owing to the unusual vigor of his constitution, soon recovered.

During the administration of John Tyler, himself a slaveholder, the gigantic scheme of annexing Texas to the Union was introduced by Southern members into Congress. This republic, which had declared itself free from Mexican rule in 1835, embraced an area of 237,500 square miles, extending from the Sabine and Red Rivers on the east, to the Rio Grande (as some held), separating it from Mexico, on the west. The acquisition of such a vast extent of territory would give the slave states the command of the Gulf of Mexico, and insure to them the balance of political power. "It would give," said Gen. James Hamilton, "a Gibraltar to the South;" and "Texas or disunion!" became the Southern war-cry. Mr. Webster, with the Whig party, opposed the annexation; and Mr. Van Buren said it would "in all human probability draw after it a war with Mexico." On this question turned the election of James K.

Polk, in 1844; and three days previous to the expiration of his term of office, John Tyler signed the bill for the annexation of Texas to the United States. On the 4th of July, 1845, the Texan legislature approved the bill of annexation; and on the same day Charles Sumner first came into the political arena by the delivery of his great speech on the THE TRUE GRANDEUR OF NATIONS before the authorities of the city of Boston. In this celebrated address — prepared to meet the impending war with Mexico, and the consequent extension of the slave power — Mr. Sumner argues against the ordeal of war, from a Christian stand-point; and establishes his positions by a remarkable affluence of learning, presented with a warm enthusiasm and in a most felicitous diction. The address produced a profound sensation, and was sharply criticised by the advocates of the war-policy, but the English patriot Richard Cobden did not hesitate to pronounce it "the most noble contribution made by any modern writer to the cause of peace."

In a letter to Mr. Sumner, Mr. Justice Story says of the oration, "It is certainly a very striking production, and will fully sustain your reputation for high talents, various reading, and exact scholarship. There are a great many passages in it which are wrought out with an exquisite finish and elegance of diction and classical beauty."

From Theodore Parker, Mr. Sumner received the following characteristic note, which opened the way to a permanent friendship between these two intrepid advocates of human rights : —

" I hope you will excuse one so nearly a stranger to you as myself, for addressing you this note. But I cannot forbear writing. I have just read your oration on the 'True Grandeur of Nations' for the second time, and write to express to you my sense of the great value of that work, and' my gratitude to you for delivering it on such an occasion. Boston is a queer little city. The public is a desperate tyrant there ; and it is seldom that one dares disobey the commands of public opinion. I know the reproaches you have already received from your friends, who will now perhaps become your foes. I have heard all sorts of ill motives attributed to you, and know that you must suffer attack from men of low morals, who can only swear by their party, and who live only in public opinion.

" I hope you will find a rich reward in the certainty that you have done a duty and service to mankind."

The oration abounds in narratives and illustrations of remarkable beauty and impressiveness, as for example : —

" In our age, there can be no peace that is not

honorable: there can be no war that is not dishonorable. The true honor of a nation is to be found only in deeds of justice and beneficence, securing the happiness of its people,—all of which are inconsistent with war. In the clear eye of Christian judgment, vain are its victories, infamous are its spoils. He is the true benefactor, and alone worthy of honor, who brings comfort where before was wretchedness; who dries the tear of sorrow; who pours oil into the wounds of the unfortunate; who feeds the hungry, and clothes the naked; who unlooses the fetter of the slave; who does justice; who enlightens the ignorant; who, by his virtuous genius, in art, in literature, in science, enlivens and exalts the hours of life; who, by words or actions, inspires a love for God and for man. This is the Christian hero: this is the man of honor in a Christian land. He is no benefactor, nor deserving of honor, whatever his worldly renown, whose life is passed in acts of brute force; who renounces the great law of Christian brotherhood; whose vocation is blood. Well may old Sir Thomas Browne exclaim, 'The world does not know its greatest men!' for thus far it has chiefly discerned the violent brood of battle, the armed men springing up from the dragon's teeth sown by hate; and cared little for the truly good men, children of love, guiltless of their country's blood, whose steps on earth have been noiseless as an angel's wing."

One of the most remarkable passages, however, in this eloquent speech, is Mr. Sumner's declaration of his opposition to the system of slavery. It has been said that he commenced the reading of " The Liberator," the guiding star of freedom, anterior to Mr. Wendell Phillips, whose eloquent voice had long before been heard in anti-slavery assemblages; but it appears that this was Mr. Sumner's first open, public avowal of his sentiments in respect to the rights of the colored race. He was led, undoubtedly, to espouse their cause, not from any desire of political advancement or emolument, but simply from his profound sense of justice, and his love of human right and liberty. In reference to the liberation of the slave, he says, —

" What glory of battle in England's annals will not fade by the side of that great act of justice by which her parliament, at a cost of one hundred million dollars, gave freedom to eight hundred thousand slaves! And when the day shall come (may those eyes be gladdened by its beams!) that shall witness an act of greater justice still, — the peaceful emancipation of three millions of our fellow-men, 'guilty of a skin not colored as our own,' now, in this land of jubilant freedom, held in gloomy bondage, — then shall there be a victory, in comparison with which that of Bunker Hill shall be as a farthing candle held up to the sun. That victory shall need no monument of stone. It shall be written on the grateful hearts of uncounted multitudes, that shall proclaim it to the latest generation. It shall be one of the famed landmarks of civilization; nay, more, it shall be one of the links in the golden chain by which humanity shall connect itself with the throne of God."

This masterly production, though containing some views upon the war-question which Mr. Sumner himself afterwards was led to modify, brought him at once to the front rank of the great orators of his time.

It has been said, that, in making researches for this speech, Mr. Sumner's thoughts were first directed to the dreadful iniquity of the slave system. He found that it implied a state of continual war, and therefore came to the determination to employ in its overthrow whatever ability he possessed.

Although the conditions of annexation had been accepted by its legislature, Texas had not yet actually become a State of the Republic. Strenuous efforts were therefore made by the friends of freedom to prevent the consummation of this slaveholding scheme. Conventions were held, petitions

signed, in various sections of our State, and eloquent
speeches made by Edmund Quincy, Henry Wilson,
Theodore Parker, William Henry Channing, R. W.
Emerson, and others, with the design of influencing
Congress on the final vote. On the 4th of November,
1845, a large meeting was held in Faneuil Hall in
Boston, at which resolutions drawn up by Mr. Sumner were presented, setting forth that the annexation
of Texas was sought for the purpose of increasing
the market in human flesh, of extending and perpet-
uating slavery, and of securing political power, and
in the name of God, of Christ, and of humanity,
protesting against its admission as a slave State.
These resolutions were eloquently and earnestly supported by Mr. Sumner, Mr. John G. Palfrey, Mr.
Wendell Phillips, Mr. W. L. Garrison, and other
able advocates of freedom.

During his remarks Mr. Sumner eloquently exclaimed : —

" God forbid that the votes and voices of the free-
men of the North should help to bind anew the fetter of the slave ! God forbid that the lash of the
slave-dealer should be nerved by any sanction from
New England ! God forbid that the blood which
spurts from the lacerated, quivering flesh of the
slave should soil the hem of the white garments of
Massachusetts ! "

He also introduced into this speech, as descriptive of a Northern man with Southern principles, his apt comparison of the iron bolts of the ship drawn out by the magnetic mountain of the Arabian story.

" Let Massachusetts continue to be known as foremost in the cause of freedom ; and let none of her children yield to the fatal dalliance with slavery. You will remember the Arabian story of the magic mountain, under whose irresistible attraction the iron bolts which held together the strong timbers of a stately ship were drawn out, till the whole fell apart and became a disjointed wreck. Do we not find in this story an image of what happens to many Northern men under the potent magnetism of Southern companionship or Southern influence ? Those principles which constitute the individuality of the Northern character, which render it staunch, strong, and seaworthy, which bind it together as with iron, are drawn out one by one, like the bolts from the ill-fated vessel ; and out of the miserable, loosened fragments is formed that human anomaly, — *a Northern man with Southern principles.* Such a man is no true son of Massachusetts."

" This," says Mr. Henry Wilson in his invaluable " History of the Rise and Fall of the Slave Power in America," " was the first public participation of Mr. Sumner in that great conflict in which he subsequently bore a part so important and honorable. His speech and the resolutions from his pen were based on the fixed and indestructible principles of justice, humanity, and moral rectitude. Stating that the object of the meeting was to strengthen the hearts and hands of those opposed to the admission of Texas into the family of States, and referring to the voices of discouragement they heard, that all exertion would be in vain, he declared that their efforts could not fail to accomplish great good, as no act of self-sacrifice and devotion to duty can ever be without its reward. Such an act as theirs, he said, must ever stand as a landmark; and 'future champions of equal rights and human brotherhood will derive new strength from these exertions.' 'Massachusetts,' he said, 'must continue foremost in the cause of freedom; nor can her children yield to dalliance with slavery. They must resist it at all times, and be fore-armed against its fatal influence.' He closed by expressing the hope that it might be hereafter among the praises of Massachusetts that on this occasion she knew so well how to say 'No!'"

Mr. Sumner here stood boldly forth, and announced the course he had elected; and to it he adhered, with the unwavering steadiness of one whose feet are planted on the everlasting rock of TRUTH, until the termination of his life. He had made the liberation of the slave a most profound constitutional and legal study. He had prepared himself to invest the question with the charms of eloquence and poetry. He had access to the halls of learning. He had gained position as an orator and a scholar; and therefore his assumption of the advocacy of human freedom was of immense importance to the cause. In him the prophet saw the leader of the young men of culture and of learning in the coming crusade against oppression; and through his voice the advanced heralds of human freedom spoke. Bitter opposition he encountered; but his course was chosen.

CHAPTER VI.

"*Et magis, magisque viri nunc gloria claret.*"

"Rest not ! life is sweeping by:
Go and dare before you die.
Something mighty and sublime
Leave behind to conquer time."

GOETHE.

IN the autumn of this year (1845), Mr. Sumner was called to mourn the loss by death of his beloved friend and counsellor, Chief Justice Story, whom Lord Campbell characterized in the House of Lords as "the first of living writers on the law." In "The Boston Daily Advertiser," Sept. 16, 1845, there appeared from Mr. Sumner's hand a most eloquent and discriminating eulogy of this great

74

American jurist. In it he says, " It has been my fortune to know or see the chief jurists of our times in the classical countries of jurisprudence, — France and Germany. . I remember well the pointed and effective style of Dupin, on the delivery of one of his masterly opinions in the highest court of France; I recall the pleasant converse of Pardessus, to whom commercial and maritime law is under a larger debt, perhaps, than to any other mind, while he descanted on his favorite theme; I wander in fancy to the gentle presence of him with flowing silver locks, who was so dear to Germany, — Thibaut, the expounder of the Roman law, and the earnest and successful advocate of a just scheme for the reduction of the unwritten law to the certainty of a written text; from Heidelberg I fly to Berlin, where I listen to the grave lecture and mingle in the social circle of Savigny, so stately in person and peculiar in countenance, whom all the continent of Europe delights to honor: but my heart and my judgment, untrammelled, fondly turn to my Cambridge teacher and friend. Jurisprudence has many arrows in her golden quiver; but where is one to compare with that which is now spent in the earth? . . . I remember him in my childhood; but I first knew him after he came to Cambridge as professor while I was yet an undergraduate; and remember freshly, as if the words were of yesterday, the eloquence and animation with which at that time, to a youthful circle, he enforced the beautiful truth that no man stands in the way of another. 'The world is wide enough for all,' he said, 'and no success which may crown our neighbor can affect our own career.'"

Mr. Sumner prepared for "The Law Reporter" of June, 1846, another beautiful tribute, to the memory of the eminent scholar John Pickering, who died on the 5th of May preceding; and, in the course of the eulogy of his friend, indicates the magic of his own success: "His talisman," said he, "was industry. He was pleased in referring to those rude inhabitants of Tartary, who placed idleness in the torments of the world to come; and often remembered the beautiful proverb in his Oriental studies, that by labor the leaf of the mulberry-tree is turned to silk. His life is a perpetual commentary on those words of untranslatable beauty in the great Italian poet:—

'Seggendo in piuma,
In fama non si vien, nè sotto coltre:
Senza la qual chi sua vita consuma
Cotál vestigio in terra di se lascia,
Qual fumo in áere ed in acqua la schiuma.'"

DANTE, *Inferno*, Canto xxv.

On the twenty-seventh day of August, 1846, Mr. Sumner pronounced his splendid oration on "The

Scholar, the Jurist, the Artist, the Philanthropist,"
before the Phi Beta Kappa Society of Harvard University; in which he eloquently portrays the characters, and commemorates the names, of his illustrious
friends, John Pickering, Joseph Story, Washington
Allston, and William Ellery Channing, each of whom
had but recently finished his career. This oration
abounds with singular affluence of illustration, and
with glowing thoughts clothed in choice and elegant
language. From it the authors of our best school
reading-books have drawn several passages as models
for the student. At the dinner following the delivery of this admirable discourse, John Quincy Adams
justly gave this sentiment: "The memory of the
scholar, the jurist, the artist, the philanthropist; and
not the memory, but the long life, of the kindred
spirit who has this day embalmed them all."

In characterizing the eloquence of Channing, the
orator unconsciously described himself: "His eloquence had not the character and fashion of forensic
efforts or parliamentary debates. It ascended above
these, into an atmosphere as yet unattempted by the
applauded orators of the world. Whenever he
spoke or wrote, it was with the loftiest aims, — not
for display, not to advance himself, not for any
selfish purpose, not in human strife, not in any
question of pecuniary advantage; but in the service

of religion and benevolence, to promote the love of God and man.   In these exalted themes are untried founts of truest eloquence."

His peroration glows with hope, and seems almost prophetic : —

" Go forth into the many mansions of the house of life.   Scholars, store them with learning ; jurists, build them with justice ; artists, adorn them with beauty ; philanthropists, let them resound with love. Be servants of truth, each in his vocation ; doers of the word, and not hearers only.   Be sincere, pure in heart, earnest, enthusiastic. . . . Like Pickering, blend humility with learning.   Like Story, ascend above the present in place and time.   Like Allston, regard fame only as the eternal shadow of excellence. Like Channing, bend in adoration of the right.   Cultivate alike the wisdom of experience, and the wisdom of hope.   Mindful of the future, do not neglect the past : awed by the majesty of antiquity, turn not with indifference from the future.   True wisdom looks to the ages before us as well as behind us. Like the Janus of the Capitol, one front thoughtfully regards the past, rich with experience, with memories, with the priceless traditions of virtue : the other is earnestly directed to the All Hail Hereafter, richer still with its transcendent hopes and unfulfilled prophecies.

" We stand on the threshold of a new age, which is preparing to recognize new influences.   The ancient divinities of violence and wrong are retreating to their kindred darkness.   The sun of our moral universe is entering a new ecliptic, no longer deformed by those images Cancer, Taurus, Leo, Sagittarius, but beaming with mild radiance of those heavenly signs, Faith, Hope, and Charity.

> ' There's a fount about to stream:
> There's a light about to beam:
> There's a warmth about to glow;
> There's a flower about to blow :
> There's a midnight blackness changing
>   Into gray :
> Men of thought and men of action,
>   Clear the way !
>
> Aid the dawning, tongue and pen ;
> Aid it, hopes of honest men ;
> Aid it, paper; aid it, type ;
> Aid it, for the hour is ripe.
> And our earnest must not slacken
>   Into play :
> Men of thought and men of action,
>   Clear the way ! '

" The age of chivalry has gone.   An age of humanity has come.   The horse, whose importance, more than human, gave the name to that early period of gallantry and war, now yields his foremost place to man. In serving him, in promoting his elevation, in contributing to his welfare, in doing him good, there are fields of bloodless triumph nobler far than any in which Bayard or Du Guesclin ever conquered. Here are spaces of labor wide as the world, lofty as heaven. Let me say, then, in the benison once bestowed upon the youthful knight: Scholars, jurists, artists, philanthropists, heroes of a Christian age, companions of a celestial knighthood, 'Go forth; be brave, be loyal, and successful.'"

In a letter to Mr. Sumner dated September, 1846, Theodore Parker says: —

"I thank you most heartily for your noble and beautiful Phi Beta Kappa Address. It did me good to read it. I like it, like it all, all over and all through. I like especially what you say of Allston and Channing. That sounds like the Christianity of the nineteenth century, the application of religion to life. You have said a strong word, and a beautiful, — planted a seed 'out of which many and tall branches shall arise,' I hope. *The people are always true to a good man who truly trusts them.* You have had opportunity to see, hear, and feel the truth of that oftener than once. I think you will have enough more opportunities yet: men will look for deeds noble as the words *a man speaks.* I take these words as an earnest of a life full of deeds of that heroic sort." — *See Life and Correspondence of Theodore Parker*, vol. i., p. 316.

Mr. Sumner was no revolutionist. He held in profound reverence the organic law of the land. He would meet the commanding question of slavery on constitutional grounds alone. He believed that the provisions of the constitution in favor of the slaveholder were merely temporary, and that the instrument itself, which nowhere speaks of the slave as a chattel or recognized slavery as an institution, was framed in the expectation that the inhuman traffic in flesh and blood would be soon abandoned.

"There is," said he, in an able speech before the Whig State Convention at Faneuil Hall, Sept. 23, 1846, "no compromise on the subject of slavery, of a character not to be reached *legally and constitutionally*, which is the only way in which I propose to reach it. Wherever power and jurisdiction are secured to Congress, they may unquestionably be exercised in conformity with the constitution. And even in matters beyond existing powers and jurisdiction, there is a constitutional method of action. The constitution contains an article pointing out, how, at any time, amendments may be made thereto. This is an important element, giving to the constitution a *progressive* character, and allowing it to be moulded to suit new exigencies and new conditions of feeling. The wise framers of this instrument did not treat the country as a Chinese foot, — never to grow after its infancy, — but anticipated the changes incident to its growth."

Assuming as a watchword, " REPEAL OF SLAVERY UNDER THE CONSTITUTIONAL LAWS OF THE FEDERAL GOVERNMENT," he said: "The time has passed when this can be opposed on constitutional grounds. It will not be questioned by any competent authority that Congress may by express legislation abolish slavery, first in the District of Columbia; second in the Territories, if there should be any; third, that it may abolish the slave-trade on the high seas between the States; fourth, that it may refuse to admit any new State with a constitution sanctioning slavery. Nor can it be questioned that the people of the United States may, in the manner pointed out by the Constitution, proceed to its amendment. It is, then, by constitutional legislation, and even by amendment of the Constitution, that slavery may be reached."

Mr. Sumner then paid this brief, but memorable compliment to John Quincy Adams, "the old man eloquent," who, as a true representative of the anti-slavery sentiment of the North, was fearlessly opposing the aggressions of the slaveholding power:

" Massachusetts has a venerable representative,
whose aged bosom still glows with inextinguishable
fires, like the central heats of the monarch mountain of the Andes beneath its canopy of snow.   To
this cause he dedicates the closing energies of a
long and illustrious life.   Would that all would join
him ! "   He then, in this bold apostrophe, addresses
Daniel Webster of the Senate, and points out a
policy which it had been well for the imperious
leader of the old Whig party to have heeded:
" Dedicate, sir," said Mr. Sumner, " the golden years
of experience happily in store for you, to the grand
endeavor, in the name of freedom, to remove from
your country its greatest evil.   In this cause you
shall find inspirations to eloquence higher than any
you have yet confessed.

' To heavenly themes sublimer strains belong.'

" Do not shrink from the task.   With your marvellous powers, and the auspicious influences of an
awakened public sentiment, under God, who always
smiles upon conscientious labors for the welfare of
man, we may hope for beneficent results.

" Assume, then, these unperformed duties.   The
aged shall bear witness to you ; the young shall kin-
dle with rapture as they repeat the name of ' Webster ; ' and the large company of the ransomed shall

teach their children's children, to the latest generation, to call you blessed; while all shall award to you yet another title, which shall never be forgotten on earth or in heaven, — *Defender of Humanity;* by the side of which that earlier title shall fade into insignificance, as the constitution, which is the work of mortal hands, dwindles by the side of man, who is created in the image of God."

In a characteristic letter to Robert C. Winthrop, dated Oct. 25, 1846, Mr. Sumner sharply criticises that gentleman's course in respect to the Mexican War; charging him with want of sympathy " with those who seek to carry into our institutions that practical conscience which declares it to be equally wrong in individuals and in states to sanction slavery." " Through you," continues Mr. Sumner, "they [the Bostonians] have been made to declare an unjust and cowardly war with falsehood in the cause of slavery. Through you they have been made partakers in the blockade of Vera Cruz, in the seizure of California, in the capture of Santa Fé, in the bloodshed of Monterey. It were idle to suppose that the poor soldier or officer only, is stained by this guilt. It reaches far back, and incarnadines the halls of Congress; nay, more, — through you it reddens the hands of your constituents in Boston;" and he concludes the letter by the assertion that

more than one of his neighbors will be obliged to
say, —

> " Cassio, I love thee,
> But never more be officer of mine."

In this forcible letter, the writer uses these memorable words indicating the eternal source of rectitude
as the guide for the settlement of the great political
question: " Aloft on the throne of God, and not
below in the footprints of a trampling multitude of
men, are to be found the sacred rules of right, which
no majorities can displace or overturn."

In a speech against the Mexican War at a public
meeting in November following, when Dr. Samuel
G. Howe was brought forward as a Congressional
candidate in opposition to Mr. Winthrop, Mr.
Sumner said, " It is with the Whigs that I have
heretofore acted, and may hereafter act; always confessing a loyalty to principles higher than any party
ties."

On this solid platform of conscience and of duty,
dealing his blows against the peculiar institution,
Mr. Sumner proudly stood. He clearly saw and
openly rebuked the subservience of his party to the
slaveocracy of the South; and though not then an
aspirant for political power, he caught prophetic
glimpses of a rupture in the Whig organization, and
of the ultimate triumph of the right. With the

uncompromising Garrison he had not yet come into sympathy; but within the constitution of the United States, he declared himself an eternal foe to slavery. His wing of the party soon received the title of "Conscience Whigs;" and conscience over might or cotton will eventually prevail.

Mr. Sumner was not for a moment idle. In January, 1847, he made a very able argument before the Supreme Court of Massachusetts, against the validity of enlistments in the regiment of volunteers raised by the State for the Mexican War. As counsel for one of the petitioners, he argued that the act of Congress of 1846, providing for the officering of the companies, was in some of the provisions unconstitutional, that the enlistments were not in accordance with that act, that the militia acts of Massachusetts had been fraudulently used in forming the regiment, and also that a minor could not be held by his contract of enlistment under the act. The validity of proceedings was sustained; but the minors were discharged. On the 4th of February following, he made a short but telling speech in Faneuil Hall, for the withdrawal of the American troops from Mexico, in which he said, "The war is not only unconstitutional: it is unjust; it is vile in its object and character. It has its origin in a well-known series of measures to extend and perpetuate slavery.

It is a war which must ever be odious in history, beyond the common measure allotted to the outrages of brutality which disfigure other nations and times. It is a slave-driving war. In its principle, it is only a little above those miserable conflicts between the barbarian chiefs of Central Africa, to obtain slaves for the inhuman markets of Brazil. Such a war must be accursed in the sight of God. Why is it not accursed in the sight of man?"

"Let a voice," he eloquently closing said, "go forth from Faneuil Hall to-night, awakening fresh echoes throughout the kindly valleys of New England, swelling as it proceeds, and gathering new reverberations in its ample volume, traversing the whole land, and still receiving other voices, till it reaches our rulers at Washington, and in tones of thunder demands the cessation of this unjust war."

On the 17th of the same month he read before the Boston Mercantile Library Association a curious and brilliant paper on "White Slavery in the Barbary States."

Taking up its origin, history, and character, he brings into his subject a surprising wealth of learning and of illustration, drawn from English, French, and Spanish literature, and traces with a masterly hand the iniquities of slavery in the Barbary States from the earliest times until its final extinction by Lord Exmouth, under the direction of His Royal Highness the Prince Regent of England, in 1816. In this discourse he adroitly aims a blow at slavery at home. The theme was new, the speaker's heart in sympathy with it : his researches were exhaustive ; and he so graphically portrays the horrors of the slave system, and so breathes the spirit of humanity and Christian love into his lecture, as to render it a study worthy of the enlightened philanthropist and historian.

As gleams of golden light upon the thunder-cloud, so Mr. Sumner's tender sympathies relieved the gloomy scenes which he presents. Thus glowingly, in a charming passage, his kind regard for the unfortunate breaks forth : " Endeavors for freedom are animating ; nor can any honest nature hear of them without a throb of sympathy. As we dwell on the painful narrative of the unequal contest between tyrannical power and the crushed captive or slave, we resolutely enter the lists on the side of freedom ; and as we behold the contest waged by a few individuals, or perhaps by one alone, our sympathy is given to his weakness as well as to his cause. To him we send the unfaltering succor of our good wishes. For him we invoke vigor of arm to defend, and fleetness of foot to escape. The enactments of human laws are vain to restrain the warm tides of the heart. We pause with rapture on those historic scenes in which freedom has been attempted or pre- served through the magnanimous self-sacrifice of friendship or Christian aid. With palpitating bosom we follow the midnight flight of Mary of Scotland from the custody of her stern jailers; we accompany Grotius in his escape from prison in Holland, so adroitly promoted by his wife; we join with Lava- lette in France in his flight, aided also by his wife; and we offer our admiration and gratitude to Huger and Bollman, who, unawed by the arbitrary ordi- nances of Austria, strove heroically, though vainly, to rescue Lafayette from the dungeons of Olmutz."

This admirable production, every page of which proclaims the scholar and the friend of human liberty, was beautifully printed in 1853, by John P. Jewett and Company, in a volume with elegant illustrations by Edwin T. Billings, and should find a place in every library.

While abroad, Mr. Sumner's attention was natu- rally drawn to the condition of European prisons; and he availed himself of the opportunities afforded him by intercourse with distinguished friends of humanity, to study their various systems of disci- pline. On returning he continued his investigations on this subject; and in connection with Dr. Samuel

8*

G. Howe, the Rev. Francis Wayland, and other gentlemen, became deeply interested in the course of the Boston Prison Discipline Society, and in the improvement of the condition of the prisons of our own country. Of the various systems in vogue, Mr. Sumner deprecated that of the promiscuous commingling of prisoners in one company, and also that of absolute solitude, endangering the health and preventing reformation. With the distinguished M. de Tocqueville, he favored the Pennsylvania system, which embraced these elements, — separation, labor in the cell, exercise in the open air, visits, and books, together with moral and religious instruction. In a speech of much power before the Boston Prison Discipline Society, at the Tremont Temple, June 18, 1847, he criticised the partial and inefficient course of that body, and presented his enlightened views upon the subject, which gave fresh impulse to the efforts made for the amelioration of the systems of our penal institutions.

The next notable literary effort of Mr. Sumner was an address entitled "Fame and Glory," delivered before the literary societies of Amherst College, at their anniversary, Aug. 11, 1847. Although the theme was commonplace, the genius of the speaker unfolded it from such a lofty standpoint, and so affluently illustrated it with classic lore, as to impart

to it the charm of novelty, and to secure the warm
approval of the college and the public. As in his
oration on "The True Grandeur of Nations," so in
this, he condemned the art and the atrocities of war,
and breathed forth his aspirations for the reign of
universal peace and brotherhood. His positions,
founded on the eternal principles of good-will to
man, of truth and justice, were in advance of time,
and by some persons deemed Utopian; but he was
introduced into the world to be a leader, not a fol-
lower; and, as William Cullen Bryant nobly says, —

> "Truth crushed to earth shall rise again:
> The eternal years of God are hers:
> But Error, wounded, writhes in pain,
> And dies among his worshippers."

After passing in review the career of warriors, as
Alexander, drunk with victory and wine; Cæsar,
trampling on the liberties of Rome; Frederick of
Prussia, playing the game of robbery with human
lives for dice, — he beautifully says, "There is
another and a higher company, who thought little of
praise or power, but whose lives shine before men
with those good works which truly glorify their
authors. There is Milton, poor and blind, but 'ba-
ting not a jot of heart or hope;' in an age of ignorance, the friend of education; in an age of servility

and vice, the pure and uncontaminated friend of freedom, tuning his harp to those magnificent melodies which angels might stoop to hear, and confessing his supreme duties to humanity in words of simplicity and power. 'I am long since persuaded,' was his declaration, 'that to say or do aught worth memory and imitation, no purpose or respect should sooner move us than love of God and mankind.' There is St. Vincent de Paul of France, once in captivity in Algiers. Obtaining his freedom by a happy escape, this fugitive slave devoted himself with divine success to labors of Christian benevolence, to the establishment of hospitals, to visiting those in prison, to the spread of amity and peace. Unknown, he repaired to the galleys at Marseilles, and, touched by the story of a poor convict, personally assumed his heavy chains, that he might be excused to visit his wife and children. And, when France was bleeding with war, this philanthropist appears in a different scene. Presenting himself to her powerful minister, the Cardinal Richelieu, on his knees he says, 'Give us peace : have pity upon us ; give peace to France.' There is Howard, the benefactor of those on whom the world has placed its brand, whose charity, — like that of the Frenchman, inspired by the single desire of doing good — penetrated the gloom of the dungeon as with angelic presence. 'A

person of more ability,' he says with sweet simplicity, ' with my knowledge of facts, would have written better; but the object of my ambition was not
the fame of an author. *Hearing the cry of the miserable, I devoted my time to their relief.*' And, lastly,
there is Clarkson, who while yet a pupil of the
university commenced those life-long labors against
slavery and the slave-trade, which have embalmed
his memory. Writing an essay on the subject as a
college-exercise, his soul warmed with the task; and
at a period when even the horrors of the 'middle
passage' had not excited condemnation, he entered
the lists, the stripling champion of the right. He has
left a record of the moment when this duty seemed
to flash upon him. He was on horseback, on his way
from Cambridge to London. ' Coming in sight of
Wade's Mill, in Hertfordshire,' he says, ' I sat down
disconsolate on the turf by the roadside, and held my
horse. Here a thought came over my mind, that, if
the contents of my essay were true, *it was time some
person should see these calamities to their end.*' Pure
and noble impulse to a beautiful career!'"

After such exalted models Mr. Sumner formed
the ideal for his own life. In the Whig State Convention at Springfield, Sept. 29, 1847, he made a
stirring speech against supporting any pro-slavery
man for the presidential chair, and urging uncom-

promising resistance against the extension of slavery to any territory to be acquired from Mexico.

"The Missouri compromise, the annexation of Texas, the war with Mexico," said he, "are only a portion of the troubles caused by the slave-power. It is an ancient fable, that the eruptions of Etna were produced by the restless movements of the giant Enceladus, who was imprisoned beneath. As he turned on his side, or stretched his limbs, or struggled, the conscious mountain belched forth flames, fiery cinders, and red-hot lava, carrying destruction and dismay to all who dwelt upon its fertile slopes. The slave-power is the imprisoned giant of our constitution. It is there confined and bound to the earth. But its constant and strenuous struggles have caused, and ever will cause, eruptions of evil to our happy country, in comparison with which the flames, the fiery cinders, and red-hot lava, of the volcano are trivial and transitory. The face of nature may be blasted; the land may be struck with sterility; villages may be swept by floods of flame, and whole families entombed alive in its burning embrace: but all these evils shall be small by the side of the deep, abiding, unutterable curse of an act of national wrong.

"Let us, then, pledge ourselves in the most solemn form, by united exertions at least to restrain this destructive influence within its original constitutional bounds. Let us at all hazards prevent the extension of slavery, and the strengthening of the slave-power. Our opposition must keep right on, and not look back.

> ' Like to the Pontic Sea,
> Whose icy current and compulsive course
> Ne'er feels retiring ebb, but keeps due on
> To the Propontic and the Hellespont.'

In this contest, let us borrow from the example of the ancient Greek, who when his hands were cut off fought with his stumps, and even with his teeth. . . .

"Loyalty to principle is higher than loyalty to party. The first is a heavenly sentiment, from God : the other is a device of this earth. Far above any flickering light or mere battle-lantern of party is the everlasting sun of truth, in whose beams are displayed the duties of men."

CHAPTER VII.

The Formation of the Free-soil Party. — Defection of the Whig Party. — Mr. Sumner's Speech announcing his Withdrawal from that Party. — Aggressions of the Slaveholding Power. — The Duty of Massachusetts. — The Commanding Question. — Mr. Sumner's Oration on "The Law of Human Progress." — Greek and Roman Civilization. — The Power of the Press. — Signs of Progress. — The Course of the True Reformer. — His Speech at Faneuil Hall on the New Party. — His Leading Ideas, Freedom, Truth, and Justice. — Opposition to his Views. — The Unity of Aim and the Advanced Standing of Mr. Sumner and Mr. Garrison.

"He put to the hazard his ease, his interests, his friendship, even his darling popularity, for the benefit of a race of men he had never seen, who could not even give him thanks. He hurt those who were able to requite a benefit or punish an injury. He well knew the snares that might be spread about his feet by political intrigue, personal animosity, and possibly by popular delusion. This is the path that all heroes have trod before him. He was traduced and maligned for his supposed motives. He well knew, that, as in the Roman triumphal processions, so in public service, obloquy is an essential ingredient in the composition of all true glory." — EDMUND BURKE.

ARLY in 1848, a small company of reformers, among whom were Henry Wilson, Stephen C. Phillips, John A. Andrew, and Horace Mann, used to assemble frequently in the rooms of Mr. Sumner in Court Street to discuss the encroach-

ments of the slaveocracy, and the duties and delinquencies of the Whig party. Here indeed was
taken the first real political anti-slavery stand; and
here, in view of the subserviency of prominent
Whigs to Southern rule, was inaugurated the intrepid Free-soil party, whose leading policy was
free soil, free labor, free speech, free men, and opposition to the extension of slavery and of the slaveholding power. As the South became more and
more intent on domination, the Whig party yielded
more and more to its arrogant demands, and, in the
national convention held in Philadelphia on the first
day of June, united with the advocates of slavery in
the nomination of Zachary Taylor — a slaveholder,
and known to be adverse to the Wilmot Proviso — for
the presidential chair. Henry Wilson and Charles
Allen, delegates from this State, denounced the
action of the body; and returning home held with
their associates, in the city of Worcester, on the
28th of June, a grand mass-meeting, over which
Charles Francis Adams presided. Able speeches
were made, calling for a union of men of all parties
to resist the aggression of the slaveholding power.
Mr. Sumner here came forward, and, in a speech of
signal force and earnestness, announced in these
words his separation from the Whig party: "They
[referring to Mr. Giddings and Mr. Adams, who

5

had just spoken] have been Whigs; and I, too,
have been a Whig, though 'not an ultra Whig.'
I was so because I thought this party represented
the moral sentiments of the country, — that it was
the party of humanity. It has ceased to sustain this
character. It does not represent the moral sentiments of the country. It is not the party of
humanity. A party which renounces its sentiments
must itself expect to be renounced. For myself, in
the coming contest, I wish it to be understood that
I belong to the party of freedom, — to that party
which plants itself on the Declaration of Independence, and the Constitution of the United States.

"As I reflect upon the transactions in which we
are now engaged, I am reminded of an incident in
French history. It was late in the night at Versailles that a courtier of Louis XVI., penetrating
the bed-chamber of his master, and arousing him
from his slumbers, communicated to him the intelligence — big with gigantic destinies — that the people of Paris, smarting under wrong and falsehood,
had risen in their might, and, after a severe contest
with hireling troops, destroyed the Bastile. The
unhappy monarch, turning upon his couch, said,
'It is an *insurrection*.' 'No, sire,' was the reply
of the honest courtier: 'it is a *revolution*.' And
such is our movement to-day. It is a revolution,

not beginning with the destruction of a Bastile, but
destined to end only with the overthrow of a
tyranny differing little in hardship and audacity
from that which sustained the Bastile of France:
I mean the slave-power of the United States.
Let not people start at this similitude. I intend no
unkindness to individual slaveholders, many of
whom are doubtless humane and honest. And such
was Louis XVI.; and yet he sustained the Bastile,
with the untold horrors of its dungeons, where
human beings were thrust into companionship with
toads and rats."

"In the pursuit of its purposes," he continued,
"the slave-power has obtained the control of both
the great political parties of the country. Their
recent nominations have been made with a view to
serve its interests, to secure its supremacy, and
especially to promote the extension of slavery. The
Whigs and Democrats — I use the old names still —
professing to represent conflicting sentiments, yet
concur in being the representatives of the slave-
power. Gen. Cass, after openly registering his
adhesion to it, was recognized as the candidate of
the Democrats. Gen. Taylor, who owns slaves on a
large scale, though observing a studious silence on
the subject of slavery, as on all other subjects, is not
only a representative of the slave-power, but an

important and constituent part of the power itself. . . . And now the question occurs, What is the true line of duty with regard to these two candidates? Mr. Van Buren (and I honor him for his trumpet-call to the North) sounded the true note when he said he could not vote for either of them. Though nominated by different parties, they represent, as I have said, substantially the same interest, — the slave-power. The election of either would be a triumph of the slave-power, and entail upon the country, in all probability, the sin of extending slavery. How, then, shall they be encountered? It seems to me in a very plain way. The lovers of freedom, of all parties, and irrespective of all party association, must unite, and, by a new combination congenial with the constitution, oppose both candidates. This will be the FREEDOM POWER, whose single object shall be to resist the SLAVE POWER. We will put them face to face, and let them grapple. Who can doubt the result? . . .

"But it is said that we shall throw away our votes, and that our opposition will fail. Fail, sir! No honest, earnest effort in a good cause ever fails. It may not be crowned with the applause of man; it may not seem to touch the goal of immediate worldly success, which is the end and aim of so much of life: but still it is not lost. It helps to strengthen the weak with new virtue, to arm the irresolute with proper energy, to animate all with devotion to duty, which in the end conquers all. Fail! Did the martyrs fail when with their precious blood they sowed the seed of the Church? Did the discomfited champions of freedom fail, who have left those names in history which can never die? Did the three hundred Spartans fail when, in the narrow pass, they did not fear to brave the innumerable Persian hosts, whose very arrows darkened the sun? No! Overborne by numbers, crushed to earth, they have left an example which is greater far than any victory. And this is the least we can do. Our example shall be the source of triumph hereafter. It will not be the first time in history that the hosts of slavery have outnumbered the champions of freedom. But where is it written that slavery finally prevailed?

"Let Massachusetts, then," he says, — "nurse of the men and principles which made our earliest revolution, — vow herself anew to her early faith. Let her elevate once more the torch which she first held aloft. Let us, if need be, pluck some fresh coals from the living altars of France. Let us, too, proclaim. 'Liberty, equality, fraternity!' — liberty to the captive, equality between the master and his slave, fraternity with all men, the whole comprehended in that sublime revelation of Christianity, — the brotherhood of mankind."

By the treaty of peace with Mexico, proclaimed July 4, 1848, that vast extent of territory north of the Rio Grande, together with New Mexico and California, embracing more than 500,000 square miles, was relinquished to the United States; and over these immense regions the slave propagandists sought to extend their abominable system. The stake in the political game between them and the friends of freedom was a virgin territory more than four times as large as the British Isles, and more than twice as large as France and Switzerland. Shall it be opened to free or servile labor? Shall peace and plenty, or bondage and poverty, reign therein? Life or death?— this was the commanding question of the day. The new organization saw the magnitude of the issue, and said, "Life!" The old party, bending to the arrogant dictation of the South, said, "Death!" Daniel Webster doubtless drank his brandy with his eye turned toward the North, then towards the South, then towards the White House, and said, "Death!" And this was his finality!

Although hard names, forbidding frowns, and gibe and jest and social ostracism, were to be accepted by the men who dared to leave the domi-

nant party, Mr. Sumner and his compeers had a
grand idea; they had a sentiment of humanity, deep-
seated in the heart of the people, to sustain them:
and they thus went boldly forward, turning neither
to the right nor left, to the accomplishment of one of
the most transcendently beneficent political under-
takings of these modern times.

In a hopeful and well-written oration on THE LAW
OF HUMAN PROGRESS, pronounced before the Phi
Beta Kappa Society of Union College, Schenectady,
on the 25th day of July, 1848, Mr. Sumner, sweeping with an eagle eye over the various social systems
of the past, indicates their points of weakness, but
still acknowledges the steady march of civilization;
and, under the benignant influences of Christianity
and the printing-press, ardently anticipates a brighter
day for science, art, literature, freedom, and humanity. Of the anomaly of Greek and Roman civilization, he thus eloquently discourses: —

"There are revolutions in history which may seem,
on a superficial view, inconsistent with this law.
Our attention, from early childhood, is directed to
Greece and Rome; and we are sometimes taught
that these two states reached heights which subsequent nations cannot hope to equal, much less sur-
pass. Let me not disparage the triumphs of the
ancient mind. The eloquence, the poetry, the phil-

osophy, the art, of Athens still survive, and bear no mean sway upon the earth. Rome, too, yet lives in her jurisprudence, which, next after Christianity, has exerted a paramount influence over the laws of modern states.

" But, exalted as these productions may be, it is impossible not to perceive that something of their present importance is derived from the peculiar method in which they appeared ; something from the habit of unquestioning the high-flown admiration with regard to them, which has been transmitted through successive generations ; and something also from the disposition, still prevalent, blindly to elevate antiquity at the expense of subsequent ages. Without here undertaking to decide the question of the supremacy of Greek or Roman genius, as displayed in individual minds, it would be easy to show that the ancient standard of civilization never reached the heights of many modern states. The people were ignorant, vicious, and poor, or degraded to abject slavery, — slavery itself, the sum of all injustice and all vice. And even the most illustrious characters, whose names still shine from that distant night with stellar brightness, were little more than splendid barbarians. Architecture, sculpture, painting, and vases of exquisite perfection, attested their appreciation of the beauty of form ; but they were

strangers to the useful arts, as well as to the comforts and virtues of home. Abounding in what to
us are luxuries of life, they had not what to us are
its necessaries.

" Without knowledge there can be no sure progress.
Vice and barbarism are the inseparable companions
of ignorance. Nor is it too much to say, that, except in rare instances, the highest virtue is attained
only through intelligence. And this is natural; for,
in order to do right, we must first understand what
is right. But the people of Greece and Rome, even
in the brilliant days of Pericles and Augustus, were
unable to arrive at this knowledge. The sublime
teachings of Plato and Socrates — calculated in many
respects to promote the best interests of the race —
were restrained in their influence to the small company of listeners, or to the few who could obtain a
copy of the costly manuscript in which they were
preserved. Thus the knowledge and virtue acquired
by individuals failed to be diffused in their own age,
or secured to posterity.

" But now at last, through an agency all unknown
to antiquity, knowledge of every kind has become
general and permanent. It can no longer be confined to a select circle. It cannot be crushed by
tyranny, or lost by neglect. It is immortal as the
soul from which it proceeds. This alone renders all

relapse into barbarism impossible, while it affords unquestionable distinction between ancient and modern times. The press, watchful with more than the hundred eyes of Argus, strong with more than the hundred arms of Briareus, not only guards all the conquests of civilization, but leads the way to future triumphs. Through its untiring energies, the meditations of the closet or the utterances of the human voice, which else would die away within the precincts of a narrow room, are prolonged to the most distant nations and times, with winged words circling the globe. We admire the genius of Demosthenes, of Sophocles, of Plato, and of Phidias; but the printing-press is a higher gift to man than the eloquence, the drama, the philosophy, and the art of Greece."

The power even of the rudest people to advance in civilization under the law of progress, and the auspicious influences to this end conspiring, are well set forth in this hopeful passage : —

"Look at the cradles of the nations and races which have risen to grandeur; and learn from the barbarous wretchedness by which they were originally surrounded, that no lot can be removed from the influence of the law of progress. The Feejee Islander, the Bushman, the Hottentot, the Congo negro, cannot be too low for its care. No term of imagined 'finality' can arrest it. The polished Briton, whose civilization we now admire, is a descendant, perhaps, of one of those painted barbarians whose degradation still lives in the pages of Julius Cæsar. Slowly and by degrees he has reached the position where he now stands; but he cannot be stayed here. The improvement of the past is the earnest of still further improvement in the long ages of the future. And who can doubt, that, in the lapse of time, as the Christian law is gradually fulfilled, the elevation which the Briton may attain will be shared by all his fellow-men?

"The signs of improvement may appear at a special period, in a limited circle only, among the people, favored of God, who have enjoyed the peculiar benefits of commerce and of Christianity; but the blessed influence cannot be restrained to any time, to any place, or to any people. Every victory over evil rebounds to the benefit of all. Every discovery, every humane thought, every truth, when declared, is a conquest of which the whole human family are partakers. It extends by so much their dominion, while it lessens by so much the sphere of their future struggles and trials. Thus it is, while nature is always the same, the power of man is ever increasing. Each day gives him some new advantage.

The mountains have not grown in size; but man has broken through their passes. The winds and waves are capricious ever, as when they first beat upon the ancient Silurian rocks; but the steamboat

'Against the wind, against the tide,
Now steadies on with upright keel.'

The distance between two places upon the surface of the globe is the same to-day as when the continents were first heaved from their ocean-bed; but the inhabitants can now, by the art of man, commune together.

"Much still remains to be done; but the Creator did not speak in vain when he blessed his earliest children, and bade them 'to multiply, and replenish the earth, and *subdue it*.'

"But there shall be nobler triumphs than any over inanimate nature. Man himself shall be subdued, — subdued to abhorrence of vice, of injustice, of violence; subdued to the sweet charities of life; subdued to all the requirements of duty and religion; subdued, according to the law of human progress, to the recognition of that gospel law by the side of which the first is as the scaffolding upon the sacred temple, — the law of human brotherhood. To labor for this end was man sent forth into the world; not in the listlessness of idle perfections, but en-

dowed with infinite capacities, inspired by infinite
desires, and commanded to strive perpetually after
excellence, amidst the encouragements of hope, the
promises of final success, and the inexpressible
delights which spring from its pursuit. Thus does
the law of human progress

> 'Assert eternal Providence,
> And justify the ways of God to men,'

by showing evil no longer as a gloomy mystery,
binding the world into everlasting thrall, but as an
accident, destined, under the laws of God, to be
slowly subdued by the works of men as they press
on to the promised goal of happiness."

In Mr. Sumner's closing words on future progress,
its certainty, and the means of making it, may be
seen his lofty ideal of humanity, the leading motive
of his life, which was the liberation of the captive,
the upraising of the masses; and also his idea of a
true reformer: " Be it, then, our duty and our encouragement to live and to labor ever mindful of the
future; but let us not forget the past. All ages have
lived and labored for us. From one has come art, from
another jurisprudence, from another the compass,
from another the printing-press: from all have proceeded priceless lessons of truth and virtue. The
earliest and most distant times are not without a

present influence on our daily lives. The mighty stream of progress, though fed by many tributary waters and hidden springs, derives something of its force from the earlier currents which leap and sparkle in the distant mountain-recesses, over precipices, among rapids, and beneath the shade of the primeval forest.

"Nor should we be too impatient to witness the fulfilment of our aspirations. The daily increasing rapidity of discovery and improvement, and the daily multiplying efforts of beneficence, in later years outstripping the imaginations of the most sanguine, furnish well-grounded assurance that the advance of man will be with a constantly accelerating speed. The extending intercourse among the nations of the earth, and among all the children of the human family, gives new promises of the complete diffusion of truth, penetrating the most distant places, chasing away the darkness of night, and exposing the hideous forms of slavery, of war, of wrong, which must be hated as soon as they are clearly seen. And yet, while confident of the future, and surrounded by heralds of certain triumph, let us learn to moderate our anticipations, nor imitate those children of the crusaders, who, in their long journey from Western Europe, —

'To seek
In Golgotha Him dead, who lives in heaven,'

hailed each city and castle which they approached as the Jerusalem that was to be the end of their wanderings. No: the goal is distant, and ever advancing; but the march is none the less certain. As well attempt to make the sun stand still in his course, or to restrain the sweet influence of the Pleiades, as to arrest the incessant, irresistible movement which is the appointed destiny of man.

" Cultivate, then, a just moderation: learn to reconcile order with change, stability with progress. This is a wise conservatism: this is a wise reform. Rightly understanding these terms, who would not be a conservative? who would not be a reformer? — a conservative of all that is good, a reformer of all that is evil; a conservative of knowledge, a reformer of ignorance; a conservative of truths and principles, whose seat is the bosom of God; a reformer of laws and institutions, which are but the wicked or imperfect work of man: a conservative of that divine order which is found only in movement; a reformer of those earthly wrongs and abuses which spring from a violation of the great law of human progress. Blending these two characters in one, let us seek to be at the same time *Reforming Conservatives, and Conservative Reformers.*"

Martin Van Buren having been nominated as a

presidential candidate by the Free-soil party at the Buffalo Convention, a meeting to ratify the same was held at Faneuil Hall on the twenty-second day of August, when Mr. Sumner said, " It is no longer banks and tariffs which are to occupy the foremost place in our discussions, and to give their tone, sounding always with the chink of dollars and cents, to the policy of the country. Henceforward PROTECTION TO MAN shall be the true AMERICAN SYSTEM. . . . The old and ill-compacted party organizations are broken: from their ruins is now formed a new party, — *The Party of Freedom.* There are good men who longed for this, and have died without the sight. John Quincy Adams longed for it. William Ellery Channing longed for it. Their spirits hover over us, and urge us to persevere. Let us be true to the moral grandeur of our cause. Have faith in truth, and in God who giveth the victory.

> ' Oh ! a fair cause stands firm and will abide:
> Legions of angels fight upon its side.'

It is said that we have but one idea. This I deny ; but, admitting that it is so, are we not, with our one idea, better than a party with no ideas at all ? And what is our one idea ? It is the idea which combined our fathers on the heights of Bunker Hill. It

is the idea which carried Washington through a
seven-years' war; which inspired Lafayette; which
touched with coals of fire the lips of Adams, Otis,
and Patrick Henry. Ours is an idea which is at
least noble and elevating: it is an idea which draws
in its train virtue, goodness, and all the charities of
life, all that makes earth a home of improvement
and happiness.

> ' Her path, where'er the goddess roves,
>   Glory pursues, and generous shame,
> The unconquerable mind, and freedom's holy flame.'

We found now a new party. Its corner-stone is
freedom. Its broad, all-sustaining arches are truth,
justice, and humanity. Like the ancient Roman
Capitol, at once a temple and a citadel, it shall be the
fit shrine of the genius of American institutions."

" He is radical, an agitator, a rabid abolitionist,
scattering fire-brands and death amongst us," said
the old conservatives who were indirectly storing
their magazines of merchandise with the gains
derived from the unceasing toil of those in bondage: " he must be silenced, or bought up for our
conciliatory purposes." They mistook their man.
They set political power and money-making above
principle. Mr. Sumner had come up abreast of
the progressive spirit of the age. He saw that a

grand question, touching the interests of more than three million human beings in the chains of servitude, was to be met; that it could be done on constitutional grounds; and while Mr. Garrison, aiming grandly at the same result, and fighting manfully on a moral basis, was dealing out gigantic blows for freedom, Mr. Sumner came up with equal vigor to the political arena, and determined to meet the issue under the ægis of the constitution. Both were battling for the same victory; and the strong blows of both alike were needed. Buy cotton, buy men intent on office, the old *régime* with gold could do: Mr. Sumner and Mr. Garrison had ascended to a plane above the reach of gold.

CHAPTER VIII.

Mr. Sumner's Literary Pursuits. — His Political Views. — His Remarks on Utopian Ideas. — His Position defined. — Oration before the American Peace Society. — Encomium on Peace. — War Pictures. — A Beautiful Peroration. — The Free-soil Party. — Convention at Worcester. — Address to the Citizens of Massachusetts. — Argument in Respect to Colored Schools. — Equality of All Men before the Law. — Daniel Webster's Subserviency to the South. — The Fugitive-Slave Law. — Mr. Sumner's Effective Speech thereon. — Demands of the Free-soil Party. — Mr. Sumner's Future Course indicated. — Death of his Brother Horace Sumner, and the Ossoli Family.

"Veuillez seulement, et les lois iniques disparoîtront soudain, et la violence des oppresseurs se brisera contre votre fermeté inflexible et juste. Rien ne resiste à l'union du droit et du devoir." — *Livre du Peuple*, par F. Lamennais.

> "For what avail
>   The plough and sail,
>   Or land or life,
>   If Freedom fail ? "
>   R. W. Emerson.

R. SUMNER neither had nor cared to have much legal practice at this period. His time was, for the most part, spent either among his books — in close communion with the liberty-loving John Milton, with Nature's darling child William Shakspeare, with that glorious Florentine, the God-gifted Dante, with the genial, quick-eyed Horace, with the blind old Homer, and other grand classical authors, from whom he drew fresh inspiration for the conduct of his life — in writing lectures for literary associations, or in the consideration of the commanding civil and political questions of the day. Occasionally he prepared an article for "The Christian Examiner," or addressed a lyceum; but he had no desire to enter into the struggle for political place. His ambition was to be an independent thinker, entirely free from the trammels of office, and, in his own private way, to do something for the liberation of his fellow-men from bondage. He was called a theorizer and a visionary; but his thoughts were in advance of his age; and his opinions rested on the solid basis of eternal truth and equity. He had reached a higher level than the mercenary politicians of his time; and hence they could not understand him. "Much learning doth make thee mad," said they; and so, alike unmindful of the ground-swell underneath and of the stars above, they went on drifting hard against the fatal breakers.

"If our aims," said Mr. Sumner, in speaking of his views on peace, "are visionary, impracticable, Utopian, then the unfulfilled promises of the prophecies are vain; then the Lord's Prayer, in which we ask that God's kingdom shall come on earth, is a mockery; then Christianity is an Utopia. Let me not content myself by reminding you that all the great reforms by which mankind have been advanced have encountered similar objections; that the abolition of the punishment of death for theft was first suggested in the 'Utopia' of Sir Thomas More; that the efforts to abolish the crime of the slave-trade were opposed, almost in our day, as impracticable and visionary: in short, that all the endeavors for human improvement, for knowledge, for freedom, for virtue, that all the great causes which dignify human history, which save it from being a mere protracted war-bulletin, a common sewer, a *Cloaca Maxima*, flooded with perpetual uncleanliness, have been pronounced Utopian; while, in spite of distrust, of prejudice, of enmity, all these causes have gradually found acceptance as they gradually became understood; and the Utopias of one age have become the realities of the next."

In a letter dated Oct. 26, 1848, in which he most reluctantly accepts the nomination as the congressional candidate of the Free-soil party, Mr. Sumner says, "I have never held political office of any kind, nor have I ever been a candidate for any such office. It has been my desire and determination to labor in such fields of usefulness as are open to every private citizen, without the honors, the emoluments, or the constraints of office. I would show by my example (might I so aspire!) that something may be done for the welfare of our race without the support of public sanction, or the accident of popular favor. In this course I hoped to be allowed to persevere unto the end. . . . The principles of Washington, of Jefferson, and of Franklin; the security of our constitution; the fair fame of our country; the interests of labor; the cause of freedom, of humanity, of right, of morals, of religion, of God, — all these are now at stake. Holier cause has never appeared in history. Let me offer to it, not my vows only, but my best efforts, wherever they can be most effectual."

An ardent advocate of peace and good-will, Mr. Sumner delivered before the American Peace Society, on the 28th of May, 1849, a splendid oration on "The War Systems of the Commonwealth of Nations." In this celebrated effort he displays the riches of a ripe scholarship, and a highly-cultivated imagination, to great advantage. Though some lack of logical method in arrangement, as in almost all his speeches, is observable, the positions taken are in harmony with the teachings of Christianity, and illustrated by a wealth of learning truly admirable. His pictures of the blessings attendant on peace, as well as of the horrors of land and naval warfare, are drawn with the skill of a master. They are beautiful poems in prose, and are considered models in this kind of style. In his eloquent exordium he thus refers to the felicities of peace : —

" Peace is the grand Christian charity, the fountain and parent of all other charities. Let peace be removed, and all other charities shall sicken and die. Let peace exert her gladsome sway, and all other charities shall quicken into celestial life. Peace is a distinctive promise and possession of Christianity : so much is this the case, that, where peace is not, Christianity cannot be. There is nothing elevated which is not exalted by peace. There is nothing valuable which does not contribute to peace. Of Wisdom herself it has been said, that all her ways are pleasantness, and all her paths are peace. Peace has ever been the longing and aspiration of the noblest souls, whether for themselves or for their country. In the bitterness of exile, away from the Florence which he has immortalized by his divine poem, pacing the cloisters of a convent, in response to the inquiry of the monk, 'What do you seek?' Dante said, in words distilled from his heart, ' Peace, peace.' In the struggles of civil war in England, while king and parliament were rending the land, a gallant supporter of the monarchy, renowned for the bravery of battle, the chivalrous Falkland, cried, in words which consecrate his memory more than any feat of arms, ' Peace, peace, peace ! ' Not in aspiration only, but in benediction, is this word uttered. As the apostle went forth on his errand, as the son left his father's roof, the choicest blessing was, ' Peace be with you.' As the Saviour was born, angels from heaven, amidst quiring melodies, let fall that supreme benediction, never before tasted by the heathen tribes, addressed to all nations, and to all children of the human family, ' Peace on earth, and good-will towards men.' "

He thus vividly portrays the atrocities of war upon the land : —

" I need not dwell now on the waste and cruelty of war. These stare us wildly in the face like lurid meteor-lights, as we travel the page of history. We see the desolation and death that pursue its demoniac footsteps. We look upon sacked towns, upon ravaged territories, upon violated homes : we behold all the sweet charities of life changed to wormwood and gall. Our soul is penetrated by the sharp moan of mothers, sisters, and daughters, of fathers, brothers, and sons, who, in the bitterness of their bereavement, refuse to be comforted. Our eyes rest at last upon one of those fair fields where Nature in her abundance spreads her cloth of gold, spacious and apt for the entertainment of mighty multitudes; or, perhaps, from the curious subtlety of its position, like the carpet in the Arabian tale, seeming to contract so as to be covered by a few only, or to dilate so as to receive an innumerable host. Here, under a bright sun, such as shone at Austerlitz or Buena Vista, amidst the peaceful harmonies of nature, on the sabbath of peace, we behold bands of brothers, children of a common Father, heirs to a common happiness, struggling together in the deadly fight with the madness of fallen spirits; seeking with murderous weapons the lives of brothers who have never injured them or their kindred. The havoc rages. The ground is soaked with their commingling blood: the air is rent by their commingling cries. Horse and rider are stretched together on the earth. More revolting than the mangled victims, than the gashed limbs, than the lifeless trunks, than the spattering brains, are the lawless passions which sweep tempest-like through the fiendish tumult.

' Nearer comes the storm and nearer, rolling fast and frightful on.
Speak, Ximena, speak and tell us, who has lost and who has won ? '
' Alas! alas! I know not: friend and foe together fall.
O'er the dying rush the living: pray, my sister, for them all.'

"Horror-struck, we ask, Wherefore this hateful contest? The melancholy but truthful answer comes, that this is the *established* method of determining justice between nations."

His word-painting of warfare on the sea is still more vivid : —

"The scene changes. Far away on the distant pathway of the ocean two ships approach each other, with white canvas broadly spread to receive the flying gales. They are proudly built. All of human art has been lavished in their graceful proportions and in their well-compacted sides, while they look in dimensions like floating happy islands of the sea. A numerous crew, with costly appliances of comfort, hives in their secure shelter. Surely these two travellers shall meet in joy and friendship : the flag at the mast-head shall give the signal of fellowship ; the happy sailors shall cluster in the rigging, and even on the yard-arms, to look each other in the face, while the exhilarating voices of both crews shall mingle in accents of gladness uncontrollable. It is not so. Not as brothers, not as friends, not as wayfarers of the common ocean, do they come together, but as enemies. The gentle vessels now bristle fiercely with death-dealing instruments. On their spacious decks, aloft on all their masts, flashes the deadly musketry. From their sides spout cataracts of flame, amidst the pealing thunders of a fatal artillery. They who had escaped 'the dreadful touch of merchant-marring rocks,' who had sped on their long and solitary way unharmed by wind or wave, whom the hurricane had spared, in whose favor storms and seas had intermitted their immitigable war, — now at last fall by the hand of each other. The same spectacle of horror greets us from both ships. On their decks reddened with blood, the murderers of St. Bartholomew and of the Sicilian Vespers, with the fires of Smithfield, seem to break forth anew, and to concentrate their rage. Each has now become a swimming Golgotha. At length these vessels — such pageants of the sea, once so stately, so proudly built, but now rudely shattered by cannon-balls, with shivered masts and ragged sails — exist only as unmanageable wrecks, weltering on the uncertain waves whose temporary lull of peace is now their only safety. In amazement at this strange, unnatural contest away from country and home, where there is no country or home to defend, we ask again, Wherefore this dismal duel? Again the melancholy but truthful answer promptly comes, that this is the *established* method of determining justice between nations."

In his peroration these grand and hopeful ideas are most eloquently presented : —

" Tell me not, then, of the homage which the world yet offers to the military chieftain. Tell me not of the glory of war: tell me not of the honor or fame that is won on its murderous fields. All is vanity. It is a blood-red phantom, sure to fade and disappear. They who strive after it, Ixion-like, embrace a cloud. Though seeming for a while to fill the heavens, cloaking the stars, it must, like the vapors of earth, pass away. Milton has likened the early contests of the Heptarchy to the skirmishes of crows and kites; but God, and the exalted Christianity of the future, shall regard all the bloody feuds of men in the same likeness; and Napoleon and Alexander, so far as they were engaged in war, shall seem to be monster crows and kites. Thus shall it be as mankind ascend from the thrall of brutish passions by which they are yet degraded. Nobler aims, by nobler means, shall fill the soul; a new standard of excellence shall prevail; and honor, divorced from all deeds of blood, shall become the inseparable attendant of good works alone. Far better, then, shall it be, even in the judgment of this world, to have been a door-keeper in the house of peace, than the proudest dweller in the tents of war.

" There is a legend of the early Church, that the Saviour left his image miraculously impressed upon a napkin which he placed upon his countenance. The napkin has been lost; and men now attempt to portray that countenance from the heathen models of Jupiter and Apollo. But the image of Christ is not lost to the world. Clearer than in the precious napkin, clearer than in the colors of the marble of modern art, it appears in every virtuous deed, in every act of self-sacrifice, in all magnanimous toil, in every recognition of the brotherhood of mankind. It shall yet be supremely manifest, in unimagined loveliness and serenity, when the commonwealth of nations, confessing the true grandeur of peace, shall renounce the wickedness of the war system, and shall dedicate to labors of beneficence all the comprehensive energies which have been so fatally absorbed in its support. Then, at last, shall it be seen that *there can be no peace that is not honorable; and there can be no war that is not dishonorable.*"

Planted on the solid ground of opposition, under and within the constitution, to slavery and its extension, the Free-soil party commended itself more and more to the profound convictions of the Northern people, and, under the direction of such clear-headed men as Henry Wilson, Stephen C. Phillips, Charles A. Phelps, and Charles Sumner, gradually acquired position and commanding influence. At a convention of the party held at Worcester, Sept. 12,

1849, Mr. Sumner, calling the members to order, said, —

" It was the sentiment of Benjamin Franklin, that great apostle of freedom, uttered during the trials of the Revolution, that ' Where liberty is, there is my country.' I doubt not that each member of this convention will be ready to respond, in a similar strain, ' Where liberty is, there is my party.' "

A long and able address by Mr. Sumner to the citizens of Massachusetts on the Free-soil movement, was adopted by this convention, and widely circulated. Contrasting its position with the double dealing of the Whig party, he says, " Wherever we exist, in all parts of the country, East and West, North and South, we are truly a NATIONAL party. We are not compelled to assume one face at the South, and another at the North; to blow hot in one place, and blow cold in another; to speak loudly of freedom in one region, and vindicate slavery in another, — in short, to present a combination in which the two extreme wings profess opinions on the great issue before the country, diametrically opposed to each other. We are the same everywhere; and the reason is, because our party, unlike the other parties, is bound together in support of certain fixed and well-defined principles. It is not a combination fixed by partisan zeal, and kept together, as with mechanical force, by considerations of political expediency only; but a sincere, conscientious, inflexible union for the sake of freedom."

Of the leading question of the party, he remarks, "It is an everlasting link in the golden chain of human progress. It is a cause which, though long kept in check throughout our country, as also in Europe, now confronts the people and their rulers, demanding to be heard. It can no longer be avoided or silenced. To every man in the land it now says, with clear, penetrating voice, 'Are you for freedom, or are you for slavery?' And every man in the land must answer this question when he votes."

Towards the close of the year (Dec. 4) Mr. Sumner made a strong argument before the Supreme Court of the State, against the constitutionality of separate colored schools, establishing his positions both by the constitution and the legislation of the State, as well as by the decisions of the bench. In the course of the argument he said, in reference to the distinction between the Ethiopian and Caucasian races: "Each has received from the hand of God certain characteristics of color and form. The two may not readily intermingle; although we are told by Homer that Jupiter

'Did not disdain to grace

One may be uninteresting or offensive to the other, precisely as different individuals of the same race and color may be uninteresting or offensive to each other; *but this distinction can furnish no ground for any discrimination before the law.*

"We abjure nobility of all kinds; but here is a nobility of the skin. We abjure all hereditary distinctions; but here is an hereditary distinction, founded not on the merit of the ancestor, but on his color. We abjure all privileges derived from birth; but here is a privilege which depends solely on the accident, whether an ancestor is black or white. We abjure all inequality before the law; but here is an inequality which touches not an individual, but a race. We revolt at the relation of caste; but here is a caste which is established under a constitution declaring that *all men are born equal.*"

Closing his earnest plea for the rights of the slave, he nobly said, " Which way soever we turn, we are brought back to one single proposition, —*the equality of men before the law.* This stands as the mighty guardian of the rights of the colored children in this case. It is the constant, ever-present, tutelary genius of this Commonwealth, frowning upon every privilege of birth, upon every distinction of race, upon every institution of caste. You cannot slight it or avoid it. You cannot restrain it. God grant that you may welcome it! Do this, and your words will be a 'charter and freehold of rejoicing' to a race which, by much suffering, has earned a title to much regard. Your judgment will become a sacred landmark, not in jurisprudence only, but in the history of freedom, giving precious encouragement to all the weary and heavy-laden wayfarers in this great cause. Massachusetts will then, through you, have a fresh title to regard, and be once more, as in times past, an example to the whole land."

The South was steadily pressing for dominion; the Whig party of the North, weakened by the desertion from its ranks of many of the advocates of freedom, step by step gave way; and Daniel Webster, led on by a hope which dotage only could have entertained, of rising to the chief executive chair, in his fatal senatorial speech of March 7, 1850, bowed in most abject submission to the slaveholding interest. Keenly it was said by an honest farmer, as this mighty leader of the Whigs went down, "The masters never pay their slaves;" and never, after that false play for power, could his words, once so grandly eloquent, reach the Northern heart.

By the death of President Taylor, July 9 of the same year, the executive power devolved on Millard Fillmore, who called Mr. Webster from the Senate to his cabinet. On the 18th of September following Mr.

Fillmore signed the infamous Fugitive-Slave Bill. " The North," said one, " will never submit to this; and we shall make the breaking-point." The sentiment of the lovers of freedom was aroused; and as a pent-up stream breaks through the dam arresting it, so the full torrent of indignation came rolling forth. In a speech at the Free-soil State Convention, held in Boston on the third day of October, 1850, Mr. Sumner denounced, in words of scathing power, the iniquity of this bill. The walls of Faneuil Hall had never echoed to more impassioned strains of eloquence. The words came from the heart, as winged with a celestial fire. A prophet greater than Daniel had come to judgment. " The soul sickens," exclaimed Mr. Sumner, " in the contemplation of this outrage. In the dreary annals of the past there are many acts of shame; there are ordinances of monarchs, and laws, which have become a by-word and a hissing to the nations. But, when we consider the country and the age, I ask fearlessly, What act of shame, what ordinance of monarch, what law, can compare in atrocity with this enactment of an American Congress? I do not forget Appius Claudius, the tyrant decemvir of ancient Rome, condemning Virginia as a slave; nor Louis XIV. of France, letting slip the dogs of religious persecution by the revocation of the Edict of Nantes; nor Charles I. of

England, arousing the patriot-rage of Hampden by the extortion of ship-money; nor the British Parliament, provoking in our country spirits kindred to Hampden, by the tyranny of the Stamp Act and the tea-tax. I would not exaggerate; I wish to keep within bounds: but I think no person can doubt that the condemnation now affixed to all these transactions and to their authors must be the lot hereafter of the Fugitive-Slave Bill, and of every one, according to the measure of his influence, who gave it his support. Into the immortal catalogue of national crimes this has now passed, drawing after it, by an inexorable necessity, its authors also, and chiefly him who as president of the United States set his name to the bill, and breathed into it that final breath without which it would have no life. Other presidents may be forgotten; but the name signed to the Fugitive-Slave Bill can never be forgotten. There are depths of infamy, as there are heights of fame. I regret to say what I must; but truth compels me. Better for him had he never been born! Better far for his memory, and for the good name of his children, had he never been president! Under this detestable, Heaven-defying bill, not the slave only, but the colored freeman of the North, may be swept into ruthless captivity; and there is no white citizen, born among us, bred in our schools, partaking in our affairs, voting in our elections, whose liberty is not assailed also. Without any discrimination of color, the bill surrenders all who may be claimed as 'owing service or labor' to the same tyrannical judgment. And mark once more its heathenism : by unrelenting provisions it visits with bitter penalties of fine and imprisonment the faithful men and women who may render to the fugitive that countenance, succor, and shelter which Christianity expressly requires. Thus, from beginning to end, it sets at nought the best principles of the constitution, and the very laws of God.

"I will not dishonor the home of the Pilgrims and of the Revolution by admitting, nay, I cannot believe, — that this bill will be executed here. Individuals among us, as elsewhere, may forget humanity in a fancied loyalty to law; but the public conscience will not allow a man who has trodden our streets as a freeman to be dragged away as a slave. By his escape from bondage, he has shown that true manhood which must grapple to him every honest heart. He may be ignorant and rude, as he is poor; but he is of a true nobility. The fugitive slaves of the United States are among the heroes of our age. In sacrificing them to this foul enactment of Congress, we should violate every sentiment of hospitality, every whispering of the heart, every

dictate of religion. . . . But let me be understood:
I counsel no violence.   There is another power,
stronger than any individual arm, which I invoke:
I mean that invincible public opinion, inspired by
love of God and man, which, without violence or
noise, gently as the operations of nature, makes and
unmakes laws.   Let this opinion be felt in its Christian might, and the Fugitive-Slave Bill will become
everywhere upon our soil a dead-letter.   No lawyer
will aid it by counsel: no citizen will become its
agent.   It will die of inanition, like a spider beneath an exhausted receiver.   Oh! it were well the
tidings should spread throughout the land, that here
in Massachusetts this accursed bill has found no
servants.   'Sire, I have found in Bayonne honest
citizens and brave soldiers only, but not one execu-
tioner,' was the reply of the governor of that place
to the royal mandate of Charles IX. of France,
ordering the massacre of St. Bartholomew.

"But it rests with you, my fellow-citizens, by
your works and your words and your example, by
your calm determinations and your devoted lives, to
do this work.   From a humane, just, and religious
people shall spring up a public opinion, to keep
perpetual guard over the liberties of all within our
borders.   Nay, more: like the flaming sword of the
cherubim at the gates of Paradise, turning on every

side, it shall prevent any slave-hunter from ever setting foot in this Commonwealth. Elsewhere he may pursue his human prey, he may employ his congenial blood-hounds, and exult in his successful game; but into Massachusetts he must not come. And yet, again I say, I counsel no violence. I would not touch his person. Not with whips and thongs would I scourge him from the land. The contempt, the indignation, the abhorrence, of the community shall be our weapons of offence. Wherever he moves, he shall find no house to receive him, no table spread to nourish him, no welcome to cheer him. The dismal lot of the Roman exile shall be his. He shall be a wanderer without roof, fire, or water. Men shall point at him in the streets, and on the highways.

> 'Sleep shall neither night nor day
> Hang on his pent-house lid;
> He shall live a man forbid.
> Weary seven nights, nine times nine,
> Shall he dwindle, peak, and pine.'

The villages, towns, and cities shall refuse to receive the monster: they shall vomit him forth, never again to disturb the repose of our community. . . .

"We demand, first and foremost," continued he, "the instant repeal of the Fugitive-Slave Law.

" We demand the abolition of slavery in the District of Columbia.

" We demand the exercise by Congress, in all Territories, of the time-honored power to prohibit slavery.

" We demand of Congress to refuse to receive into the Union any new slave State.

" We demand the abolition of the domestic slave-trade so far as it can be constitutionally reached, but particularly on the high seas under the national flag.

" And, generally, we demand from the federal government the exercise of all its constitutional power to relieve itself from the responsibility for slavery.

" And yet one thing further must be done : the slave-power must be overturned, so that the federal government may be put openly, actively, and perpetually on the side of freedom." These demands he lived to see fairly and squarely met.

Referring to his own future course, he indicates that line of action which he undeviatingly pursued until the close of life : —

" To vindicate freedom, and to oppose slavery, so far as I might constitutionally, with earnestness, and yet, I trust, without any personal unkindness on my part, has been the object near my heart. Would that I could impress upon all who now hear me something of the strength of my own conviction of the importance of this work! Would that my voice, leaving this crowded hall to-night, could traverse the hills and valleys of New England, that it could run along the rivers and the lakes of my country, lighting in every humane heart a beacon-flame to arouse the slumberers throughout the land! In this cause I care not for the name by which I may be called. Let it be 'Democrat' or 'Loco-foco,' if you please: no man who is in earnest will hesitate on account of a name. I shall rejoice in any associates from any quarter, and shall ever be found with that party which most truly represents the principles of freedom. Others may become indifferent to these principles, bartering them for political success, vain and short-lived, or forgetting the visions of youth in the dreams of age. Whenever I shall forget them, whenever I shall become indifferent to them, whenever I shall cease to be constant in maintaining them, through good report and evil report, in any future combinations of party, — then may my tongue cleave to the roof of my mouth! — may my right hand forget its cunning!"

In the summer of this year, Mr. Sumner was called to lament the loss of his brother Horace, who was drowned in his endeavor to escape from the wreck of the ship " Elizabeth," which was driven by a violent gale upon the beach of Fire Island early in the morning of the 16th of July. He was of a poetical temperament, and had been residing at Rome and Florence, for the sake of regaining his health, in the family of the gifted Margaret Fuller d'Ossoli, who, on the 17th of May, with her husband, their child Angelo, and Mr. Sumner, embarked at Leghorn for New York. On the 15th of July the ship arrived in sight of land on the Jersey coast; but, the wind arising during the night, it was driven past Rockaway, and, early the next morning, struck upon the sand, and soon went to pieces in full sight of the people on the shore. In attempting to reach the land upon a plank, Mr. Sumner was lost; while the Ossoli family, remaining in the vessel, shared the same melancholy fate.

CHAPTER IX.

> "Oh great design,
> Ye sons of mercy! Oh! complete your work;
> Wrench from Oppression's hand the iron rod,
> And bid the cruel feel the wounds they give.
> Man knows no master save creating Heaven,
> Or those whom choice and common good ordains."
>
> *Liberty*, by JAMES THOMSON.

> "Hear him, ye senates! Hear this truth sublime, —
> He who allows oppression shares the crime."
>
> *Botanic Garden*, by ERASMUS DARWIN.

BY a famous coalition of the Free-soil and Democratic parties, effected mainly through the agency of Henry Wilson in the legislature, 1851, Mr. Sumner was elected, over Robert C.

Winthrop, the Whig candidate, to the Senate of the United States. The contest, commencing on .the 16th day of January, was long and acrimonious. Mr. Winthrop had much experience in public affairs, and was an intimate friend of Daniel Webster. Mr. Sumner would make no pledges: he had never held, nor did he desire to hold, any political office.* He was deemed an idealist, and, as such, unsuited to the practical duties of a senatorial career. It was, at any rate, too long a step from his private student-life to the Senate-chamber of the United States.

But the sense of Massachusetts had been outraged by the recreant course of Mr. Webster; and the far-sighted saw that the aggressions of the slave-power must be squarely met. Mr. Sumner had shown himself an orator of no mean order, a statesman qualified to discuss constitutional questions from the highest stand-point, and, more than all, an invincible defender of the colored race. Accordingly, on the 24th day of April he was elected, for six years from the 4th of March following, as the successor of Mr.

---

* Mr. Sumner said in a conversation with James Redpath, written at the time, that committee after committee waited on him during the election, to get even verbal promises relative to tariff, and to "ease off on the slave-question;" but he uniformly declined to satisfy them, saying that the office must seek him, and that he would not walk across the room to secure the election.

Webster to the senatorial chair; having had, on the twenty-fifth and last ballot in the House, a hundred and ninety-three votes, the exact number necessary to a choice. It is said that the turning vote was cast by the late Capt. Israel Haynes of Sudbury, a life-long Democrat, who voted for Mr. Sumner only on the day of his election, and then simply, as he affirmed, "on principle, and because he believed him to be the better man." The votes used at this twenty-fifth ballot were preserved by the Hon. Otis Clapp, who, in April, 1873, presented them to the New-England Historic-Genealogical Society, where they now remain.

Although some thought this triumph of the progressive party would carry with it serious disaster to the Union, "The Evening Transcript" very sensibly remarked: —

"We are not prepared to proclaim the *country ruined* in consequence of this event. Mr. Sumner is a forcible and eloquent speaker, an apt scholar, a man of superior abilities, of polished address, and extensive acquaintance with the men and events of his times; and he may become a statesman of mark in the political arena. He will probably act and work with the Whig party on all questions but one, — a vital and momentous one, it is true, as he will find when he gets to Washington. Massachusetts might have seated in the Senate a man far more objectionable than Charles Sumner. *Vive la République!*"

The world swung forward by this victory; and unusual demonstrations signalized the joy of the triumphant party. On the next day Mr. Sumner frankly avowed his indebtedness for his success to Henry Wilson.

CRAGIE HOUSE, CAMBRIDGE, April 25, 1851.

MY DEAR WILSON,—I have this moment read your remarks of last night, which I think peculiarly happy. You touched the right chord. I hope not to seem cold or churlish in thus withdrawing from all the public manifestations of triumph to which our friends are prompted. In doing so, I follow the line of reserve which you know I have kept to throughout the contest; and my best judgment at this moment satisfies me that I am right. You, who have seen me familiarly and daily from the beginning to the end, will understand me, and, if need be, can satisfy those who, taking counsel of their exultation, would have me mingle in the display. But I shrink from imposing any thing more upon you. To your ability, energy, determination, and fidelity, our cause owes its present success. For weal or woe, you must take the responsibility of having placed me in the Senate of the United States. I am prompted also to add, that, while you have done all this, I have never heard from you a single suggestion of a selfish character, looking in any way to any good to yourself: your labors have been as disinterested as they have been effective. This consideration increases my personal esteem and gratitude. I trust that you will see that Mr. B.'s resolves are passed at once *as they are,* and the bill as soon as possible. Delay will be the tactics of the enemy.

Sincerely yours,

CHARLES SUMNER.

THE HON. HENRY WILSON.

In a letter to me dated Amesbury, 3d month. 1874, John G. Whittier, in reference to Mr. Sumner's election, says, " I am inclined to believe that I was the first to suggest to him, in the summer of 1850, the possibility of his election to the Senate. He thought it impracticable, and stated with emphasis, that he desired no office, that his plans of life did not contemplate any thing of the kind, and that he greatly doubted his natural fitness for political life. He made no pledges nor explanations of any kind to insure his election when it took place. His statement in the exordium of his speech against the Fugitive-Slave Law is, to my knowledge, true to the letter."

In his letter of acceptance Mr. Sumner thus indicates the broad national policy which he intended to pursue : —

" Acknowledging the right of my country to the service of her sons wherever she chooses to place them, and with a heart full of gratitude that a sacred cause has been permitted to triumph through me, I now accept the post as senator.

" I accept it as the servant of Massachusetts; mindful of the sentiments uttered by her successive legislatures, of the genius which inspires her history, and of the men, her perpetual pride and ornament, who breathed into her that breath of liberty which early made her an example to her sister States. In such a service, the way, though new to my footsteps, will be illumined by lights which cannot be missed.

"I accept it as a servant of the Union; bound to study and maintain, with equal patriotic care, the interests of all parts of our country; to discountenance every effort to loosen any of those ties by which our fellowship of States is held in fraternal company; and to oppose all *sectionalism*, whether it appears in unconstitutional efforts by the North to carry so great a boon as freedom into the slave States, or in unconstitutional efforts by the South (aided by Northern allies) to carry the *sectional* evil of slavery into the free States, or in whatsoever efforts it may make to extend the *sectional* domination of slavery over the national government. With me the Union is twice blessed: first, as the powerful guardian of the repose and happiness of thirty-one sovereign States clasped by the endearing name of 'country;' and next, as the model and beginning of that all-embracing federation of States, by which unity, peace, and concord will finally be organized among the nations. Nor do I believe it possible, whatever may be the delusion of the hour, that any part thereof can be permanently lost from its well-compacted bulk. *E Pluribus Unum* is stamped upon the national coin, the national territory, and the national heart. Though composed of many parts united into one, the Union is separable only by a crash which shall destroy the whole."

His closing words are as follows: —

"Let me borrow, in conclusion, the language of another: 'I see my duty, — that of standing up for the liberties of my

country; and, whatever difficulties and discouragements lie in
my way, I dare not shrink from it; and I rely on that Being
who has not left us the choice of duties, that, whilst I shall
conscientiously discharge mine, I shall not finally lose my
reward.' These are the words of Washington, uttered in the
early darkness of the American Revolution. The rule of duty
is the same for the lowly and the great; and I hope it may not
seem presumptuous in one so humble as myself to adopt his
determination, and to avow his confidence.

    " I have the honor to be, fellow-citizens,

        " With sincere regard,

           " Your faithful friend and servant,

                " CHARLES SUMNER.
"BOSTON, May 14, 1851."

Massachusetts had found her man. He had now
arrived at that period which Dante calls

    "Mezzo del cammin di nostra vita,"

and was in person tall, dignified, and commanding.
His frame was solid and compact; his features were
strongly marked; and his clear, dark eye, deeply set
beneath his heavy brow and massive forehead, shone
when he was engaged in speaking, with peculiar
brilliancy. His voice was strong and musical, his
gesticulation unconstrained and graceful. Nature
had set on him her imperial seal of greatness, which
a generous and untiring culture had developed.
Few men of the day possessed a broader scholarship,

and none a loftier patriotism, or a profounder sympathy for the sufferings of humanity. In the
strength and beauty of manhood, he came to public
office as a splendid representative of the advanced
ideas of his time. A battle was before him, — hail-
stones and coals of fire; but well could he affirm, —

> " What stronger breastplate than a heart untainted?
> Thrice is he armed who hath his quarrel just;
> And he but naked, though locked up in steel,
> Whose conscience with unjustice is corrupted."

Though unpractised in debate, he had studied his
subject *à profond :* his integrity was unimpeachable,
his armor closely welded, and his position the impregnable rock of truth. What, then, had he to
fear?

The arrest of Thomas Sims as a fugitive slave, in
Boston, April 3 of this year, and his mock trial, with
the decision of the court remanding him to slavery,
threw the city into an intense excitement. On
receiving Theodore Parker's Fast-Day sermon, which
in no measured terms rebuked this outrage, Mr.
Sumner addressed to him the following letter : —

COURT STREET, BOSTON, April 19, 1851.

May you live a thousand years, always preaching the
truth of Fast Day! That sermon is a noble effort. It stirred
me to the bottom of my heart, at times softening me almost to

7

tears, and then again filling me with rage. I wish it could be read everywhere throughout the land. . . .

I have had no confidence from the beginning, as I believe you know, in our courts. I was persuaded that with solemn form they would sanction the great enormity: therefore I am not disappointed. My appeal is to the people; and my hope is to create in Massachusetts such a public opinion as will render the law a dead-letter. It is in vain to expect its repeal by Congress till the slave-power is overthrown.

It is, however, with a rare *dementia* that this power has staked itself on a position which is so offensive, and which cannot for any length of time be tenable. In enacting that law, it has given to the free States a sphere of discussion which they would otherwise have missed. No other form of the slavery question, not even the Wilmot Proviso, would have afforded equal advantages.

Very truly yours,

CHARLES SUMNER.

In another letter written to Mr. Parker, Mr. Sumner declares his disinclination to office, and that his election is to be regarded not by any means as a reward, but as a call to duty and to labor for the welfare of his country: —

COURT STREET, July 9, 1851.

Your last speech in "The Liberator" I have read with the interest and instruction with which I read all that you say; but pardon me if I criticise one point.

You speak of me as having "an early reward for good deeds." This language remainds me of "The Atlas," which did not see what I had done "to be thus rewarded."

Now, I am not conscious of doing any thing to deserve "reward," nor am I conscious of receiving any "reward." The office recently conferred upon me, and to which you probably refer, I regard as any thing but a reward. In my view, it is an imposition of new duties and labors, in a field which I never selected, and to which I do not in the least incline. . .

Ever yours,

CHARLES SUMNER.

Mr. Sumner entered the United-States Senate on Monday, the first day of December, 1851; and, in the absence of John Davis, Gen. Lewis Cass rose, and said, "I have been requested to present the credentials of Charles Sumner, a senator elect from the State of Massachusetts." The credentials having been read, William R. King of Alabama administered the oath of office. On the same day Henry Clay, after a brief speech, made his final retirement from that hall in which his eloquent voice had so many times been heard in the defence of constitutional liberty. In his own language, used a few years previously, he departed as "a wounded stag, pursued by the hunters on a long chase, scarred by their spears, and worried by their wounds, who had at last escaped to drag his mutilated body to his lair, and lie down and die." Mr. Sumner occupied the seat that had just been vacated by Jefferson Davis, and formerly occupied by John C. Calhoun, and which was thus associated with the most daring arrogance and effrontery of the slaveholding power. His rooms at Gardner's, on New-York Avenue, were soon stored with books from the Congressional Library, and honored by visits from Mr. Crampton, the British minister, Don Calderon de la Barca, minister from Spain, and other foreign celebrities, in whose society he received instruction and delight. "I remember, that winter," says an agreeable writer, "meeting Messrs. Chase and Sumner at a dinner-party given by Mr. Crampton; and, as they entered the parlor together, I was struck by their manlike appearance, as I was subsequently charmed by their dinner-table chat."

By the Southern members the anti-slavery agitator who had succeeded Daniel Webster was viewed with supercilious contempt: he was placed at the foot of the unimportant committees on revolutionary claims and on roads and canals; and no one then discerned in him the grand and fearless leader of a slowly-rising power that was to change the political destiny of the nation, and establish, over the ruins of a tyrannous and cruel servile system, the freedom of the slave from shore to shore. Few now can fully understand the ordeal of fire then opening before him. With the exception of the dauntless John P. Hale and the indomitable Joshua R. Giddings, he stood almost alone in front of the gigantic force combined for the support of slavery; and, as the latter said, it took "more courage to stand up in one's seat in Congress and say the right thing, than to walk up to the cannon's mouth." This courage Mr. Sumner had. On Wednesday, Jan. 10, he delivered his maiden speech on a resolution introduced by Senator H. S. Foote, tendering a welcome to the exiled patriot, Gov. Louis Kossuth, during which he used the celebrated expression, " equality before the law."

" I would join in this welcome, not merely because it is essential to complete and crown the work of the last Congress. but because our guest deserves it at our hands. The distinction is great, I know; but it is not so great as his deserts. He deserves it as the early, constant, and incorruptible champion of the liberal cause in Hungary. who, yet while young. with unconscious power girded himself for the contest, and, by a series of masterly labors. with voice and pen. in parliamentary debates. and in the discussions of the press, breathed into his country the breath of life. He deserves it by the great principles of true democracy which he caused to be recognized, — representation of the people without distinction of rank or birth. and *equality before the law.* He deserves it by the trials he has undergone in prison and in exile. He deserves it by the precious truth, which he now so eloquently proclaims, of the fraternity of nations."

The speaker also beautifully said, "Such a character, thus grandly historic, a living Wallace, a living Tell, I had almost said a living Washington, deserves our homage. Nor am I tempted to ask if there be any precedent for the resolution now under consideration. There is a time for all things; and the time has come for us to make precedent in harmony with his unprecedented career. The occasion is fit: the hero is near: let us speak our welcome. It is true, that, unlike Lafayette, he has never directly served our country; but I cannot admit that on this account he is less worthy. Like Lafayette, he has done penance in an Austrian dungeon: like Lafayette, he has served the cause of freedom; and whosoever serves this cause, wheresoever he may be, in whatever land, is entitled, according to his works, to the gratitude of every true American bosom, of every true lover of mankind."

For this eloquent speech Mr. Sumner received the hearty commendation of Rufus Choate and other gentlemen. In his next speech (on the Iowa Railroad Bill, taken up in the senate Jan. 27 and afterwards) occurs this elegant passage: " By roads, religion and knowledge are diffused; intercourse of all kinds is promoted; the producer, the manufac-

turer, and the consumer are all brought nearer
together; commerce is quickened; markets are
opened; property, wherever touched by these lines,
is changed as by a magic rod into new values; and
the great current of travel, like that stream of classic
fable, or one of the rivers of our own California,
hurries in a channel of golden sand. The roads,
together with the laws, of ancient Rome, are now
better remembered than her victories. The Flamin-
ian and Appian Ways, once trod by returning pro-
consuls and tributary kings, still remain as beneficent
representatives of her departed grandeur. Under
God, the road and the schoolmaster are the two
chief agents of human improvement. The education begun by the schoolmaster is expanded, liberal-
ized, and completed by intercourse with the world;
and this intercourse finds new opportunities and inducements in every road that is built. . . . The true
Golden Age is before us, not behind us; and one of
its tokens will be the completion of those long ways,
by which villages, towns, counties, states, provinces,
nations, are all to be associated and knit together in
a fellowship that can never be broken."

" Read my speech," says he in a letter to Theodore
Parker, dated Senate-Chamber, Feb. 6, 1852, " on
Lands. The Whig press is aroused; but I challenge

it. I have the satisfaction of knowing that my argument has been received as original and unanswerable. The attack of 'The Advertiser' attests its importance. I shall always be glad to hear from you, and shall value your counsels.

" Ever yours,

CHARLES SUMNER."

On the 8th of March he made a brief speech on cheap ocean-postage, which he declared would be a bond of peace among the nations of the earth, and which would extend peace and good-will among men.

On the 14th of May following he submitted an able argument, on the pardoning-power, to President Fillmore; and on the 26th of the same month he presented a memorial from the Society of Friends (a body noted for their active sympathy for the suffering of the colored race) against the Fugitive-Slave Bill, respecting which the Southern members steadily endeavored to prevent discussion. He succeeded, however, in gaining the floor to offer the following remarks, in which his future course regarding slavery was clearly indicated: —

" I desire simply to say, that I shall deem it my duty on some proper occasion hereafter to express myself at length on the matter to which it relates. Thus far, during this session, I have forborne. With the exception of an able speech from my colleague (Mr. Davis), the discussion of this all-absorbing question has been mainly left with senators from another quarter of the country, by whose mutual difference it has been complicated, and between whom I have not cared to interfere. But there is a time for all things. Justice, also, requires that both sides should be heard; and I trust not to expect too much when at some fit moment I bespeak the clear and candid attention of the Senate, while I undertake to set forth frankly and fully, and with entire respect for this body, convictions deeply cherished in my own State, though disregarded here, to which I am bound by every sentiment of the heart, by every fibre of my being, by all my devotion to country, by my love of God and man. But upon these I do not now enter. Suffice it for the present to say, that when I shall undertake that service, I believe I shall utter nothing which, in any just sense can be called *sectional*, unless the constitution is *sectional*, and unless the sentiments of the fathers were *sectional*. It is my happiness to believe, and my hope to be able to show, that, according to the true spirit of the constitution, and according to the sentiments of the fathers, FREEDOM, and not *slavery*, is NATIONAL; while SLAVERY, and not *freedom*, is SECTIONAL. In duty to the petitioners, and with the hope of promoting their prayer, I move the reference of their petition to the Committee on the Judiciary.''

On the 9th of August he paid a fitting tribute to Robert Rantoul, jun., characterizing him as ''a reformative conservative, and a conservative reformer.''

''As a debater,'' said Mr. Sumner, ''he rarely met

his peer. Fluent, earnest, rapid, sharp, incisive, his words came forth like a flashing cimeter. Few could stand against him. He always understood his subject; and then, clear, logical, and determined, seeing his point before him, pressed forward with unrelenting power."

To the complaint of some of his supporters, that he too long delayed the discussion of the mighty question of the day, he replied, that his time was occupied in making himself acquainted with the business coming before the Senate; but at the proper moment he should not fail to fulfil his duty as a representative of the anti-slavery sentiment of the nation. That moment on the twenty-sixth day of August came. By adroitly introducing an amendment that the Fugitive-Slave Bill should be repealed, on Mr. Hunter's amendment to the Civil and Diplomatic Appropriation Bill, then under consideration, he at length succeeded in gaining the unwilling ear of the Senate.

Taking for his theme, "Freedom National, and Slavery Sectional," he went into the question with gigantic force, unfolding the principles of liberty as if the whole heart of the North were throbbing in his breast alone, and nerving his arm to bring the great "Northern hammer" down with terrific blows upon the iniquitous institution of the South. He argued that slavery and the Fugitive-Slave Bill had no support whatever under the constitution, which does not recognize the right of property in man; that it was contrary to the wishes of the framers of that instrument, to the acts of the early Congress, to the decisions of the courts, to the spirit of the Church, of the colleges, of literature, to the right of trial by jury, to the natural law of man, and to the progress of the nation. "It was," remarks a vigorous writer, "a perfect land-slide of history and argument, an avalanche under which the opposing party were logically buried; and it has been a magazine from which catapults have been taken to beat down their fortresses."

Referring to himself, in his exordium, he says, —

"Sir, I have never been a politician. The slave of principles, I call no party master. By sentiment, education, and conviction, a friend of human rights in their utmost expansion, I have ever most sincerely embraced the democratic idea; not, indeed, as represented or professed by any party, but according to its real significance, as transfigured in the Declaration of Independence and in the inspiration of Christianity. In this idea I saw no narrow advantages merely for individuals or classes, but the sovereignty of the people, and the greatest happiness of all secured by equal laws. Amidst the vicissitudes of public affairs, I trust always to hold fast to this idea, and to. any political party which truly embraces it.

"Party does not constrain me; nor is my independence lessened by any relations to the office which gives me a title to be heard on this floor. And here, sir, I may speak proudly. By no effort, by no desire, of my own, I find myself a senator of the United States. Never before have I held public office of any kind. With the ample opportunities of private life I was content. No tombstone for me could bear a fairer inscription than this: 'Here lies one who, without the honors or emoluments of public station, did something for his fellow-man.' From such simple aspirations I was taken away by the free choice of my native Commonwealth, and placed in this responsible post of duty, without personal obligation of any kind beyond what was implied in my life and published words. The earnest friends by whose confidence I was first designated asked nothing from me, and, throughout the long conflict which ended in my election, rejoiced in the position which I most carefully guarded. To all my language was uniform, that I did not desire to be brought forward; that I would do nothing to promote the result; that I had no pledges or promises to offer; that the office should seek me, and not I the office; and that it should find me in all respects an independent man, bound to no party and to no human being, but only, according to my best judgment, to act for the good of all. Again, sir, I speak with pride, both for myself and others, when I add that these avowals found a sympathizing response. In this spirit I have come here; and in this spirit I shall speak to-day.

"Rejoicing in my independence, and claiming nothing from party ties, I throw myself upon the candor and magnanimity of the Senate. I now ask your attention; but I trust not to abuse it. I may speak strongly; for I shall speak openly, and from the strength of my convictions. I may speak warmly;

for I shall speak from the heart. But in no event can I forget the amenities which belong to debate, and which especially become this body. Slavery I must condemn with my whole soul; but here I need only borrow the language of slaveholders themselves; nor would it accord with my habits or my sense of justice to exhibit them as the impersonation of the institution (Jefferson calls it the 'enormity') which they cherish. Of them I do not speak; but without fear and without favor, as without impeachment of any person, I assail this wrong. Again, sir, I may err; but it will be with the fathers. I plant myself on the ancient ways of the Republic; with its grandest names, its surest landmarks, and all its original altar-fires about me."

. On the freedom of speech he makes this bold assertion, —

"To sustain slavery, it is now proposed to trample on *free speech*. In any country this would be grievous; but here, where the constitution expressly provides against abridging freedom of speech, it is a special outrage. In vain do we condemn the despotisms of Europe, while we borrow the rigors with which they repress liberty, and guard their own uncertain power. For myself, in no factious spirit, but solemnly, and in loyalty to the constitution, as a senator of Massachusetts, I protest against this wrong. On slavery, as on every other subject, I claim the right to be heard. That right I cannot, I will not, abandon. 'Give me the liberty to know, to utter, and to argue freely, above all liberties:' these are the glowing words which flashed from the soul of John Milton, in his struggles with English tyranny. With equal fervor they should be echoed now by every American not already a slave.

"But, sir, this effort is impotent as tyrannical. The convictions of the heart cannot be repressed. The utterances of conscience must be heard. They break forth with irrepressible might. As well attempt to check the tides of ocean, the currents of the Mississippi, or the rushing waters of Niagara. The discussion of slavery will proceed wherever two or three are gathered together, — by the fireside, on the highway, at the public meeting, in the church. The movement against slavery is from the Everlasting Arm. Even now it is gathering its forces, soon to be confessed everywhere. It may not yet be felt in the high places of office and power; but all who can put their ears humbly to the ground will hear and comprehend its incessant and advancing tread."

His main proposition he thus announces, —

"The relations of the Government of the United States (I speak of the national government) to slavery, though plain and obvious, are constantly misunderstood. A popular belief at this moment makes slavery a national institution, and, of course, renders its support a national duty. The extravagance of this error can hardly be surpassed. An institution which our fathers most carefully omitted to name in the constitution; which, according to the debates in the convention, they refused to cover with any 'sanction;' and which, at the original organization of the government, was merely sectional, existing nowhere on the national territory, — is now, above all other things, emblazoned as national. Its supporters plume themselves as national. The old political parties, while upholding it, claim to be national. A national Whig is simply a slavery Whig; and a national Democrat is simply a slavery Democrat, — in contradistinction to all who regard slavery as a sectional institu-

tion, within the exclusive control of the States, and with which
the nation has nothing to do. As slavery assumes to be national, so, by an equally strange perversion, freedom is degraded
to be sectional; and all who uphold it under the national
constitution share the same epithet. The honest efforts to
secure its blessings everywhere within the jurisdiction of Congress are scouted as sectional; and this cause which the founders of our national government had so much at heart is
called "sectionalism." These terms, now belonging to the com-
monplaces of political speech, are adopted and misapplied by
most persons without reflection. But herein is the power of
slavery. According to a curious tradition of the French language, Louis XIV., the Grand Monarch, by an accidental error
of speech, among supple courtiers, changed the gender of a
noun. But slavery has done more than this: it has changed word
for word. It has taught many to say "national" instead of
"sectional," and "sectional" instead of "national." Slavery
national! Sir, this is all a mistake and absurdity, fit to take a
place in some new collection of vulgar errors by some other Sir
Thomas Browne, with the ancient but exploded stories that
the toad has a stone in its head, and that ostriches digest iron.
According to the true spirit of the constitution, and the sentiments of the fathers, slavery and not freedom is sectional,
while freedom and not slavery is national. On this unanswerable proposition I take my stand."

To the free spirit of our literature he makes this
reference : —

"The literature of the land, such as then existed, agreed
with the nation, the church, and the college. Franklin, in the
last literary labor of his life; Jefferson, in his 'Notes on Vir-

ginia;' Barlow, in his measured verse; Rush, in a work which
inspired the praise of Clarkson; the ingenious author of 'The
Algerine Captive' (the earliest American novel, and, though
now but little known, one of the earliest American books
republished in London), were all moved by the contemplation
of slavery. 'If our fellow-citizens of the Southern States are
deaf to the pleadings of nature,' the latter exclaims in his
work, 'I will conjure them, for the sake of consistency, to cease
to deprive their fellow-creatures of freedom, which their
writers, their orators, representatives, and senators, and even
their constitution of government, have declared to be the
inalienable birthright of man.'"

In an admirable review of the course of argument, he says, —

"And now, sir, let us review the field over which we have
passed. We have seen that any compromise, finally closing
the discussion of slavery under the constitution, is tyrannical,
absurd, and impotent; that, as slavery can exist only by virtue
of positive law, and as it has no such positive support in the constitution, it cannot exist within the national jurisdiction; that
the constitution nowhere recognizes property in man; and that,
according to its true interpretation, freedom and not slavery is
national, while slavery and not freedom is sectional; that in
this spirit the national government was first organized under
Washington, himself an abolitionist, surrounded by abolitionists, while the whole country, by its church, its colleges, its
literature, and all its best voices, was united against slavery,
and the national flag at that time nowhere within the national
territory covered a single slave; still further, that the national

government is a government of delegated powers; and, as among these there is no power to support slavery, this institution cannot be national, nor can Congress in any way legislate in its behalf; and, finally, that the establishment of this principle is the true way of peace and safety for the republic. Considering next the provision for the surrender of fugitives from labor, we have seen that it was not one of the original compromises of the constitution; that it was introduced tardily and with hesitation, and adopted with little discussion, and then and for a long period after was regarded with comparative indifference; that the recent Slave Act, though many times unconstitutional, is especially so on two grounds, — *first* as a usurpation by Congress of powers not granted by the constitution, and an infraction of rights secured to the States; and *secondly* as a denial of trial by jury in a question of personal liberty and a suit at common law; that its glaring unconstitutionality finds a prototype in the British Stamp Act, which our fathers refused to obey as unconstitutional on two parallel grounds, — *first* because it was a usurpation by parliament of powers not belonging to it under the British constitution, and an infraction of rights belonging to the colonies; and *secondly* because it was a denial of trial by jury in certain cases of property; that, as liberty is far above property, so is the outrage perpetrated by the American Congress far above that perpetrated by the British Parliament; and, finally, that the Slave Act has not that support in the public sentiment of the States where it is to be executed, which is the life of all law, and which prudence and the precept of Washington require."

He closes his great speech by this effective peroration : —

" Finally, sir, for the sake of peace and tranquillity, cease to shock the public conscience; for the sake of the constitution, cease to exercise a power which is nowhere granted, and which violates inviolable rights expressly secured. Leave this question where it was left by our fathers at the formation of our national government, — in the absolute control of the States, the appointed guardians of personal liberty. Repeal this enactment. Let its terrors no longer rage through the land. Mindful of the lowly whom it pursues, mindful of the good men perplexed by its requirements, in the name of charity, in the name of the constitution, repeal this enactment totally and without delay. Be inspired by the example of Washington. Be admonished by those words of Oriental piety — ' Beware of the groans of the wounded souls. Oppress not to the utmost a single heart; for a solitary sigh has power to overset a whole world.' "

In reply to a letter from Dr. Horatio Stebbins thanking him for this speech, Mr. Sumner thus wrote from Newport, R.I., Oct. 12, 1852: —

MY DEAR SIR, — I cannot receive the overflowing sympathy of your letter without response. . . . I went to the Senate determined to do my duty, but in my own way. Anxious for the cause, having it always in mind, I knew that I could not fail in loyalty, though I might err in judgment. All my instincts prompted delay. But meanwhile I was taunted and attacked at home. Had I been less conscious of the rectitude of my course, I might have sunk under these words; but I persevered in my own way.

As I delivered the part to which you refer, I remember well

the intent looks of the Senate, and particularly of Mr. King [president *pro tem* of the senate]. It was already dinner-time, but all were silent and attentive; and Hale [John P. Hale, of N.H.] tells me that Mr. Underwood of Kentucky, by his side, was in tears.

From many leading Southern men I have received the strongest expressions of interest awakened in our cause, and a confession that they did not know before the strength of the argument on our side. Polk of Tennessee said to me, "If you should make that speech in Tennessee you would compel me to emancipate my niggers." But enough of this. I have been tempted to it by the generosity of your letter.

Thankfully and truly yours,

CHARLES SUMNER.

CHAPTER X.

> " Still groan the suffering millions in their chains;
> Still is the arm of the oppressor strong;
> Still Liberty doth bleed at all her veins;
> And few are they who side not with the wrong:
> Consider, then, your work as just begun,
> Until the last decisive act be done."
>
> WILLIAM LLOYD GARRISON.

" If any man thinks that the interest of these nations and the interest of Christianity are two separate and distinct things, I wish my soul may never enter into his secret." —OLIVER CROMWELL.

M R. SUMNER steadily availed himself of every opportunity to alleviate human suffering, and to promote the cause of freedom. As the needle to the pole, his eye turned to the tear

164

of sorrow.   On the twenty-fifth day of August, 1852, he made a touching appeal in the Senate on behalf of the widow of the accomplished landscape-gardener Andrew Jackson Downing, who was lost in his noble efforts to save the passengers of the ill-fated steamer " Henry Clay," burned on the Hudson River on the twenty-eighth day of the month preceding. He closed his remarks by this just tribute to the memory of the lamented artist: " Few men in the public service have vindicated a title to regard above Mr. Downing. At the age of thirty-seven he has passed away, ' dead ere his prime,' like Lycidas, also, ' stretched on a watery bier,' leaving behind a reputation above that of any other citizen in the beautiful department of art to which he was devoted. His labors and his example cannot be forgotten. I know of no man among us, in any sphere of life, so young as he was at his death, who has been able to perform services of such true, simple, and lasting beneficence. By his wide and active superintendence of rural improvements, by his labors of the pen, and by the various exercise of his genius, he has contributed essentially to the sum of human happiness. And now, sir, by practical services here in Washington, rendered at the call of his country, he has earned, it seems to me, this small appropriation, not as a charity to this desolate widow, but as a compensation for labor done. I hope the amendment will be agreed to."

At the State Convention of the Free-soil party held in Lowell on the 15th of September following, Mr. Sumner was received with demonstrations of the heartiest enthusiasm, and delivered a thrilling speech on the necessity and practicability of that organization. Capt. Drayton, the "hero of 'The Pearl,'" who, through the exertions of Mr. Sumner, had just been liberated from his long imprisonment, sat upon the platform. In the course of his remarks, the senator said, amidst tremendous cheering, —

"The rising public opinion against slavery cannot now flow in the old political channels. It is strangled, clogged, and dammed back. But, if not *through* the old parties, then *over* the old parties, this irresistible current *shall* find its way. It cannot be permanently stopped. If the old parties will not become its organ, they must become its victim. The party of freedom will certainly prevail. It may be by entering into and possessing one of the old parties, filling it with our strong life; or it may be by drawing from both to itself the good and true, who are unwilling to continue members of any political combination when it ceases to represent their convictions. But in one way or the other, its ultimate triumph is sure: of this let no man doubt."

Closing, he used these hopeful and prophetic words: —

" With such a cause and such candidates, let no man be disheartened. The tempest may blow; but ours is a life-boat, which cannot be harmed by wind or wave. The genius of Liberty sits at the helm. I hear her voice of cheer saying, ' Whoso sails with me comes to shore.' "

He sat down amidst prolonged shouts of applause; and the people of this industrial city still speak with admiration of the splendor of his eloquence on that occasion.

In a brief speech in the Senate Feb. 23, 1853, in favor of appointing civil instead of military superintendence of our armories, he closed, contrary to his usual custom, with a humorous quotation which gave much point to his fine argument.

" The manufacture of arms," said he, " is a mechanical pursuit; and for myself, I can see no reason why it should not be placed in charge of one bred to the business. Among the intelligent mechanics of Massachusetts, there are many fully fit to be at the head of the arsenal at Springfield; but all these by the existing law are austerely excluded from any such trust. The idea which has fallen from so many senators, that the superintendent of an armory ought to be a military man, that a military man only is competent, or even that a military man is more competent than a civilian, seems to me as illogical as the jocular fallacy of Dr. Johnson, that 'He who drives fat oxen must himself be fat.'"

Mr. Sumner was an admirable correspondent. He wrote his letters with rapidity, ease, and elegance. Sometimes he received as many as fifty communications in a day; and his replies, however brief, invariably contain some strong and elevating sentiment; as, for example, in a short letter to a Rhode-Island committee, dated March 26, 1853, he says, —

"It becomes all good citizens to unite in upholding freedom; nor should any one believe that his single vote may not exert an influence in the struggle." So, again, in a letter to Lewis Tappan, dated Boston, May 17, 1853, encouraging the establishment of a German newspaper at Washington, he writes, —

" The German emigrant who is not against slavery here leads us to doubt the sincerity of his opposition to the tyranny he has left behind in his native land." Also in a letter to the mayor of Boston, dated Boston, July 1, 1853, he presents this sentiment in respect to the Pacific Railroad, —

" Traversing a whole continent, and binding together two oceans, this mighty thoroughfare, when completed, will mark an epoch of human progress second only to that of our Declaration of Independence. May the day soon come ! "

His view of the secrecy of proceedings of the Senate may be seen from the following extract from his speech in the debate on that question, April 6, 1853 : " The general rule will be publicity. The executive sessions with closed doors, shrouded from the public gaze and from public criticism, constitute an exceptional part of our system, too much in harmony with the proceedings of other governments less liberal in character. The genius of our institutions requires publicity. The ancient Roman who bade his architect so to construct his house that his guests and all that he did could be seen by the world is a fit model for the American people."

Mr. Sumner was elected by the town of Marshfield to the convention for the revision of the constitution of the State, which assembled in the State House, Boston, on the fourth day of May, 1853. In this body, embracing many of the ablest men of the State, he took an active part, and made several speeches evincing a profound knowledge of constitutional law, as well as of our political history. In the debate on the powers of the State over the militia, on the 21st and 22d of June, he said, in opposition to conservative opinions, —

" Massachusetts may proudly declare, that, in her

own volunteer military companies, marshalled under her own local laws, there shall be no distinction of color or race."

In his speech, July 7, on the basis of the representative system, he ably advocated that arrangement which has since been adopted. "I cannot doubt," said he, " that the district-system, as it is generally called, whereby the representative power will be distributed in just proportion, according to the Rule of Three, among the voters of the Commonwealth, is the true system, destined at no distant day to prevail; and gladly would I see this convention hasten the day by presenting it to the people for adoption in the organic law."

As chairman of the committee on the Bill of Rights, he addressed the convention on the 25th of July, and presented a very lucid exposition of the origin and nature of these instruments, which he thus concludes : —

" The preamble, wherein the body politic is founded on the fiction of the social compact, was doubtless inspired by the writings of Sidney and Locke, and by the English discussions at the period of the revolution of 1688, when this questionable theory did good service in response to the assumptions of Filmer, and as a shield against arbitrary power. Of the different provisions in the Bill of

Rights, some are in the very words of Magna Charta : others are derived from the ancient common law, the Petition of Right, and the Bill of Rights of 1688, while no less than sixteen may be found substantially in the Virginia Bill of Rights ; but these again are in great part derived from earlier fountains.

"And now, sir, you have before you for revision and amendment, this early work of our fathers. I do not stop to consider its peculiar merits. With satisfaction I might point to special safeguards by which our rights have been protected against usurpations, whether executive, legislative, or judicial. With pride I might dwell on those words which banished slavery from our soil, and rendered the Declaration of Independence here with us a living letter. But the hour does not require or admit any such service. You have a practical duty which I seek to promote ; and I now take leave of the whole subject, with the simple remark, that a document proceeding from such a pen, drawn from such sources, with such an origin in all respects, speaking so early for human rights, and now for more than threescore years and ten a household word to the people of Massachusetts, should be touched by the convention only with extreme care."

An ardent admirer of the stern virtues, and of the heroism, of the Pilgrim Fathers, Mr. Sumner always referred to them with pleasure, as the grand leaders in the cause of civil and political freedom. In a speech at the festival held in Plymouth on the 1st of August, 1853, commemorating the embarkation of the fathers, he most eloquently eulogizes these invincible defenders of "a cherished principle" and "a lofty faith." In reference to its covert bearing on the prominent question of the day (for he could not then speak openly), he entitled this address a "Finger-point from Plymouth Rock." He concluded it in this eloquent and suggestive strain : —

"These outcasts, despised in their own day by the proud and great, are the men whom we have met in this goodly number to celebrate ; not for any victory of war, not for any triumph of discovery, science, learning, or eloquence ; not for worldly success of any kind. How poor are all these things by the side of that divine virtue which made them, amidst the reproach, the obloquy, and the hardness of the world, hold fast to freedom and truth ! Sir, if the honors of this day are not a mockery; if they do not expend themselves in selfish gratulation ; if they are a sincere homage to the character of the Pilgrims (and I cannot suppose otherwise), then is it well for us to be here. Standing on Plymouth Rock, at their great anniversary, we cannot fail to be elevated by their example. We see clearly what it has done for the world, and what it has done for their fame. No pusillanimous soul here to-day will declare their self-sacrifice, their deviation from received opinions, their unquenchable thirst for liberty, an error or illusion. From gushing multitudinous hearts we now thank these lowly men that they dared to be true and brave. Conformity or compromise might, perhaps, have purchased for them a profitable peace, but not peace of mind: it might have secured place and power, but not repose: it might have opened a present shelter, but not a home in history and in men's hearts till time shall be no more. All will confess the true grandeur of their example, while, in vindication of a cherished principle, they stood alone, against the madness of men, against the law of the land, against their king. Better be the despised pilgrim, a fugitive for freedom, than the halting politician forgetful of principle, ' with a senate at his heels.'

"Such, sir, is the voice from Plymouth Rock, as it salutes my ears. Others may not hear it; but to me it comes in tones I cannot mistake. I catch its noble words of cheer,—

'New occasions teach new duties: time makes ancient good uncouth:
They must upward still and onward, who would keep abreast of Truth.

Lo! before us gleam her camp-fires: we ourselves must pilgrims be,
Launch our "Mayflower," and steer boldly through the desperate
winter sea.' "

But a battle was impending. Encouraged by the
timid servility of the Northern Congressmen, the
advocates of slavery brought forward, in the famous
Nebraska and Kansas Bill, the iniquitous scheme of
abrogating the Missouri Compromise of 1820, prohibiting slavery, that State alone excepted, from all
the territory ceded by France to the United States,
lying north of 36° 30′ north latitude. After various
modifications, the bill came before the Senate on the
30th of January, 1854, when Stephen A. Douglas
made a violent attack on Mr. Chase of Ohio, and
Mr. Sumner, for having signed a document, entitled
" Shall Slavery be permitted in Nebraska?" and
appealing to the people to withstand the aggressions
of the propagandists of the servile institution. Mr.
Sumner replied to Mr. Douglas, characterizing the
measure before the Senate as " not only subversive
of an ancient landmark, but hostile to the peace, the
harmony, and the best interests of the country."
The debate went on, bringing front to front the stern
contestants, and assuming daily greater vehemence.
Mr. Everett and other New-England senators, John
P. Hale excepted, had yielded to the administra-

tion, favoring the abrogation of the Missouri Compromise, and to the plan of what was termed the "squatter sovereignty" of Mr. Douglas. Before the confederated host, two or three senators only stood up fearless and unterrified for the defence of freedom. This was a day that tried men's souls; and seldom has a public body witnessed a scene of more sublimity than when Charles Sumner rose, almost single-handed and alone, on the twenty-first day of February, to pronounce, in front of a solid mass of frowning and malignant senators, his masterly defence of human right. Undaunted by the fearful odds against him, or by the menace of assassination, he, like an old hero of Thermopylæ, sent home blow after blow into the dark columns bearing down upon him, and set up on that day a "landmark of freedom" that will serve to guide the coming generations. In clear, concise, and trenchant diction he depicted the wrongs of slavery, and with most persuasive tongue plead for the salvation to freedom of a range of virgin soil, of vast extent and of unsurpassed fertility. Never had he so exhibited the fire of liberty that burned within his breast: never had he so vindicated his title to the front rank of living orators. While the temporizing speeches even of an Everett are now forgotten, this "landmark," founded on the eternal principles of right, still lives; for *magna est veritas et prævelabit.*

After an eloquent introduction he said, —

"The question presented for your consideration is not surpassed in grandeur by any which has occurred in our national history since the Declaration of Independence. In every aspect it assumes gigantic proportions, whether we simply consider the extent of territory it concerns, or the public faith and national policy which it assails, or that higher question — that *question of questions*, as far above others as liberty is al.ove the common things of life — which it opens anew for judgment.

"It concerns an immense region, larger than the original thirteen States, vieing in extent with all the existing free States, stretching over prairie, field, and forest, interlaced by silver streams, skirted by protecting mountains, and constituting the heart of the North-American continent; only a little smaller, let me add, than three great European countries combined, — Italy, Spain, and France, — each of which in succession has dominated over the globe. This territory has already been likened on this floor to the Garden of God. The similitude is found, not merely in its present pure and virgin character, but in its actual geographical situation, occupying central spaces on this hemisphere, which in their general relations may well compare with that early Asiatic home. We are told that

'Southward through Eden went a river large;'

sc here a stream flows southward which is larger than the Euphrates. And here, too, amidst all the smiling products of nature lavished by the hand of God, is the lofty tree of Liberty, planted by our fathers, which, without exaggeration, or even imagination, may be likened to

' The tree of life,
High eminent, blooming ambrosial fruit
Of vegetable gold.'

"It is with regard to this territory that you are now called to
exercise the grandest function of the lawgiver, by establishing
those rules of polity which will determine its future character.
As the twig is bent the tree inclines; and the influences
impressed upon the early days of an empire, like those upon a
child, are of inconceivable importance to its future weal or
woe. The bill now before us proposes to organize and equip
two new territorial establishments, with governors, secretaries,
legislative councils, legislators, judges, marshals, and the
whole machinery of civil society. Such a measure, at any
time, would deserve the most careful attention; but at the
present moment it justly excites a peculiar interest, from the
effort made — on pretences unsustained by facts, in violation
of solemn covenant and of the early principles of our fathers
— to open this immense region to slavery."

He then proceeded to argue against the measure,
first in the "name of public faith, as an infraction
of solemn obligations, and secondly in the name of
freedom, as a departure from the anti-slavery policy
of our fathers."

The iniquity of the slave-system he characterized in
these strong words : —

"Slavery is the forcible subjection of one human being, in
person, labor, and property, to the will of another. In this
simple statement is involved its whole injustice. There is no
offence against religion, against morals, against humanity,

which may not, in the license of this institution, stalk 'unwhipt of justice.' For the husband and wife there is no marriage; for the mother there is no assurance that her infant child will not be ravished from her breast; for all who bear the name of 'slave' there is nothing that they can call their own. Without a father, without a mother, almost without a God, the slave has nothing but a master. It would be contrary to that rule of right which is ordained by God, if such a system, though mitigated often by a patriarchal kindness and by a plausible physical comfort, could be otherwise than pernicious in its influences. It is confessed that the master suffers not less than the slave. And this is not all: the whole social fabric is disorganized; labor loses its dignity; industry sickens; education finds no schools; and all the land of slavery is impoverished. And now, sir, when the conscience of mankind is at last aroused to these things; when throughout the civilized world a slave-dealer is a by-word and a reproach, — we, as a nation, are about to open a new market to the traffickers in flesh that haunt the shambles of the South."

In the course of his remarks he made this forcible appeal on behalf of the Missouri Compromise: —

"The Missouri compact, in its unperformed obligations to freedom, stands at this day as impregnable as the Louisiana purchase.

"I appeal to senators about me not to disturb it. I appeal to the senators from Virginia to keep inviolate the compact made in their behalf by James Barbour and Charles Fenton Mercer. I appeal to the senators from South Carolina to guard the work of John Gaillard and William Lowndes. I appeal to the senators from Maryland to uphold the compromise which elicited the constant support of Samuel Smith, and was first triumphantly pressed by the unsurpassed eloquence of Pinkney. I appeal to the senators from Delaware to maintain the landmark of freedom in the Territory of Louisiana, early espoused by Louis McLane. I appeal to the senators from Kentucky not to repudiate the pledges of Henry Clay. I appeal to the senators from Alabama not to break the agreement sanctioned by the earliest votes in the Senate of their late most cherished fellow-citizen William Rufus King. Sir, I have heard of an honor that felt a stain like a wound. If there be any such in this chamber, — as surely there is, — it will hesitate to take upon itself the stain of this transaction."

In respect to the future of his cause he used this bold, prophetic language : —

"I am not blind to the adverse signs; but this I see clearly: amidst all seeming discouragements, the great omens are with us. Art, literature, poetry, religion, every thing which elevates man, — all are on our side. The plough, the steam-engine, the railroad, the telegraph, the book, every human improvement, every generous word anywhere, every true pulsation of every heart which is not a mere muscle and nothing else, gives new encouragement to the warfare with slavery. The discussion will proceed. The devices of party can no longer stave it off. The subterfuges of the politician cannot escape it. The tricks of the office-seeker cannot dodge it. Wherever an election occurs, there this question will arise. Wherever men come together to speak of public affairs, there again will it be. No political Joshua now, with miraculous power, can stop the sun in his course through the heavens. It is even now rejoicing, like a strong man, to run its race, and will yet send its beams into the most distant plantations, — ay, sir, and melt the chains of every slave."

The grandeur of his peroration well accords with the sublimity of his theme : —

"The North and the South, sir, as I fondly trust, amidst all differences, will ever have a hand and heart for each other; and, believing in the sure prevalence of almighty truth, I confidently look forward to the good time when both will unite, according to the sentiments of the fathers and the true spirit of the constitution, in declaring freedom and not slavery *national*, to the end that the flag of the Republic, wherever it floats, on sea or land, within the *national* jurisdiction, may not cover a single slave. Then will be achieved that Union contemplated at the beginning, against which the storms of faction and the assaults of foreign power shall beat in vain, as upon the Rock of Ages; and LIBERTY, seeking a firm foothold, WILL HAVE AT LAST WHEREON TO STAND AND MOVE THE WORLD."

This speech was read by millions. It sunk deeply into the heart of the nation. It was the Sumter shot, that roused anew the spirit of freedom. It met with bitterest opposition. It stirred the embers of that fire that was to try and purify — as gold is tried and purified — the nation. "I am unused to flatter any one, least of all one whom I love and honor," said John G. Whittier in a letter to Mr. Sumner;

"but I must say in all sincerity that there is no orator or statesman living in this country or in Europe, whose fame is so great as not to derive additional lustre from such a speech. It will live the full life of American history." Prof. C. S. Henry characterized it as "in every quality of nobleness transcendently noble;" and Pierre Soulé said, in a letter to the senator, "Que je profite de cette occasion pour vous dire combien j'ai été heureux du succès, et pour mieux dire, du triomphe éclatant que vous avez obtenu à l'occasion de votre discours sur le Nebraska Bill. Courage! *Sic itur ad astra.*"

On the night of the passage of the Kansas and Nebraska Bill, May 25, 1854, Mr. Sumner presented, in addition to memorials from the Society of Friends and other bodies, twenty-five separate remonstrances from clergymen of every Protestant denomination in the six New-England States, and said with solemn earnestness : —

"Like them, sir, I do not hesitate to protest here against the bill yet pending before the Senate, as a great moral wrong, as a breach of public faith; as a measure full of danger to the peace and even existence of our Union. And, sir, believing in God as I profoundly do, I cannot doubt that the opening of an immense region to so great an enormity as slavery is calculated to draw down upon our country his righteous judgments.

"'In the name of Almighty God, and in his presence,' these remonstrants protest against the Nebraska Bill. In this solemn language, which has been strangely pronounced blasphemous on this floor, there is obviously no assumption of ecclesiastical power, as has been perversely charged, but simply a devout observance of the Scriptural injunction, 'Whatsoever ye do, in word or deed, do all in the name of the Lord.' Let me add, also, that these remonstrants, in this very language, have followed the example of the Senate, which at our present session nas ratified at least one important treaty beginning with these precise words, 'In the name of Almighty God.' Surely, if the Senate may thus assume to speak, the clergy may do likewise without imputation of blasphemy or any just criticism, at least in this body.

"But I am unwilling, particularly at this time, to be betrayed into any thing that shall seem like a defence of the clergy. They need no such thing at my hands. There are men in this Senate, justly eminent for eloquence, learning, and ability; but there is no man here competent, except in his own conceit, to sit in judgment on the clergy of New England. Honorable senators who have been so swift with criticism and sarcasm might profit by their example. Perhaps the senator from South Carolina [Mr. Butler], who is not insensible to scholarship, might learn from them something of its graces. Perhaps the senator from Virginia [Mr. Mason], who finds no sanction under the constitution for any remonstrance from clergymen, might learn from them something of the privileges of an American citizen. And perhaps the senator from Illinois [Mr. Douglas], who precipitated this odious measure upon the country, might learn from them something of political wis dom. Sir, from the first settlement of these shores, from those early days of struggle and privation, through the trials of the Revolution, the clergy have been associated, not only

with the piety and the learning, but with the liberties, of the
country. For a long time New England was governed by
their prayers more than by any acts of the legislature; and, at
a later day, their voices aided even the Declaration of Independence. The clergy of our time may speak, then, not only from
their own virtues, but from the echoes which yet live in the
pulpits of their fathers.

"For myself, I desire to thank them for their generous inter-
position. They have already done much good in moving the
country. They will not be idle. In the days of the Revolution, John Adams, yearning for independence, said, 'Let the
pulpits thunder against oppression!' and the pulpits thundered. The time has come for them to thunder again.

"Sir," said he most pertinently in this midnight protest,
"the bill which you are now about to pass is at once the worst
and the best bill on which Congress ever acted. Yes, sir,
WORST and BEST at the same time.

"It is the worst bill, inasmuch as it is a present victory of
slavery. In a Christian land, and in an age of civilization, a
time-honored statute of freedom is struck down, opening the
way to all the countless woes and wrongs of human bondage.
Among the crimes of history another is about to be recorded,
which no tears can blot out, and which, in better days, will be
read with universal shame. Do not start. The tea tax and
Stamp Act, which aroused the patriot rage of our fathers, were
virtues by the side of your transgression; nor would it be easy
to imagine, at this day, any measure which more openly and
perversely defied every sentiment of justice, humanity, and
Christianity. Am I not right, then, in calling it the worst bill
on which Congress ever acted?

"But there is another side to which I gladly turn. Sir, it is the best bill on which Congress ever acted; for it prepares the way for that 'All hail hereafter,' when slavery must disappear. It annuls all past compromises with slavery, and makes all future compromises impossible. Thus it puts freedom and slavery face to face, and bids them grapple. Who can doubt the result? It opens wide the door of the future, when, at last, there will really be a North, and the slave-power will be broken; when this wretched despotism will cease to dominate over our government, no longer impressing itself upon every thing at home and abroad; when the national government shall be divorced in every way from slavery, and, according to the true intention of our fathers, freedom shall be established by Congress everywhere, at least beyond the local limits of the States.

"Slavery will then be driven from its usurped foothold here in the District of Columbia, in the national Territories, and elsewhere beneath the national flag; the Fugitive-Slave Bill, as vile as it is unconstitutional, will become a dead-letter; and the domestic slave-trade, so far as it can be reached, but especially on the high seas, will be blasted by Congressional prohibition. Everywhere within the sphere of Congress, the great *northern hammer* will descend to smite the wrong; and the irresistible cry will break forth, 'No more slave States!'"

"Thus, sir, now standing at the very grave of freedom in Kansas and Nebraska, I lift myself to the vision of that happy resurrection by which freedom will be secured hereafter, not only in these Territories, but everywhere under the national government. More clearly than ever before, I now see 'the beginning of the end' of slavery. Proudly I discern the flag of my country, as it ripples in every breeze, at last become in reality, as in name, the flag of freedom, undoubted, pure, and irresistible. Am I not right, then, in calling this bill the best on which Congress ever acted ?

"Sorrowfully I bend before the wrong you are about to enact: joyfully I welcome all the promises of the future."

Such was the intense excitement of the country at this time, that these bold utterances, which expressed the sober sentiment of the people of the North, threw Mr. Sumner into great personal danger. This was heightened by a tragical event which then occurred in Boston. On the day preceding this midnight speech, Anthony Burns was arrested as a fugitive slave, and held a prisoner in the Court-House. Many of the citizens were fired with indignation ; and on the evening of the 26th instant, after an excited meeting in Faneuil Hall, an attack was made upon the Court-House, during which James Batchelder, acting as a guard, was killed. This resistance to the iniquitous Fugitive-Slave Law was attributed to the late speech of Mr. Sumner, in which he had said, "In passing this bill, as is now threatened, you scatter from this dark midnight-hour no seeds of harmony and good-will, but broadcast through the land dragons' teeth, which haply may not spring up in direful crops of armed men ; but yet I am assured, sir, will they fructify in civil strife and feud."

"He is a murderer!" said the organs of the administration. "Down with this fanatical abolitionist!"

"Let Sumner and his infamous gang," said "The Star," an official paper at Washington, "feel that he cannot outrage the fame of his country, counsel treason to its laws, incite the ignorant to bloodshed and murder, and still receive the support and countenance of the society of this city, which he has done so much to vilify." The obnoxious speech of the "fanatical abolitionist" was not, however, read in Boston until the day after the *émeute*, and the death of James Batchelder; and this the partisans of slavery well knew. "Put a ball through his head!" cried the infuriated slaveholders of Alexandria. "A strenuous and systematized effort is making here and in Alexandria," wrote a correspondent, May 31, to "The New-York Times," "to raise a mob against Senator Sumner, in retaliation for the Boston difficulty." But, though menaced on every hand, and once threatened and insulted at a restaurant; though counselled by his friends to leave Washington, — Mr. Sumner continued to walk unattended and unarmed, as usual, through the streets. He knew no fear. "Let the minions of the administration and of the slaveocracy harm one hair of your head," wrote to him his friend George Livermore of Cambridge, "and they will raise a whirlwind that will sweep them to destruction."

This word was verified.

CHAPTER XI.

" Where is charity? Where is the love of God? Where is the zeal for his glory? Where is desire for his service? Where is human pity, and the compassion of man for man? Certainly, to redeem a captive, to liberate him from wretched slavery, is the highest work of charity, of all that can be done in this world." — *Topografia y Historia de Argel* por FRA ILAEDO.

"And 'tis for this we live, —
To smite the oppressor with the words of power;
To bid the tyrant give
Back to his brother Heaven's allotted hour."

WILLIAM HOWITT.

OVED by a lofty purpose, — the redemption of the slave, — sustained by the rectitude of his intentions, and by the generous sympathies of many advocates of freedom both in

187

America and Europe, the inflexible patriot pursued his course with giant stride; and, though the dominant party held him in contempt, it trembled when he struck.

The rendition of Anthony Burns to servitude, and the violent scenes thereon attendant, served to deepen the anti-slavery sentiment in Massachusetts; and a petition for the repeal of the Fugitive-Slave Bill, signed by two thousand nine hundred citizens of Boston, many of whom had hitherto opposed the course of Mr. Sumner, was on the twenty-second day of June, 1854, presented to the Senate by Mr. Rockwell, who had taken the place of Mr. Everett. An exciting debate arose on the motion to refer this memorial, when Mr. Sumner took the floor in defence of himself and Massachusetts.

" So far as the arraignment touches me personally," he said, " I hardly care to speak. It is true that I have not hesitated, here and elsewhere, to express my open, sincere, and unequivocal condemnation of the Fugitive-Slave Bill. I have denounced it as at once a violation of the law of God, and of the Constitution of the United States.

" In violation of the constitution, it commits the great question of human freedom — than which none is more sacred in the law — not to a solemn trial, but to summary proceedings.

" It commits this question, not to one of the high tribunals of the land, but to the unaided judgment of a single petty magistrate.

" It commits this question to a magistrate appointed, not by the President with the consent of the Senate, but by the court; holding his office, not during good behavior, but merely during the will of the court; and receiving, not a regular salary, but fees according to each individual case.

" It authorizes judgment on *ex parte* evidence, by affidavits, without the sanction of cross-examination.

" It denies the writ of *habeas corpus*, ever known as the palladium of the citizen.

" Contrary to the declared purposes of the framers of the constitution, it sends the fugitive back ' at the public expense.'

" Adding meanness to the violation of the constitution, it bribes the commissioner by a double fee to pronounce against freedom. If he dooms a man to slavery, the reward is ten dollars; but, saving him to freedom, his dole is five dollars."

" In response for Massachusetts," he emphatically asserted, "there are other things. Something surely must be pardoned to her history. In Massachusetts stands Boston. In Boston stands Faneuil Hall, where, throughout the perils which preceded the Revolution, our patriot fathers assembled to vow themselves to freedom. Here, in those days, spoke James Otis, full of the thought that ' the people's safety is the law of God.' Here also spoke James Warren, inspired by the sentiment that ' death with all its tortures is preferable to slavery.' And here also thundered John Adams, fervid with the conviction that ' consenting to slavery is a sacrilegious breach of trust.' Not far from this venerable hall — between this temple of freedom and the very court-house to which the senator [Mr. Jones] has referred — is the street where, in 1770, the first blood was spilt in conflict between British troops and American citizens; and among the victims was one of that African race which you so much despise. Almost within sight is Bunker Hill: farther off, Lexington and Concord. Amidst these scenes a slave-hunter from Virginia appears; and the disgusting rites begin by which a fellow-man is to be doomed to bondage. Sir, can you wonder that the people were moved?

'Who can be wise, amazed, temperate, and furious,
     Loyal and neutral, in a moment? No man.'

"It is true that the Slave Act was with difficulty executed, and that one of its servants perished in the effort. On these grounds the senator from Tennessee charges Boston with fanaticism. I express no opinion on the conduct of individuals; but I do say that the fanaticism which the senator condemns is not new in Boston. It is the same which opposed the execution of the Stamp Act, and finally secured its repeal. It is the same which opposed the tea tax. It is the fanaticism which finally triumphed on Bunker Hill. The senator says that Boston is filled with traitors. That charge is not new. Boston, of old, was the home of Hancock and Adams. Her traitors now are those who are truly animated by the spirit of the American Revolution. In condemning them, in condemning Massachusetts, in condemning these remonstrants, you simply give a proper conclusion to the utterance on this floor, that the Declaration of Independence is 'a self-evident lie.'"

This manly speech, as the last one on the Kansas and Nebraska Bill, hit the vulnerable point of his opponents, and was followed by a torrent of vituperation and abuse. Said Mr. Mason of Virginia in a most contemptuous tone: " I am speaking of a fanatic, one whose reason is dethroned. Can such a one expect to make impressions upon the American people from his rabid, vulgar declamation here, accompanied by a declaration that he would violate his oath now recently taken ? "

In spite of bitter opposition, Mr. Sumner on the 28th instant again obtained the floor, and made a masterly reply to his assailants, and a glorious defence of the Commonwealth he represented. Though his reason were " dethroned," enough was left to annihilate the arguments and meet the taunts of Messrs. Mason, Butler, Petitt, and other domineering and abusive senators.

At the conclusion of this splendid speech, Mr. Chase said to him, " You have struck slavery the strongest blow it ever received: you have made it reel to the centre." Said Mr. Giddings, " Sumner stood inimitable, and hurled back the taunts of his assailants with irresistible force." " Your recent encounter with the wild beasts of Ephesus," wrote John A. Andrew to him, " has been a brilliant success." " Sumner," wrote Edward T. Channing to a friend, " has done nobly. He is erect, and a man of authority among the slave holders, dealers, and hunters. He has made an historical era for the North."

He had done so; for thousands of the temporizing saw, by this masterly exposition of the weakness of the slave-power, and by the ferocity manifested in this debate, that the dark wave of human servitude must be stayed; that there was business to be done; and that it was time to wheel into the line of those who had the will and backbone to go forward. Among the many cordial tributes Mr. Sumner received for this massive argument in defence of Northern principles, none was more welcome than these elegant lines of John G. Whittier: —

TO CHARLES SUMNER.

If I have seemed more prompt to censure wrong
Than praise the right; if seldom to thine ear
My voice hath mingled with the exultant cheer,
Borne upon all our Northern winds along;
If I have failed to join the fickle throng,
In wide-eyed wonder that thou standest strong
In victory, surprised in thee to find
Brougham's scathing power with Channing's grace combined,
That he for whom the ninefold Muses sung,
From their twined arms a giant athlete sprung,
Barbing the arrows of his native tongue
With the spent shafts Latona's archer flung
To smite the Python of our land and time,
Fell as the monster born of Crissa's slime,
Like the blind bard who in Castalian springs
Tempered the steel that clove the crest of kings,
And on the shrine of England's freedom laid
The gifts of Cumæ and of Delphi's shade, —

Small need hast thou of words of praise from me.
Thou knowest my heart, dear friend, and well canst guess
That, even though silent, I have not the less
Rejoiced to see thy actual life agree
With the large future which I shaped for thee,
When, years ago, beside the summer sea,
White in the moon, we saw the long waves fall,
Baffled and broken, from the rocky wall,
That to the menace of the brawling flood
Opposed alone its massive quietude,
Calm as a fate, with not a leaf nor vine
Nor birch-spray trembling in the still moonshine,
Crowning it like God's peace.   I sometimes think
That night-scene by the sea prophetical,
(For Nature speaks in symbols and in signs,
And through her pictures human fate divines), —
That rock wherefrom we saw the billows sink
In mumuring rout, uprising clear and tall
In the white light of heaven, the type of one
Who, momently by error's host assailed,
Stands strong as Truth, in greaves of granite mailed,
And, tranquil-fronted, listening over all
The tumult, hears the angels say, "Well done!"

J. G. W.

11th MONTH, 25th, 1854.

Bravely and persistently Mr. Sumner pressed the
question of slavery upon the attention of the Senate;
but he met at every point malignant opposition.
Parliamentary practice was boldly set aside to thwart
his purposes.   "The miscreant must be silenced!"
was the general cry.   A specimen of the debate on
the thirty-first day of July will exhibit the tactics of
the partisans of slavery.

During the passage of two unimportant measures, Mr. Sumner endeavored to present a proposition for the repeal of the Fugitive-Slave Act; and, having gained the floor, this interesting scene occurred: —

Mr. SUMNER. In pursuance of notice, I now ask leave to introduce a bill.

Mr. STUART (of Michigan). I object to it, and move to take up the River and Harbor Bill.

THE PRESIDING OFFICER (Mr. Cooper of Pennsylvania). The other bill is not disposed of, — the third reading of a Bill for the Relief of Betsey Nash.

The bill was then read a third time, and passed.

Mr. SUMNER. In pursuance of notice, I ask leave to introduce a bill which I now send to the table.

Mr. STUART. Is that in order?

Mr. SUMNER. Why not?

Mr. BENJAMIN (of Louisiana). There is a pending motion of the senator from Michigan to take up the River and Harbor Bill.

THE PRESIDING OFFICER. That motion was not entertained, because the senator from Massachusetts had and has the floor.

Mr. STUART. I make the motion now.

THE PRESIDING OFFICER. The Chair thinks it is in order to give the notice.

Mr. SUMNER. Notice has been given; and I now,

in pursuance of notice, introduce the bill. The question is on its first reading.

THE PRESIDING OFFICER. The first reading of a bill.

Mr. NORRIS (of New Hampshire). I rise to a question of order.

Mr. SUMNER. I believe I have the floor.

Mr. NORRIS. But I rise to a question of order. I submit that that is not the question. The senator from Massachusetts has given notice that he would ask leave to introduce a bill. He now asks that leave. If there be objection, the question must be decided by the Senate, whether he shall have leave or not. Objection is made; and the bill cannot be read.

Mr. SUMNER. Very well; the first question, then, is on granting leave; and the title of the bill will be read.

THE PRESIDING OFFICER (to the Secretary). Read the title.

The Secretary read it as follows: "A Bill to repeal the Act of Congress, approved Sept. 18, 1850, for the Surrender of Fugitives from Service or Labor."

THE PRESIDING OFFICER. The question is on granting leave to introduce the bill.

Mr. SUMNER. And I have the floor.

THE PRESIDING OFFICER. The senator from Massachusetts is entitled to the floor.

Mr. Sumner. I shall not occupy much time, nor shall I debate the bill. Some time ago, Mr. President, after the presentation of the memorial from Boston, signed by twenty-nine hundred citizens, without distinction of party, I gave notice that I should, at a day hereafter, ask leave to introduce a bill for the repeal of the Fugitive-Slave Act. Desirous, however, not to proceed prematurely, I awaited the action of the Committee on the Judiciary, to which the memorial, and others of a similar character, were referred. At length an adverse report was made, and accepted by the Senate. From the time of that report down to this moment, I have sought an opportunity to introduce this bill. Now, at last, I have it. At a former session, sir, in introducing a similar proposition, I considered it at length, in an argument which I fearlessly assert —

Mr. Gwin (of California). I rise to a point of order. Has the senator a right to debate the question, or say any thing on it, until leave be granted?

The Presiding Officer. My impression is that the question is not debatable.

Mr. Sumner. I propose simply to explain my bill, — to make a statement, not an argument.

Mr. Gwin. I make the point of order.

The Presiding Officer. I am not aware precisely what the rule of order on the subject is; but I have the impression that the senator cannot debate —

Mr. Sumner. The distinction is this —

Mr. Gwin. I insist upon the application of the decision of the Chair.

Mr. Mason (of Virginia). Mr. President, there is one rule of order that is undoubted, — that, when the Chair is stating a question of order, he must not be interrupted by a senator. There is no question about that rule of order.

The Presiding Officer. The senator did not interrupt the Chair.

Mr. Sumner. The Chair does me justice, in response to the injustice of the senator from Virginia.

The Presiding Officer. Order! order!

Mr. Mason. The senator is doing that very thing at this moment. I am endeavoring to sustain the authority of the Chair, which certainly has been violated.

The Presiding Officer. It is the opinion of the Chair that the debate is out of order. I am not precisely informed of what the rule is; but such is my clear impression.

Mr. Walker (of Wisconsin). If the senator from Massachusetts will allow me, I will say a word here.

Mr. Sumner. Certainly.

Thus, fearful of the truth, and fencing off the question, the slaveocracy prolonged the struggle through the entire day; and, at the close, the Senate determined not to introduce the bill. But the elements were in commotion; the breast of the nation was heaving; a spirit was abroad which neither senatorial manœuvrings nor unjust laws nor bannered army could intimidate or resist.

Under the persistent arrogance of the South, the anti-slavery sentiment of the North was still extending; and, in order to combine the scattered elements opposed to the servile system into one grand, compact, and solid body, the Republican party was, through the constructive power of Henry Wilson and a few other leading politicians, formed in the summer of 1854 to occupy the place of the Free-soil organization. A large convention was held in the city of Worcester on the seventh day of September, over which the Hon. Robert Rantoul of Beverly presided. As Mr. Sumner entered the convention, the whole assembly rose, and with long-continued cheering gave him welcome as their honored champion. He then made one of the most effective and brilliant speeches ever heard in that city. His theme was "The Duties of Massachusetts at the Present Crisis;" and with the skill of a master whose heart is glowing with the grandeur of his subject, whose tongue is touched with a celestial flame, he proceeded amidst continued outbursts of applause from the vast audience.

"After months," said he, "of constant, anxious service in another place, away from Massachusetts, I am permitted to stand among you, my fellow-citizens, and to draw satisfaction and strength from your generous presence. Life is full of changes and contrasts. From slave soil I have come to free soil: from the tainted breath of slavery I have passed to this bracing air of freedom; and the heated antagonism of debate, shooting forth its fiery cinders, is changed into this brimming, overflowing welcome, where I seem to lean on the great heart of our beloved Commonwealth as it palpitates audibly in this crowded assembly.

"Let me say at once, frankly and sincerely, that I have not come here to receive applause, or to give occasion for any tokens of public regard, but simply to unite with my fellow-citizens in new vows of duty. And yet I would not be thought insensible to the good-will now swelling from so many honest bosoms: it touches me more than I can tell.

"During the late session of Congress, an eminent supporter of the Nebraska Bill said to me, with great animation, in language which I give with some precision, that you may appreciate the style as well as the sentiment, 'I would not go through all that you do on *this nigger question*, for all the offices and honors of the country.' To which I naturally and promptly replied, 'Nor would I, for all the offices and honors of the country.' Not in such things can be found the true inducements to this warfare. For myself, if I have been able to do any thing in any respect not unworthy of you, it is because I thought rather of those commanding duties which are above office and honor."

In the progress of his address he said with emphasis, —

"The Fugitive-Slave Bill, monstrous in cruelty as in unconstitutionality, is a usurpation which must be opposed. The admission of new slave States, from whatsoever quarter, from Texas or Cuba, Utah or New Mexico, must be opposed. And to every scheme of slavery — whether in Cuba or Mexico, on the high seas in opening the slave-trade, in the West Indies, the valley of the Amazon, whether accomplished or merely plotted, whether pending or in prospect — we must send forth an everlasting NO!"

He concluded his grand address by these memorable words : —

"By the passage of the Nebraska Bill, and the Boston kidnapping case, the tyranny of the slave-power has become unmistakably manifest; while, at the same time, all compromises with slavery are happily dissolved, so that freedom now stands face to face with its foe. The pulpit, too, released from ill-omened silence, now thunders for freedom, as in the olden time. It belongs to Massachusetts — nurse of the men and principles which made the earliest Revolution — to vow herself anew to her ancient faith, as she lifts herself to the great struggle. Her place now, as of old, is in the van, at the head of the battle. But, to sustain this advanced position with proper inflexibility, three things are needed by our beloved Commonwealth, in all her departments of government, — the same three things which once in Faneuil Hall I ventured to say were needed by every representative of the North at Washington. The first is *backbone;* the second is BACKBONE; and the third is BACKBONE. With these Massachusetts will be respected, and felt as a positive force in the national government; while at home, on her own soil, — free at last in reality as in name, — all her people, from the islands of Boston to Berkshire Hills, and from the sands of Barnstable to the northern line, will unite in the cry, —

" No slave-hunt in our borders ! no pirate on our strand !
No fetter in the Bay State! no slave upon her land !"

Mr. Sumner was called this autumn to bear the loss of his beloved brother Albert, his wife and daughter Kate, who perished in the ill-fated steamer "Arctic" which collided with the French steamer "Vesta" off Newfoundland, Sept. 27, 1854, sending three hundred persons to an ocean-grave. Albert was an able financier, and had been of great service to his mother in her economical affairs. The Sumner family long hoped that some way of escape from the wreck had been effected; but no tidings of the unfortunate voyagers ever came.

On the evening of the 15th of November, 1854, Mr. Sumner delivered an admirable address before the Mercantile Library Association of Boston, on "The Position and Duties of the Merchant," which he illustrated by sketching the life of Granville Sharp, the earliest abolitionist of England. In portraying the character of this eminent philanthropist, he pointed out the duties of the mercantile profession, especially in respect to slavery and the practical demands of the present age.

On the tenth day of February, 1855, Henry Wilson, a fearless representative of the working-men, and of the progressive spirit, of Massachusetts, took his seat in the United-States Senate. His advent was hailed with joy by Mr. Sumner, who saw in him a combatant well girded to repel the assaults on

freedom. They were stigmatized as " Black Republicans," and held as members sent for the reception
of the ridicule and invective of the dominant party ;
but they well understood its weakness, and by a
kind of inspiration prophesied its coming dissolution. Their own cause, they as clearly saw, stood
on the immutable basis of the gospel: they heard
afar the rolling of the tidal wave ; they caught faint
glimpses of the dawn of a new day. " A forlorn
hope," said politicians on the lower plane. But
the feet of Sumner and of Wilson touched the
rock : their temples felt the breeze of an incoming
power. Shoulder to shoulder they, beneath the
ægis of the constitution, defiantly confronted their
opponents, and with burning words denounced the
usurpations of the partisans of slavery. They were
heroes ; and men now accord to them this appella-
tion.

Referring to the course pursued by Mr. Sumner in
Congress, Theodore Parker says, in a letter to Henry
Wilson, dated Feb. 15, 1855, —

" What a noble stand Sumner has taken and kept in the
Senate ! He is one of the few who have grown *morally* as well
as intellectually by his position in Congress. But his example
shows that politics do not necessarily debase a man in two
years. I hope the office may do as much for you as for your
noble and generous colleague."

Mr. Sumner's next senatorial effort, Feb. 23, 1855, was an earnest speech, during which he was frequently interrupted by Messrs. Rusk and Butler, on the repeal of the Fugitive-Slave Act. In the course of his remarks, he declared again his plan of emancipation to be, not a political revolution, but the awakening of an enlightened, generous, human, Christian, public opinion, which "should blast with contempt, indignation, and abhorrence, all who, in whatever form, or under whatever name, undertake to be agents in enslaving a fellow-man." At the close of his speech, Mr. Butler said, " I will ask the gentleman one question : If it devolved upon him as a representative of Massachusetts, all federal laws being put out of the way, would he recommend any law for the delivery of a fugitive slave under the constitution of the United States ? "

" NEVER ! " Mr. Sumner instantly replied.

The following letter to his classmate the Rev. S. B. Babcock. D.D., of Dedham, exhibits his anxiety for union at the North : —

SENATE CHAMBER, March 30, 1854.

MY DEAR BABCOCK, — Your letter has cheered and strength-ened me. It came to me, too, with pleasant memories of early life. As I read it, the gates of the past seemed to open ; and I saw again the bright fields of study in which we walked to-gether. Our battle has been severe ; and much of its brunt has fallen upon a few. For weeks my trials and anxieties were intense. It is a satisfaction to know that they have found sympathy among good men.

But the slave-power will push its tyranny yet farther; and there is but one remedy, — union among men, without distinction of party, at the North, who shall take possession of the national government, and administer it in the spirit of freedom and not of slavery. Oh! when will the North be aroused?

Ever sincerely yours,
CHARLES SUMNER.

On the 9th of May following, he delivered, at the Metropolitan Theatre, New York, a brilliant address on " The Necessity, Practicability, and Dignity of the Anti-Slavery Enterprise." In presenting him to the vast audience, the Hon. William Jay said, " I introduce him to you as a Northern senator on whom nature has conferred the unusual gift of a backbone, —a man who, standing erect on the floor of Congress amid creeping things from the North, with Christian fidelity denounces the stupendous wickedness of the Fugitive Law and Nebraska perfidy, and, in the name of liberty, humanity, and religion, demands the repeal of those most atrocious enactments."

Speaking of the outspread and power of the anti-slavery sentiment, Mr. Sumner beautifully said, " It

18

touches the national heart as it never before was
touched, sweeping its strings with a might to draw
forth emotions such as no political struggle has ever
evoked. It moves the young, the middle-aged, and
the old. It enters the family circle, and mingles
with the flame of the household hearth. It reaches
the souls of mothers, wives, sisters, and daughters,
filling all with a new aspiration for justice on earth,
and awakening not merely a sentiment against
slavery, such as prevailed with our fathers, but a
deep, undying conviction of its wrong, and a determination to leave no effort unattempted for its removal. With the sympathies of all Christendom as
allies, it has already encompassed the slave-masters
by a *moral blockade*, invisible to the eye, but more
potent than navies, from which there can be no escape except in final capitulation."

Referring to the contemptible part performed by
the slave-hunter, he made the emphatic declaration:
" For myself, let me say that I can imagine no office,
no salary, no consideration, which I would not gladly
forego rather than become in any way an agent for
the enslavement of my brother-man. Where, for
me, would be comfort or solace after such a work?
In dreams and waking hours, in solitude and in the
street, in the study of the open book, and in conversation with the world, wherever I turned, there my

victim would stare me in the face; while, from the
distant rice-fields and sugar-plantations of the South,
his cries beneath the vindictive lash, his moans at
the thought of liberty once his, now — alas! — ravished away, would pursue me, repeating the tale of
his fearful doom, and sounding, forever sounding, in
my ears, 'Thou art the man.' Mr. President, may
no such terrible voice fall on your soul or mine!'"

He concluded this magnificent address by these
strong words: —

"Face to face against the SLAVE OLIGARCHY must
be rallied the UNITED MASSES of the North, in
compact political association, planted on the everlasting base of justice, knit together by the instincts
of a common danger and by the holy sympathies of
humanity; enkindled by a love of freedom, not only
for themselves, but for others; determined to enfran-
chise the national government from degrading
thraldom; and constituting the BACKBONE PARTY,
powerful in numbers, wealth, and intelligence, but
more powerful still in an inspiring cause. Let this
be done, and victory will be ours."

Entertaining broad and catholic views of humanity and brotherhood, Mr. Sumner did not identify
himself with the American or "Know-Nothing"
organization, which he truly characterized as a "separate" and "short-lived" party. "Cut off from the

main body," said he, " it may still show a brief vitality, as a head of a turtle still bites for some days after it is severed from the neck, but can have no permanent existence."

"It is proposed," he as justly as eloquently remarked, " to attaint men for their religion, and also for their birth. If this object can prevail, vain are the triumphs of civil freedom in its many hard-fought fields, vain is that religious toleration which we all profess. The fires of Smithfield, the tortures of the Inquisition, the proscriptions of non-conformists, may all be revived. It was mainly to escape these outrages, dictated by a dominant religious sect, that our country was early settled, in one place by Quakers, who set at nought all forms; in another by Puritans, who disowned bishops; in another by Episcopalians, who take their name from bishops; and in yet another by Catholics, who look to the pope as their spiritual father. Slowly among sects was evolved the great idea of the equality of all men before the law, without regard to religious belief; nor can any party now organize a proscription merely for religious belief, without calling in question this unquestionable principle. . . .

" The history of our country in its humblest as well as most exalted spheres testifies to the merits of foreigners. Their strong arms have helped furrow our broad territory with canals, and stretch in every direction the iron rail. They have filled our workshops, navigated our ships, and tilled our fields. Go where you will, among the hardy sons of toil on land or sea, and there you will find industrious and faithful foreigners bending their muscles to the work. At the bar, and in the high places of commerce, you will find them. Enter the retreats of learning, and there you will find them too, shedding upon our country the glory of science. Nor can any reflection be cast upon foreigners claiming hospitality now, which will not glance at once upon the distinguished living and the illustrious dead; upon the Irish Montgomery, who perished for us at the gates of Quebec; upon Pulaski the Pole, who perished for us at Savannah; upon De Kalb and Steuben, the generous Germans, who aided our weakness by their military experience; upon Paul Jones the Scotchman, who lent his unsurpassed courage to the infant thunders of our navy; also upon those great European liberators, Kosciusko of Poland, and Lafayette of France, each of whom paid his earliest vows to liberty in our cause. Nor should this list be confined to military characters, so long as we gratefully cherish the name of Alexander Hamilton, who was born in the West Indies, and the name of Albert Gallatin, who was born in Switzerland, and never, to

18*

the close of his octogenarian career, lost the French accent of his boyhood, — both of whom rendered civic services which may be commemorated among the victories of peace."

CHAPTER XII.

Struggles in Kansas. — Excitement through the Country and in Congress. — Remarks of Mr. Sumner on the Reports of Messrs. Douglas and Collamer. — His Speech on the Admission of Kansas. — The Exordium. — Reference to Mr. Douglas. — The Nebraska Bill a Swindle. — Defence of Massachusetts. — The Conclusion of the Speech. — The Effect of the Speech. — Remarks of Mr. Wilson. — The Assault on Mr. Sumner. — His Account of the Same. — The Effect of this Assault on the North and South. — Mr. Brooks challenges Mr. Wilson, also Mr. Burlingame. — Mr. Sumner at Cape May; at Cresson ; at Philadelphia.

"I know no figure in history which commands more of my admiration than that of Charles Sumner in the Senate of the United States, from the hour when Douglas presented his ill-omened measure for the repeal of the Missouri Compromise until the blow of the assassin laid him low. Here was the perfection of moral constancy and daring. Here was sleepless vigilance, unwearying labor, hopefulness born only of deepest faith, buoyant resolution, caring nothing for human odds, but serenely abiding in the perfect peace which the unselfish service of truth alone can bring." — Hon. ROBERT B. ELLIOTT.

"Strike, but hear! " — *Greek Proverb.*

BY the Kansas and Nebraska Act, passed in May, 1854, a vast extent of virgin territory, in the heart of this continent, was laid open both to free and servile labor; and immigration at once began to set in from the North and South, thus

bringing freedom and slavery hand to hand and face
to face. The field was broad enough for a mighty
kingdom. Which party now shall have the mas-
tery?

The Northern Emigrant Aid Society, under the
direction of the Hon. Eli Thayer, encouraged hardy
men to take possession of the country in the name
of liberty, and to plant the institutions of the Pilgrim Fathers on those fertile plains. The South
sent forward lawless bands of marauding slaveholders, to establish there its inhuman system.
Although the Northern emigrant went with peaceful
intentions only, it was natural to suppose that colli-
sions would ensue, since it is impossible that free
and servile industry should harmoniously co-exist;
and then commenced indeed a struggle, especially
for ascendency in political affairs, which was marked
by most revolting scenes of violence and bloodshed.
" The first ballot-box that was opened upon our
virgin soil, Nov. 29, 1854," wrote Gen. Pomeroy,
" was closed to us by overpowering numbers and
impending force."

At the first election of the legislature, March 30,
1855, organized bands of armed and lawless men
from Missouri, entering the territory, exercised complete control over the ballot-box; and in the autumn
of the same year gross outrages were perpetrated

by the border ruffians at Lawrence, and several unoffending citizens murdered.

"Crush them out!" said Gen. Stringfellow: "let them vote at the point of the bowie-knife and revolver."

The whole country was aroused. "Down with the Black Republicans!" and "Disunion!" were the Southern, "No more slave territory!" "No slave-hunting!" were the Northern watchwords. To quell the outrages in Kansas, the advocates of freedom demanded of the administration immediate and decisive action; but, subservient to the slave oligarchy, it steadily fanned the flame of the aggressive party.

The contest deepened in the halls of Congress. Front to front the defenders of the two opposing systems stood, with crimination and recrimination, taunt, invective, and defiance, on their tongues. Intrenched in principle, calm and unterrified as a Roman gladiator, Mr. Sumner met the shafts of hatred, and dealt with stalwart arm his deadly blows against the servile institution. He was then the best representative of freedom living. During the winter he said to Mr. Waldo Higginson, "The session will not pass without the Senate-chamber's becoming the scene of some unparalleled outrage;" but he had no fears except that he might not fulfil his duty to his country.

Respecting the reports of Mr. Douglas and Mr. Collamer on affairs in Kansas, presented in the Senate March 13, 1856, Mr. Sumner said, " In the report of the majority (by Mr. Douglas) the true issue is smothered : in that of the minority (signed by Mr. Collamer alone) the true issue stands forth as a pillar of fire to guide the country.   I have no desire," continued he, " to precipitate the debate on this important question, under which the country already shakes from side to side, and which threatens to scatter from its folds civil war."

A short time afterwards Mr. Seward presented " A Bill for the Admission of Kansas into the Union," on which an acrimonious debate ensued.   In the course of the discussion Mr. Sumner, on the 19th and 20th of May, made his celebrated speech entitled " The Crime against Kansas."   His positions were, first, the crime against Kansas in its origin and extent ; secondly, the apologies for the crime ; and, thirdly, the true remedy.

In this masterly philippic, he disclosed the atrocities of slavery with the vigor of an intellectual athlete.   He laid under contribution for this attack on slavery the acquisitions of a ripe scholar, the wisdom of an enlightened statesman, the eloquence of an accomplished orator, and the courage of an invincible champion of liberty.   He sent with steadiest aim shot after shot into the intrenchments of the arrogant defenders of the servile institution, and triumphantly vindicated the policy of the friends of free men, free labor, and free speech.

In his exordium he thus boldly sets forth the crime, and foreshadows the great events to come : —

"But the wickedness which I now begin to expose is immeasurably aggravated by the motive which prompted it. Not in any common lust for power did this uncommon tragedy have its origin. It is the rape of a virgin Territory, compelling it to the hateful embrace of slavery; and it may be clearly traced to a depraved longing for a new slave State, the hideous offspring of such a crime, in the hope of adding to the power of slavery in the national government. Yes, sir; when the whole world, alike Christian and Turk, is rising up to condemn this wrong, and to make it a hissing to the nations, here in our Republic, *force* — ay, sir, FORCE — has been openly employed in compelling Kansas to this pollution, and all for the sake of political power. There is the simple fact, which you will vainly attempt to deny, but which in itself presents an essential wickedness that makes other public crimes seem like public virtues.

"But this enormity, vast beyond comparison, swells to dimensions of wickedness which the imagination toils in vain to grasp, when it is understood that for this purpose are hazarded the horrors of intestine feud, not only in this distant Territory, but everywhere throughout the country. Already the muster has begun. The strife is no longer local, but national. Even now, while I speak, portents hang on all the arches of the horizon, threatening to darken the broad land, which already yawns with the mutterings of civil war. The fury of the propagandists of slavery, and the calm determination of their opponents, are now diffused from the distant Territory over wide-spread communities, and the whole country in all its extent; marshalling hostile divisions, and foreshadowing a strife, which, unless happily averted by the triumph of freedom, will become war, — fratricidal, parricidal war, —with an accumulated wickedness beyond the wickedness of any war in human annals; justly provoking the avenging judgment of Providence and the avenging pen of history; and constituting a strife, in the language of the ancient writer, more than *foreign*, more than *social*, more than *civil*, but something compounded of all these strifes, and in itself more than war : *sed potius commune quoddam ex omnibus, et plus quam bellum.*"

He thus refers to Mr. Douglas, who, in subservience to the South, was moving on that fatal course in which Daniel Webster ignominiously fell :—

"The senator dreams that he can subdue the North. He disclaims the open threat; but his conduct still implies it. How little that senator knows himself, or the strength of the cause which he persecutes! He is but a mortal man : against him is an immortal principle. With finite power he wrestles with the infinite; and he must fall. Against him are stronger battalions than any marshalled by mortal arm, — the inborn, ineradicable, invincible sentiments of the human heart : against him is Nature in all her subtle forces : against him is God. Let him try to subdue these !"

The act which opened Kansas to the rule of

slavery, he characterizes in the following trenchant language : —

" Sir, the Nebraska Bill was in every respect a swindle. It was a swindle by the South of the North. It was, on the part of those who had already completely enjoyed their share of the Missouri Compromise, a swindle of those whose share was yet absolutely untouched ; and the plea of unconstitutionality set up — like the plea of usury after the borrowed money has been enjoyed — did not make it less a swindle. Urged as a bill of peace, it was a swindle of the whole country. Urged as opening the doors to slave-masters with their slaves, it was a swindle of the asserted doctrine of popular sovereignty. Urged as sanctioning popular sovereignty, it was a swindle of the asserted rights of slave-masters. It was a swindle of a broad Territory, thus cheated of protection against slavery. It was a swindle of a great cause, early espoused by Washington, Franklin, and Jefferson, surrounded by the best fathers of the republic. Sir, it was a swindle of God-given, inalienable rights. Turn it over, look at it on all sides, — and it is everywhere a swindle ; and, if the word I now employ has not the authority of classical usage, it has on this occasion the indubitable authority of fitness. No other word will adequately express the mingled meanness and wickedness of the cheat."

Of the State of Massachusetts he thus grandly speaks : —

" God be praised ! Massachusetts, honored Commonwealth that gives me the privilege to plead for Kansas on this floor, knows her rights, and will maintain them firmly to the end.

10

This is not the first time in history that her public acts have been arraigned, and that her public men have been exposed to contumely. Thus was it when, in the olden time, she began the great battle whose fruits you all enjoy. But never yet has she occupied a position so lofty as at this hour. By the intelligence of her population ; by the resources of her industry ; by her commerce, cleaving every wave ; by her manufactures, various as human skill ; by her institutions of education, various as human knowledge ; by her institutions of benevolence, various as human suffering ; by the pages of her scholars and historians ; by the voice of her poets and orators, — she is now exerting an influence more subtle and commanding than ever before ; shooting her far-darting rays wherever ignorance, wretchedness, or wrong prevail ; and flashing light even upon those who travel far to persecute her. Such is Massachusetts ; and I am proud to believe that you may as well attempt, with puny arm, to topple down the earth-rooted, heaven-kissing granite which crowns the historic sod of Bunker Hill, as to change her fixed resolves for freedom everywhere, and especially now for freedom in Kansas. I exult, too, that in this battle, which surpasses far in moral grandeur the whole war of the Revolution, she is able to preserve her just eminence. To the first she contributed a larger number of troops than any other State in the Union, and larger than all the slave States together ; and now to the second, which is not of contending armies, but of contending opinions, on whose issue hangs trembling the advancing civilization of the country, she contributes, through the manifold and endless intellectual activity of her children, more of that divine spark by which opinions are quickened into life than is contributed by any other State, or by all the slave States together ; while her annual productive industry excels in value three times the whole vaunted cotton-crop of the whole South.

Sir, to men on earth it belongs only to deserve success, not to secure it; and I know not how soon the efforts of Massachusetts will wear the crown of triumph. But it cannot be that she acts wrong for herself or children, when in this cause she thus encounters reproach. No: by the generous souls who were exposed at Lexington; by those who stood arrayed at Bunker Hill; by the many from her bosom who, on all the fields of the first great struggle, lent their vigorous arms to the cause of all; by the children she has borne whose names alone are national trophies, — is Massachusetts now vowed irrevocably to this work. What belongs to the faithful servant she will do in all things; and Providence shall determine the result."

The closing words are worthy of the speaker and the occasion : —

"In just regard for free labor in that Territory which it is sought to blast by unwelcome association with slave-labor; in Christian sympathy with the slave, whom it is proposed to task and to sell there; in stern condemnation of the crime which has been consummated on that beautiful soil; in rescue of fellow-citizens now subjugated to a tyrannical usurpation; in dutiful respect for the early fathers whose aspirations are now ignobly thwarted; in the name of the constitution, which has been outraged, of the laws trampled down, of justice banished, of humanity degraded, of peace destroyed, of freedom crushed to earth; and in the name of the heavenly Father, whose service is perfect freedom, — I make this last appeal." *

* "I have read and re-read thy speech," wrote J. G. Whittier to Mr. Sumner, "and look upon it as thy best, — a grand and terrible

Never had the slaveholding power received a
deadlier blow.   In the course of his remarks, he
had spoken somewhat freely of the chivalry of Mr.
Butler, and of the sectionalism of South Carolina.
It must be remembered, however, that for four long
years he had patiently borne the systematic assaults
of this senator, and that there is a time when " for-
bearance ceases to be a virtue."   " The senator from
South Carolina has applied to my colleague," said
Mr. Wilson, in his strong defence of Mr. Sumner
delivered in the senate on the thirteenth day of
June, " every expression calculated to wound the
sensibilities of an honorable man, and to draw down
upon him sneers, obloquy, and hatred, in and out of
the senate.   In my place here, I now pronounce
these continued assaults upon my colleague unparalleled in the history of the senate. . . . The speech
was indeed severe, — severe as truth, — but in all
respects parliamentary.   It is true that it handles
the senator from South Carolina freely; but that
senator had spoken repeatedly in the course of the
Kansas debate, once at length and elaborately, and

philippic worthy of the great occasion; the severe and awful truth
which the sharp agony of the national crisis demanded.   It is
enough for immortality.   So far as thy own reputation is concerned,
nothing more is needed; but this is of small importance.   We cannot see as yet the entire results; but every thing now indicates that
it has saved the country."

at other times more briefly foisting himself into the speeches of other senators, and identifying himself completely with the crime which my colleague felt it his duty to arraign. It was natural, therefore, that his course in the debate, and his position, should be particularly considered. And in this work Mr. Sumner had no reason to hold back, when he thought of the constant, systematic, and ruthless attacks which, utterly without cause, he had received from that senator. The only objection which the senator from South Carolina can reasonably make to Mr. Sumner is, that he struck a strong blow."

That strong blow hit the mark. "Now what is to be done with the Black Republican?" said the knights of Southern chivalry. "His words are damaging. He has the audacity of a Danton. He must be silenced. Shall we challenge him? but he will not fight. What, then, is to be done with him?" A fiendish plot was laid. Two days subsequent to the conclusion of his speech, Mr. Sumner was sitting at his narrow desk in the Senate-chamber with his head bent forward, earnestly engaged in writing. The Senate had adjourned sooner that day than usual; and several senators, as Messrs. Douglas, Geyer, Toombs, Iverson, and Crittenden, together with some strangers, were conversing near him.

Preston S. Brooks, a nephew of Mr. Butler, and member of the House from South Carolina, then entered the chamber, and remained until the friends of Mr. Sumner had retired. He had with him a gold-headed, hollow, gutta-percha cane. Coming directly up in front of Mr. Sumner's desk, and addressing to him a short remark, he suddenly struck him with his heavy cane, opening a long and fearful gash upon the back part of his head. In quick succession Brooks repeated his murderous blows until Mr. Sumner, rising, wrenched the desk from the floor, to which it was firmly screwed, and, under the fiendish pounding, which continued until the cane was shivered in pieces, fell forward, bleeding and insensible as a dead man, on the floor now covered with his blood. "Do you want the pieces of your cane, Mr. Brooks?" said a page of the Senate, picking up the bloody fragments.

"Only the gold head," replied the assailant, deliberately thrusting it into his coat-pocket.

"The next time, kill him, Brooks," said Keitt, who stood in the doorway with a pistol. "Come, let us go and take a drink." They did so; and Bright, Douglas, Edmundson, leaving the wounded man weltering in blood, immediately followed them.

Of the senators present, John J. Crittenden of Kentucky only proffered aid, and condemned the

outrage. Mr. Morgan of New York supported the
bleeding head of Mr. Sumner, and assisted in remov-
ing him to a sofa in the lobby of the Senate-chamber.
Mr. Wilson, who was in the room of Mr. Banks at
the time of the attack, came immediately to the aid
of his colleague, and with others raised him, after his
wounds had been dressed, into a carriage, — attended
him to his lodgings, placed him upon his couch, and
alleviated his pain. During the night he lay pale and
bewildered, and could scarcely speak to the few persons standing by his bedside. His brother George
Sumner soon came to Washington, and, in conversation with Senator Charles T. James, said, "What
ought I to do?" "If it were my brother," replied
the Congressman, "I would take a short, double-
barrelled shot-gun, put it under my cloak, walk up
to the house of representatives, and right in his
chair, as he attacked my brother, I would blow him
to pieces." "I shall do no such thing," returned
the brother of the wounded senator. As soon as
Mr. Sumner was able, he gave, while lying in his
bed, the following testimony in respect to the
assault : —

"I attended the Senate as usual on Thursday, the 22d of
May. After some formal business, a message was received
from the House of Representatives, announcing the death of a
member of that body from Missouri. This was followed by a

brief tribute to the deceased from Mr. Geyer of Missouri, when, according to usage and out of respect to the deceased, the Senate adjourned at once. Instead of leaving the Senate-chamber with the rest of the senators, on the adjournment, I continued in my seat occupied with my pen; and while thus intent, in order to be in season for the mail, which was soon to close, I was approached by several persons who desired to converse with me; but I answered them promptly and briefly, excusing myself for the reason that I was engaged. When the last of these persons left me, I drew my arm-chair close to my desk, and with my legs under the desk continued writing.

"My attention at this time was so entirely drawn from all other objects, that, although there must have been many persons in the Senate, I saw nobody. While thus intent, with my head bent over my writing, I was addressed by a person who approached the front of my desk. I was so entirely absorbed, that I was not aware of his presence until I heard my name pronounced. As I looked up with pen in hand, I saw a tall man, whose countenance was not familiar, standing directly over me, and at the same moment caught these words, 'I have read your speech twice over carefully: it is a libel on South Carolina, and Mr. Butler, who is a relative of mine.' While these words were still passing from his lips, he commenced a succession of blows with a heavy cane on my bare head, by the first of which I was stunned so as to lose my sight. I saw no longer my assailant, nor any other person or object in the room. What I did afterwards was done almost unconsciously, acting under the instincts of self-defence. With head already bent down, I rose from my seat, wrenching up my desk, which was screwed to the floor, and then pressing forward, while my assailant continued his blows. I had no other consciousness until I found myself ten feet forward in front of my desk, lying on the floor of the Senate, with my bleeding head supported on the knee of a gentleman whom I soon recognized, by voice and manner, as Mr. Morgan of New York. Other persons there were about me, offering me friendly assistance; but I did not recognize any of them. Others there were at a distance, looking on and offering no assistance, of whom I recognized only Mr. Douglas of Illinois, Mr. Toombs of Georgia, and I thought also my assailant standing between them. I was helped from the floor, and conducted into the lobby of the Senate, where I was placed upon a sofa. Of those who helped me here I have no recollection. As I entered the lobby, I recognized Mr. Slidell of Louisiana, who retreated; but I recognized no one else until I felt a friendly grasp of the hand, which seemed to come from Mr. Campbell of Ohio. I have a vague impression that Mr. Bright, president of the Senate, spoke to me while I was on the floor of the lobby. I make this statement in answer to the interrogatory of the committee, and offer it as presenting completely all my recollections of the assault and of the attending circumstances, whether immediately before or immediately after. I desire to add, that, besides the words which I have given as uttered by my assailant, I have an indistinct recollection of the words 'old man;' but these are so enveloped in the mist which ensued from the first blow, that I am not sure whether they were uttered or not."

"On the cross-examination of Mr. Sumner, he stated that he was entirely without arms of any kind, and that he had no notice or warning of any kind, direct or indirect, of this assault.

"In answer to a cross-question, Mr. Sumner replied that

what he had said of Mr. Butler was strictly responsive to Mr. Butler's speeches, and according to the usages of parliamentary debate."

In this dastardly assault, Preston S. Brooks struck the heart of every slave and every friend of freedom on this continent.

In his mad attempt to crush one champion of humanity, he called forth millions. In his barbarous effort to stay the fountain of liberty, he unloosed the gates; for, as Kossuth most nobly said, "Its waters will flow: every new drop of martyr-blood will increase the tide. Despots may dam its flood, but never stop it. The higher its dam, the higher the tide: it will overflow or break through."

The news of the outrage on Mr. Sumner was borne with lightning speed to every section of the country; and at the North speakers and resolutions in popular assemblies, the pulpit and the press, in earnest words, declared the public indignation. At a large meeting in Faneuil Hall, Gov. Henry J. Gardner said, "We must stand by him who is the representative of Massachusetts, under all circumstances." Peleg W. Chandler remarked that "Every drop of blood shed by him in this disgraceful affair has raised up ten thousand armed men."

At the dinner of the Massachusetts Medical Society, at the Revere House, Boston, Dr. O. W. Holmes

gave this characteristic toast: "To the surgeons of
the city of Washington. God grant them wisdom!
for they are dressing the wounds of a mighty empire,
and of uncounted generations."

At a great indignation-meeting in Albany, held on
the 6th of June, the Rev. Dr. Halley said, "We
are slaves if we permit these atrocities to go on
unchallenged."

At a mass-meeting in New-York City, Henry
Ward Beecher truly said, "Mr. Sumner had no
other weapon in his hand than his pen. Ah! gentlemen, here we have it. The symbol of the North
is the pen: the symbol of the South is the bludgeon." The voice of the slaveholders at the South
was of course in approval of the atrocious deed.
"The Richmond Enquirer" of June 12 said, "In
the main the press of the South applaud the conduct of Mr. Brooks without condition or limitation.
Sumner, in particular, ought to have nine and thirty
early every morning." "The Charleston Standard"
said of Mr. Brooks, "He will be recognized as one
of the first who struck for the vindication of the
South." On one of the banners in a procession at
Washington, these brutal words were inscribed,
"Sumner and Kansas: let them bleed!"

On the day subsequent to the assault, Mr. Wilson
called the attention of the Senate to the circumstance;

and, a committee having been appointed, he, on the morning of the 27th, while the floor and galleries were crowded with anxious listeners, rose, and characterized the attack on Mr. Sumner as "brutal, murderous, and cowardly." Mr. Butler interrupted him; and cries of "Order! order!" rang through the assembly. Two days later Mr Wilson received a challenge from Mr. Brooks, and in reply made use of these memorable words: "I have always regarded duelling as the lingering relic of a barbarous civilization, which the law of the country has branded as a crime." A resolution was introduced into the House, "that Preston S. Brooks be, and he is, forthwith expelled from this House as a representative from the State of South Carolina." This resolution was lost by a vote of 121 to 95.

Mr. Brooks immediately addressed the House; and on closing said, "I went to work very deliberately, as I am charged, — and this is admitted, — and speculated somewhat as to whether I should employ a horsewhip or a cowhide; but, knowing that the senator was my superior in strength, it occurred to me that he might wrest it from my hand, and then — for I never attempt anything I do not perform — I might have been compelled to do that which I would have regretted the balance of my natural life" [a voice was heard, "He would have killed him!"]. And now, Mr. Speaker, I announce to you and to this House, that I am no longer a member of the Thirty-fourth Congress."*

On the 21st of June Mr. Burlingame made a manly speech in the House, during which, in reference to the assault he said, "I denounce it in the name of the sovereignty of Massachusetts, which was stricken down by the blow; I denounce it in the name of humanity; I denounce it in the name of civilization, which it outraged; I denounce it in the name of that fair play which even bullies and prize-fighters respect. What! strike a man when he is pinioned, — when he cannot respond to a blow! Call you that chivalry? In what code of honor did you get your authority for that?" Mr. Brooks sent him a challenge, which he accepted, and insisted on these terms: "weapons, rifles; distance, twenty paces; place, District of Columbia; time of meeting, the next morning." Mr. Campbell, acting for Mr. Burlingame, substituted the Clifton House, Canada, for the place designated; and thus the duel was prevented. The damage done to Mr. Sumner's system was most serious and alarming; and, had not

* Mr. Brooks returned to Charleston, and was soon re-elected by his constituents to Congress. He died miserably at Washington, Jan. 27, 1857. Dr. Boyle, who dressed the wounds of Mr. Sumner in the lobby of the Senate-chamber, attended him during his last illness.

his frame and constitution been very strong and vigorous, he could not have survived the assault. As soon as he was able to sit up, he was removed to the house of his friend Francis P. Blair, at Silver Spring, near Washington, where he received the most assiduous attention. He declined to take any part in the action brought against Mr. Brooks for the assault by the District of Columbia, and is not known to have used any revengeful word respecting his assailant. On the 6th of June he was able to dictate a telegram to Boston, in regard to a recommendation made by Gov. Gardner to the General Court to assume the expense of his illness. " Whatever Massachusetts can give," said he, "let it all go to suffering Kansas." " That letter, and Mr. Wilson's answer to the challenge," wrote Mrs. L. M. Child, "have revived my early faith in human nature." Mr. Sumner also, on the 13th, wrote a letter to Carlos Pierce, declining to receive a testimonial from his friends in Boston, in approval of his Kansas speech, for which subscriptions to the amount of one thousand dollars had been made, and said in closing, "I express a desire that the contributions intended for the testimonial to me may be applied at once, and without abatement of any kind, to the recovery and security of freedom in Kansas." *

* The testimonial was to have been an elaborate and beautiful silver vase two feet in height, ornamented with the figure of Charles

On the 21st of June, he found strength sufficient to write an encouraging letter to the Republican committee at Boston in respect to the nomination of J. C. Fremont and W. L. Dayton at the Republican National Convention held at Philadelphia on the 17th of the same month.

"In this contest," said he, "there is every motive to union, and also every motive to exertion. '*Now or never! now and forever!*' — such was the ancient war-cry, which, embroidered on the Irish flag, streamed from the Castle of Dublin, and resounded through the whole island, arousing a generous people to a new struggle for ancient rights; and this war-cry may be fitly inscribed on our standard now. *Arise now, or an inexorable, slave-driving tyranny will be fastened upon you. Arise now, and liberty will·be secured forever.*"

Mr. Sumner went to Philadelphia July 9, and thence to Cape May for the benefit of the sea-breeze; but, continuing very feeble, he was advised by his

Sumner and appropriate devices. In a subsequent conversation with his friend James Redpath, written down at the time, Mr. Sumner spoke long and strongly against the habit of public men receiving gifts. He related an anecdote of the Russian prince who paid into his master's treasury the value of the present he had received; and remarked that he himself had adopted the same rule. "Webster," said he, "was injured in consequence of receiving gifts from his constituents."

physician, Dr. Caspar Wistar, to repair to Cresson on the Alleghany Mountains, in Pennsylvania, where he arrived on the 3d of August, and resided in the family, and had the medical advice, of Dr. R. M. Jackson. In the beginning of September he became again the guest of his friend J. T. Furness, Esq., in Philadelphia, where he remained till November, received many consolatory letters, and also dictated several brief communications, in which he often expressed his earnest solicitude for recovery, that he might resume his public duties, and also for the wrongs of Kansas, and the success of the Republican party. But the wound which he received was deep.

CHAPTER XIII.

> " Heed not what may be your fate ;
> Count it gain when worldlings hate ;
> Naught of hope or heart abate :
> Victory's before.
> Ask not that your toils be o'er
> Till all slavery is no more,
> No more, no more, no more ! "
>
> ELIZA LEE FOLLEN.

" If our arms at this distance cannot defend him from assassins, we confide the defence of a life so precious to all honorable men and true patriots, to the Almighty Maker of men." — RALPH WALDO EMERSON.

BOSTON deeply felt the blow received by Mr. Sumner ; and his reception by the city, on the third day of November, was a triumph. A cavalcade numbering about eight hundred horsemen, together with a long line of carriages and an immense throng of people, with enlivening strains of music, attended him from Roxbury to the Capitol.

Many of the buildings along the line of the procession were decorated with festoons, banners, and appropriate mottoes, such as, " Welcome, Freedom's Defender;" "Resistance to Tyrants is Obedience to God ; " "Massachusetts loves, honors, will sustain and defend, her noble SUMNER."

At one point in the route, a large company of elegantly-dressed young ladies with bouquets and waving handkerchiefs bade him welcome. A vast concourse of people awaited him in front of the Capitol, where he was received on a platform erected for the purpose, and presented in an eloquent speech by Prof. F. D. Huntington to Gov. Henry J. Gardner and his staff.

To words of generous welcome extended to him by the governor, he made a touching and appropriate reply, in the course of which he said, " My soul overflows, especially to the young men of Boston, out of whose hearts, as from an exuberant fountain, this broad hospitality took its rise." In referring to his colleague, Mr. Wilson, he said, " It is my special happiness to recognize his unfailing sympathies for myself, and his manly assumption of all the responsibilities of honor." His encomium on Massachusetts was remarkable for its truth and beauty. "My filial love does not claim too much," said he, "when it exhibits her as approaching the pattern of a Christian commonwealth, which, according to the great English republican, John Milton, ' ought to be but as one huge Christian personage, one mighty growth and stature of an honest man, as big and compact in virtue as in body.' Not through any worldly triumphs, not through the vaults of State Street, the spindles of Lowell, or even the learned endowments of Cambridge, is Massachusetts thus; but because, seeking to extend everywhere within the sphere of her influence the benign civilization which she cultivates at home, she stands forth the faithful, unseduced supporter of human nature."

"Terrestrial place," he beautifully said in closing, "is determined by celestial observation. Only by watching the stars can the mariner safely pursue his course; and it is only by obeying these lofty principles which are above men and human passion, that we can make our way safely through the duties of life. In such obedience I hope to live, while, as a servant of Massachusetts, I avoid no labor, shrink from no exposure, and complain of no hardship."

Mr. Sumner was then escorted to his home in Hancock Street, which was surrounded by a dense crowd of people, who rent the air with enthusiastic acclamations. With his widowed mother he appeared at the parlor window, and was again received with cheers of parting, when the multitude retired, and he himself sought that repose which his feeble system, after the demonstrations of the day, demanded.

His injuries from the assault of Mr. Brooks were much more serious than he at first anticipated. For several months he remained at home, under the treatment of Dr. Marshall S. Perry, and the unremitting care of his affectionate mother. He found, however, strength to dictate several letters, referring mostly to the interests of the Republican party and of suffering Kansas. On the 17th of November, for instance, he wrote a letter to M. F. Conway, to the effect that State legislatures should contribute to sustain the cause of liberty in Kansas, which, with a letter from Mr. Wilson to the governor of Vermont, was in a great measure instrumental in securing an appropriation of twenty thousand dollars from that State. On the 24th of the same month, to a committee in Worcester, and in reference to the recent Republican victories, he said, " All New England, with New York, Ohio, Michigan, Wisconsin, and Iowa, constitute an irresistible phalanx for freedom, while our seeming reverse in our Presidential election is only another Bunker Hill." In a letter, dated Hancock

Street, Jan. 10, 1857, to his friend James Redpath, Esq., who was heroically laboring on behalf of freedom in Kansas, he said, "I cannot believe that Massachusetts will hesitate. Her people have already opened their hearts to Kansas ; and the public treasury should be opened as wide as their hearts."

On the thirteenth day of January, 1857, he was almost unanimously re-elected to another six-years term of office; the Senate casting for him every vote; the house having already given him 333 out of the 345 votes thrown.

" It is not too much to say," justly remarked " The New-York Tribune," " that Mr. Sumner is at this moment the most popular man in the State, the opinions of which he so truly represents."   In his acceptance of the trust, Jan. 22, Mr. Sumner said, " Alike by sympathy with the slave, and by determination to save ourselves from wretched thraldom, we are all summoned to the effort now organized for the emancipation of the national government from a degrading influence, hostile to civilization, which, whenever it shows itself even at a distance, is brutal, vulgar, and mean ; an unnatural tyranny, calculated to arouse the generous indignation of good men.   Of course no person, unless ready to say in his heart that there is no God, can doubt the certain result."   His health continuing to decline, he was advised by his physicians to seek relief abroad ; and early in March following he took passage in the steamship "Fulton," at New York, for Havre. His last word before sailing was on behalf of that fair territory where the friends and the foes of the freedom of the colored race were in conflict.

In a letter to Mr. Redpath, dated on board "The Fulton," March 7, 1857, he said, "Do any sigh for a Thermopylæ? They have it in Kansas ; for there is to be fought the great battle between freedom and slavery, by the ballot-box I trust ; but I do not forget that all who destroy the *ballot-box* madly invoke the *cartridge-box*. With a farewell to my country as I seek a foreign land for health long deferred, I give my best thoughts to suffering Kansas, with devout prayers that the usurpation which now treads her down may be proudly overthrown, and that she may be lifted into the enjoyment of freedom and repose."

Soon after his arrival at Paris, a public dinner was tendered him (April 28) by the American merchants residing in that city ; and in his letter deciding, on account of the state of his health, not to accept the honor, occurs this elegant paragraph : —

"Pardon the allusion, when I add that you are the daily industrious workmen in that mighty loom whose frame stands on the coasts of opposite continents, whose threads are Atlantic voyages, whose colors are the various enterprises and activities of a beneficent commerce, and whose well-wrought product is a radiant, speaking tissue — more beautiful to the mind's eye than any fabric of rarest French skill, more marvellous than any tapestry woven for kings — where every color mingles with every thread, in completed harmony and on the grandest scale, to display the triumphs and the blessings of peace."

Still battling manfully with his disease, Mr. Sumner visited various parts of Europe during the summer. His line of travel may be seen by the following letter, dated Heidelberg, Sept. 11, 1857. "I have been ransacking Switzerland : I have visited most of its lakes, and crossed several of its mountains, muleback. My strength has not allowed me to venture upon any of those foot expeditions, the charm of Swiss travel, by which you reach places out of the way; but I have seen much, and have gained health constantly.

"I have crossed the Alps by the St. Gothard, and then recrossed by the grand St. Bernard, passing a night with the monks and dogs. I have spent a day at the foot of Mont Blanc, and another on the wonderful Lake Leman. I have been in the Pyrenees, in the Alps, in the Channel Isles. You will next hear of me in the Highlands of Scotland."

While in Edinburgh he made the acquaintance of George Combe, Esq., the distinguished phrenologist, who endeavored to dissuade him from an early return to public duties. Yet his anxiety to lend his aid to that heroic band of patriots who were struggling to resist the encroachments of the slave propagandists, induced him to return to his seat in Congress, which he resumed at the opening of the session in December. His health was, however, so much impaired, that he could only attend to some minor points of business, and vote on important questions coming before the Senate. Finding no permanent relief, he was constrained again to leave the country; and on the twenty-second day of May, 1858, he took passage at New York, by the steamship "Vanderbilt" for Havre. In a letter, dated on board "The Vanderbilt," May 22, 1858, to the people of Massachusetts, who deeply sympathized with him in his continued sufferings, he made this touching allusion: "I was often assured and encouraged to feel that to every sincere lover of civilization my vacant chair was a perpetual speech." It was a perpetual speech, which moved, as no words could have done, the national heart to sympathize with those in bondage.

In Paris he came under the treatment of the eminent physician Dr. Brown-Séquard, who, when his patient asked what was to be the remedy, replied,

"Fire." "When can you apply it?" said Mr. Sumner. "To-morrow, if you please," answered the doctor. "Why not this afternoon?" continued the other; and that afternoon it was done by the *moxa*,* and afterwards repeated, without the use of chloroform. The diagnosis and the treatment of this case are, on account of their unusual interest, here given in the words of this distinguished physiologist and practitioner as presented by him in a public lecture: —

"When, in 1857, I saw Mr. Charles Sumner for the first time, he presented to me at once symptoms which I could not but recognize as dependent upon an irritation of some fibres of a sympathetic nerve, and a paralysis of others. As you know, he received a terrible blow upon the head. His spine as he was sitting had been bent in two places, the cranium fortunately resisting. This bending of the spine in two places had produced there the effects of a sprain. When I saw him in Paris he had recovered altogether from the first effects of the blow. He suffered only from the two sprains of the spine, and perhaps a slight irritation of the spinal cord itself. He had two troubles at that time. One was that he could not make use of his brain at all. He could not read a newspaper, could not write a letter. He was in a frightful state as regards the activity of the mind, as every effort there was most painful to him. It seemed to him at times as if his head would burst: there seemed to be some great force within pushing the pieces

---

* A substance used as a counter-irritant by gradual combustion on the skin.

11

away from one another. Any emotion was painful to him. Even in conversation, any thing that called for depth of thought or feeling caused him suffering, so that we had to be very careful with him. He had another trouble, resulting from the sprain which was at the level of the lowest dorsal vertebra. The irritation produced was intense, and the result very painful. When he tried to move forward, he was compelled to push one foot slowly and gently forward but a few inches, and then drag the other foot to a level with the first, holding his back at the same time to diminish the pain that he had there. It had been thought that he was paralyzed in the lower limbs, and that he had disease of the brain; and the disease of the brain was construed as being the cause of this paralysis of the lower limbs.

"Fortunately, the discovery made of what we call the vasamotor nervous system led me at once to the conclusion that he had no disease of the brain, and had no paralysis: he had only an irritation of those vasa-motor nerves, resulting from the upper sprain in the spine. That irritation was the cause of the whole mischief as regards the function of the brain. The other sprain caused the pain which gave the appearance of paralysis. When I asked him if he was conscious of any weakness in his lower limbs, he said, 'Certainly not: I have never understood that my physicians considered me paralyzed. I only cannot walk on account of the pain.'

"What was to be done was to apply counter-irritants to those two sprains. That was done. I told him that the best plan of treatment would consist in the application of moxas, and that they produced the most painful kind of irritation of the skin that we knew. I urged him then to allow me to give him chloroform, to diminish the pain, if not take it away altogether.

I well remember his impressive accent when he replied, 'If you can say positively that I shall derive as much benefit if I take chloroform as if I do not, then of course I will take it; but if there is to be any degree whatever of amelioration in case I do not take it, then I shall not take it.'

"I did not find courage enough to deceive him. I told him the truth, — that there would be more effect, as I thought, if he did not take chloroform ; and so I had to submit him to the martyrdom of the greatest suffering that can be inflicted on mortal man. I burned him with the first moxa. I had the hope that after the first application he would submit to the use of chloroform; but for five times after that he was burned in the same way, and refused to take chloroform. I have never seen a patient who submitted to such treatment in that way.

"I cannot conceive that it was from mere heroism that he did it. The real explanation was this: Heaps of abuse had been thrown upon him. He was considered as amusing himself in Paris, as pretending to be ill. In fact, he wanted to get well and go home as quickly as possible. A few days were of great importance to him. And so he passed through that terrible suffering, the greatest that I have ever inflicted upon any being, be it man or animal.

"I mention this only to show what the man was ; and I shall only add, that, since that, I have always found him ready to submit to any thing for the sake of what he thought to be right; and in other spheres you know that such was his character." [Applause.]

At this point Dr. Brown-Séquard was so much affected, that he found himself unable to proceed, and so stopped the lecture, after having spoken one-half of the usual time.

While undergoing the painful treatment of his physicians, Mr. Sumner found some alleviation to his sufferings by continuing the study of engravings in the cabinets of Paris. In the latter part of August he visited Aix in Savoy, long noted for its thermal waters and healthful atmosphere. In a letter to a friend, dated ⅃ this place, Sept. 11, 1858, he describes his mode of life and his anxieties : —

"My life is devoted to health. I wish that I could say that I am not still an invalid; yet, except when attacked by the pain on my chest, I am now comfortable, and enjoy my baths, my walks, and the repose and *incognito* which I find here. I begin the day with *douches* hot and cold, and when thoroughly exhausted am wrapped in sheet and blanket, and conveyed to my hotel, and laid on my bed. After my walk, I find myself obliged again to take to my bed for two hours before dinner. But this whole treatment is in pleasant contrast with the protracted suffering from fire which made the summer a torment; and yet I fear that I must return to that treatment.

"It is with a pang unspeakable, that I find myself thus arrested in the labors of life and in the duties of my position. This is harder to bear than the fire.

I do not hear of friends engaged in active service, — like Trumbull in Illinois, — without a feeling of envy."

From Savoy he went through Switzerland *via* Milan to Venice, but was too great an invalid to derive much pleasure from visiting the Ducal Palace or the far-famed Rialto. He returned to Paris in November by the way of Vienna, Berlin, and Munich. By the advice of Dr. Brown-Séquard, he now abandoned his cherished purpose of returning home, and repaired to the ancient city of Montpellier, near the Mediterranean Sea, distinguished alike for the brilliancy of its atmosphere, and the richness of its scenery. Here he passed the winter months in reading, in attending the lectures at the college, and in using means for the restoration of his health. These were so far effectual, that he was able again to visit Italy in the spring. Returning thence to Paris, he still found the state of his health improving. Here he had the pleasure of meeting his friend Theodore Parker, an invalid on his way to Italy (where he died May 10, 1860), and of learning that the degree of LL.D. had been conferred on him by Harvard University.

Spending the month of August in Havre for the benefit of sea-bathing, Mr. Sumner returned to Paris in the autumn almost entirely well; and with exquisite pleasure visited La Grange, the country home of Lafayette, whose noble character and public services he held in great admiration. In his grand address on "Lafayette, the Faithful One," at Cooper Institute, New York, Nov. 30, 1860, he thus spoke of his excursion and the place: —

"On a clear and lovely day of October, in company with a friend, I visited this famous seat, which at once reminded me of the prints of it so common at shop-windows in my childhood. It is a picturesque and venerable castle, — with five round towers, a moat, a drawbridge, an arched gateway, ivy-clad walls, and a large court-yard within, — embosomed in trees, except on one side, where a beautiful lawn spreads its verdure. Every thing speaks to us. The castle itself is of immemorial antiquity, — supposed to have been built in the earliest days of the French monarchy, as far back as Louis le Gros. It had been tenanted by princes of Lorraine, and been battered by the cannon of Turenne, one of whose balls penetrated its thick masonry. The ivy, so luxuriantly mantling the gate with the tower by its side, was planted by the eminent British statesman Charles Fox, on a visit during the brief peace of Amiens. The park owed much of its beauty to Lafayette himself. The situation harmonized with the retired habits which found shelter there from the storms of fortune."

During his long absence from the Senate and the country, the impending crisis to which he had so distinctly and so often pointed was steadily approaching. Under the timid and imbecile administration of James Buchanan (inaugurated March 4, 1857), the South continued to make desperate efforts to extend the realm of human servitude; and Northern politicians, fearful of the dismemberment of the Union, but too often tamely yielded to the arrogant assumptions of the slaveholding congressmen. But more and more enlightened by the eloquent speeches of such advocates of freedom as Wendell Phillips, Henry Wilson, William H. Seward, and Joshua R. Giddings; by the pulpit, which now spoke out fearlessly; and by the public press, especially by "The Liberator" and "The New-York Tribune,"—the people came to entertain profounder convictions of the inhumanity of the servile system, of its antagonism to free labor, free speech, to social and civil progress, and also of the tremendous interests at stake. The Republican party had therefore steadily increased in strength, and now, embracing every anti-slavery element, presented an unbroken front in opposition to the Southern domination. In various sections, North and West, it had elected senators and representatives to Congress, in whose halls debates on almost every question still continued to assume a more decided partisan character. Freedom and slavery had come to the death-grapple. "Let us call our system an unmixed good," exclaimed a Southern member, "and stake our money and o r lives in its defence!" "It is an unmitigated evil," replied the North: "thus far shall it come, no far- ther." As the advocates of slavery saw the strength of the Republican party (which now had nearly twenty members in the Senate) rising, it held with more tenacity its ground, and more obstinately strove to render the administrative, the judicial, and the legislative power subservient to its control. With less parade, less demonstration, than upon the field of action afterwards, but with no less intrepidity and decision, the war was raging, and the battle for dominion rolling on.

The raid of Capt. John Brown,* which was an at-

* John Brown, with about twenty followers, under the impression that the slaves would unite in the movement, surprised Harper's Ferry on the night of the 20th of October, 1859, and took the arsenal, armory, and about forty prisoners. On the day following, two sons and nearly all his men were killed, and he himself, after receiving several wounds, was captured. He was tried in November, sentenced to death, and executed. He acted conscientiously, and evinced the heroism of an old martyr. His life was written by James Redpath, 1860. John Brown, as well as Mr. Sumner, was remarkable for his height; and, on being asked by the latter if he ever intended to live in Kansas, he replied, "No, unless I happened to find my last home there." "In that case," returned Mr. Sumner, "yours, like mine, would be a long home."

tempt, made in the autumn of 1859, to liberate the
slaves of Virginia, had greatly exasperated the
South; and on the day in which Mr. Sumner again
took his seat in the Senate (December 5), a committee
was appointed " to inquire into the facts attending the
late invasion."   This committee introduced a resolution compelling Thaddeus Hyatt to testify in regard
to this affair before the Senate; and on the question
of its passage, March 12, 1860, Mr. Sumner made a
brief but able speech, in which he clearly showed
that that body had no power to imprison a citizen.
The resolutions, however, were adopted on the 12th
of March, when Mr. Hyatt was committed to jail.
During his imprisonment he was frequently visited
by Mr. Sumner, who found the jail " neither more
nor less," as he observed, " than a mere human sty ; "
and this led to a resolution " to improve the condition of the common jail of the city of Washington."   On the 10th of April he presented the
memorial of Frank B. Sanborn, a teacher of Concord,
Mass., whom certain agents of the slaveocracy, under
the pretence that he had been in complicity with
John Brown, had on the 3d of April attempted to
kidnap, but who was rescued by his neighbors and the
deputy sheriff with a writ of *habeas corpus*.   On the
16th of April, Mr. Mason of Virginia moved that

the memorial be rejected; and in his remarks thereon Mr. Sumner made use of this severe comparison : —

" I feel it my duty to establish a precedent also in this case, by entering an open, unequivocal protest against such an attempt. Sir, an ancient poet said of a judge in hell, that he punished first, and heard afterwards (*castigatque auditque*); and permit me to say, the senator from Virginia on this occasion takes a precedent from that court."

Mr. Sumner undoubtedly sympathized with John Brown in respect to the ends he had in view, but did not agree with him as to the means employed for securing them. " I once," says James Redpath, " visited Senator Sumner in the company of John Brown. We spoke of the assault of P. S. Brooks, under which Mr. Sumner was suffering. Capt. Brown then suddenly said, 'Have you still the coat?' 'Yes,' replied Mr. Sumner: 'it is in that closet. Would you like to see it?' 'Very much indeed,' returned the captain. Mr. Sumner then, rising slowly and painfully from his bed, opened a closet-door, and handed the garment to the old hero. The scene was striking. Mr. Sumner was bending slightly, and supporting himself by resting his hand upon the bed, while Capt. Brown stood erect as a pillar, holding up the blood-besmeared coat, and intently scanning it. The old man said nothing; but his lips were compressed, and his eyes shone like polished steel."

CHAPTER XIV.

Mr. Sumner Represents the Spirit of the North. — "The Crime against Kansas." — Exordium. — Analysis of the Speech. — Slave Masters. — Freedom of Speech. — William Lloyd Garrison. — By Nature every Man is Free. — Property in Man not recognized by the Constitution. — Closing Words. — Remarks of Mr. Chestnut. — Mr. Sumner's Reply. — Reception of his Speech by the Public Press. — The Opinion of S. P. Chase. — Of Carl Schurz. — Of N. Hall. — Personal Violence attempted. — A Body-Guard. — Resolutions of the Massachusetts Legislature. — Nomination of the Presidential Candidates, 1860. — Mr. Sumner's Speeches at Cooper Institute, Worcester, and other Places.

> "No skill had he with veering winds to veer;
>   By trampling on the good, himself to rise;
>   To run for any port, indifferent where,
>   So tongue and conscience make fair merchandise."
>
> · W. W. NEWELL.

> Spiriti piu nobili del suo, io non ne avea mai conosciuti, pari al suo, pochi."
> *Le Mie Prigione* di SILVIO PELLICO.

> "Such earnest natures are the fiery pith,
>   The compact nucleus, round which systems grow;
>   Mass after mass becomes inspired therewith,
>   And whirls impregnate with the central glow."

ALTHOUGH Mr. Sumner attended to some minor senatorial duties, and watched with an eagle eye the logic of events, it was not until the fourth day of June, 1860, that he came grandly up to the work on hand, and showed the country that Richard was on his feet again. On the Bill for the Admission of Kansas as a Free State, then before the Senate, he made one of the most masterly speeches of his life, sending broadside after broadside of solid shot into the strongholds of slavery, and utterly demolishing every defence and fortress of its partisans. He had the learning, the statesmanship, the eloquence, the heroism, the *brutum fulmen*, which the exigence demanded; and with Titanic force he stood forth, mailed in the armor of truth, as the best representative of the spirit of a free people, and as the strongest champion living of the inalienable rights of the colored race. The rising of Mr. Sumner in that seat where he had four years previously been stricken down by the hand of violence, to pronounce again, in front of a vindictive power, the doom of slavery, was a spectacle of moral grandeur such as when the dauntless Mirabeau at the point of bayonet rose, in 1789, to vindicate the Third-Estate in the presence of the French Assembly. In allusion to the solemnity of the occasion, and the death of Mr. Butler and of Mr. Brooks, he said : —

"Mr. PRESIDENT, — Undertaking now, after a silence of more than four years, to address the Senate on this important subject, I should suppress the emotions natural to such an occasion, if I did not declare on the threshold my gratitude to that supreme Being through whose benign care I am enabled, after much suffering and many changes, once again to resume my duties here, and to speak for the cause which is so near my heart. To the honored Commonwealth whose representative I am, and also to my immediate associates in this body, with whom I enjoy the fellowship which is found *in thinking alike concerning the Republic*, I owe thanks which I seize this moment to express, for the indulgence shown me throughout the protracted seclusion enjoined by medical skill; and I trust that it will not be thought unbecoming in me to put on record here, as an apology for leaving my seat so long vacant, without making way, by resignation, for a successor, that I acted under the illusion of an invalid, whose hopes for restoration to his natural health constantly triumphed over his disappointments.

"When last I entered into this debate, it became my duty to expose the crime against Kansas, and to insist upon the immediate admission of that Territory as a State of this Union, with a constitution forbidding slavery. Time has passed; but the question remains. Resuming the discussion precisely where I left it, I am happy to avow that rule of moderation, which, it is said, may venture even to fix the boundaries of wisdom itself. I have no personal griefs to utter: only a barbarous egotism could intrude these into this chamber. I have no personal wrongs to avenge: only a barbarous nature could attempt to wield that vengeance which belongs to the Lord. The years that have intervened and the tombs that have been opened since I spoke have their voices too, which I cannot fail to hear. Besides, what am I? — what is any man among the living or among the dead, — compared with the question now before us? It is this alone which I shall discuss; and I open the argument with that easy victory which is found in charity."

Mr. Sumner entitled his Speech "The Crime against Kansas;" and he thus indicated the manner in which it was to be discussed : —

"Motive is to crime as soul to body; and it is only when we comprehend the motive, that we can truly comprehend the crime. Here, the motive is found in slavery and the rage for its extension. Therefore, by logical necessity, must slavery be discussed; not indirectly, timidly, and sparingly, but directly, openly, and thoroughly. It must be exhibited as it is, alike in its influence and in its animating character, so that not only its outside but its inside may be seen.

This is no time for soft words or excuses. All such are out of place. They may turn away wrath; but what is the wrath of man? This is no time to abandon any advantage in the argument. Senators sometimes announce that they resist slavery on political grounds only, and remind us that they say nothing of the moral question. This is wrong. Slavery must be resisted not only on political grounds, but on all other grounds, whether social, economical, or moral. Ours is no holiday contest; nor is it any strife of rival factions, — of White and Red Roses, of theatric Neri and Bianchi: but it is a solemn battle between right and wrong, between good and evil. Such a battle cannot be fought with excuses or with rosewater. There is austere work to be done; and Freedom cannot consent to fling away any of her weapons."

His weapons were directed against the claims put forth especially by Mr. Davis: first, that slavery is a form of civilization; and second, that property in man is placed beyond the reach of Congressional prohibition. To the first said he, —

"I oppose the essential barbarism of slavery, in all its influences, whether high or low, as Satan is Satan still, whether towering in the sky, or squatting in the toad. To the second I oppose the unanswerable, irresistible truth, that the Constitution of the United States nowhere recognizes property in man. These two assumptions naturally go together. They are 'twins' suckled by the same wolf: they are the 'couple' in the present slave-hunt; and the latter cannot be answered without exposing the former. It is only when slavery is exhibited in its truly hateful character, that we can fully appreciate the absurdity of the assumption which, in defiance of the express letter of the constitution, and without a single sentence, phrase, or word upholding human bondage, yet foists into this blameless text the barbarous idea that man can hold property in man."

He represented the barbarism of slavery under the law of slavery in five distinct elements, —

" First, assuming that man can hold property in man; secondly, abrogating the relation of husband and wife; thirdly, abrogating the parental tie; fourthly, closing the gates of knowledge; and fifthly, appropriating the unpaid labor of another."

In respect to the last element he said, —

" By such a fallacy is a whole race pauperized ; and yet this transaction is not without illustrative example. A solemn poet, whose verse has found wide favor, pictures a creature who

' With one hand put
A penny in the urn of poverty,
And with the other took a shilling out.'*

And a celebrated traveller through Russia, more than a generation ago, describes a kindred spirit, who, while on his knees before an altar of the Greek Church, devoutly told his beads with one hand, and with the other deliberately picked the pocket of a fellow-sinner by his side."

The speaker then, by a careful comparison between the industrial, social, and literary condition of the slave and the free States, presented the sad results of slavery.

In speaking of the influence of the slave-system on the characters of the slave-masters he said,—

"Barbarous standards of conduct are unblushingly avowed. The swagger of a bully is called chivalry; a swiftness to quarrel is called courage; the bludgeon is adopted as the substitute for argument; and assassination is lifted to be one of the fine arts. Long ago it was fixed certain that the day which made man a slave 'took half his worth away,'—words from the ancient harp of Homer, resounding through long generations. Nothing here is said of the human being at the other end of the chain. To aver that on this same day all his worth is taken away, might seem inconsistent with exceptions which we gladly recognize; but, alas! it is too clear, both from reason and from evidence, that, bad as slavery is for the slave, it is worse for the master."

* Pollok's Course of Time, Book VIII., 632.

In confirmation of this point, he adds these words, which Col. Mason, a slave-master from Virginia, used in debate on the adoption of the national constitution: "They produce the most pernicious effect on manners. Every master of slaves is born a petty tyrant. They bring the judgment of Heaven on a country."

In reference to suppression of freedom of speech, Mr. Sumner truly said, —

"Looking now at the broad surface of society where slavery exists, we shall find its spirit actively manifest in the suppression of all freedom of speech or of the press, especially with regard to this wrong. Nobody in the slave States can speak or print against slavery, except at the peril of life or liberty. St. Paul could call upon the people of Athens to give up the worship of unknown gods; he could live in his own hired house at Rome, and preach Christianity in this heathen metropolis: but no man can be heard against slavery in Charleston or Mobile."

He noticed in this connection the ridiculous attempt of a Southern governor to secure the person of a distinguished advocate of freedom at the North.

"A citizen," said he, "of purest life and perfect integrity, whose name is destined to fill a conspicuous place in the history of freedom, — William Lloyd Garrison. Born in Massachusetts, bred to the same profession with Benjamin Franklin, and like his great predecessor becoming an editor, he saw with instinctive clearness the wrong of slavery; and, at a period when the ardors of the Missouri Question had given way to indifference throughout the North, he stepped forward to denounce it. The jail at Baltimore, where he then resided, was his earliest reward. Afterwards, January 1, 1831, he published the first number of 'The Liberator,' inscribing for his motto an utterance of Christian philanthropy, 'My country is the world : my countrymen are all mankind,' and declaring, in the face of surrounding apathy, 'I am in earnest. I will not equivocate ; I will not retreat a single inch : and I will be heard.' In this sublime spirit he commenced his labors for the slave, proposing no intervention by Congress in the States, and on well-considered principle avoiding all appeals to the bondmen themselves. Such was his simple and thoroughly constitutional position, when, before the expiration of the first year, the legislature of Georgia, by solemn act, a copy of which I have now before me, 'approved' by Wilson Lumpkin, Governor, appropriated five thousand dollars ' to be paid to any person who shall arrest, bring to trial, and prosecute to conviction under the laws of this State, the editor or publisher of a certain paper called " The Liberator," published at the town of Boston and State of Massachusetts.' This infamous legislative act, touching a person absolutely beyond the jurisdiction of Georgia, and in no way amenable to its laws, constituted a plain bribe to the gangs of kidnappers engendered by slavery. With this barefaced defiance of justice and decency, slave-masters inaugurated the system of violence by which they have sought to crush every voice that has been raised against slavery."

Under the second claim of the slaveocracy he said : —

" This assumption may be described as an attempt to *Africanize* the constitution by introducing into it the barbarous law of slavery, derived as we have seen originally from barbarous Africa; and then, through such *Africanization* of the constitution, to *Africanize* the Territories, and to *Africanize* the national government. . . . Under what ordinance of nature or of nature's God is one human being stamped an owner, and another stamped a thing? God is no respecter of persons. Where is the sanction for this respect of certain persons to a degree which becomes outrage to other persons? God is the Father of the human family; and we are all his children. Where, then, is the sanction of this pretension by which a brother lays violent hands upon a brother? To ask these questions is humiliating; but it is clear there can be but one response. There is no sanction for such pretension, no ordinance for it, or title. On all grounds of reason, and waiving all questions of 'positive' statute, the Vermont judge was nobly right, when, rejecting the claim of a slave-master, he said, 'No; not until you show a bill of sale from the Almighty.' Nothing short of this impossible link in the chain of title would do. I know something of the great judgments by which the jurisprudence of our country has been illustrated; but I doubt if there is any thing in the wisdom of Marshall, the learning of Story, or the completeness of Kent, which will brighten with time like this honest decree."

In closing his grand argument, Mr. Sumner used these hopeful words: —

"Let the answer become a legislative act, by the admission of Kansas as a free State. Then will the barbarism of slavery be repelled, and the pretension of property in man be rebuked. Such an act, closing this long struggle by the assurance of peace to the Territory, if not of tranquillity to the whole country, will be more grateful still as the herald of that better day, near at hand, when freedom shall be installed everywhere under the national government; when the national flag, where-ever it floats, on sea or land, within the national jurisdiction, will not cover a single slave; and when the Declaration of Independence, now reviled in the name of slavery, will once again be reverenced as the American Magna Charta of human rights. Nor is this all. Such an act will be the first stage in those triumphs by which the Republic — lifted in character so as to become an example to mankind — will enter at last upon its noble 'prerogative of teaching the nations how to live.'"

This magnificent speech was unanswerable except by menace and vituperation. It struck the heart of the barbarous system, and was in respect to argument a death-blow. As soon as Mr. Sumner resumed his seat, Mr. Chestnut of South Carolina rose, and in the bitter spirit of the doomed institution said, —

"After ranging over Europe, crawling through the back doors to whine at the feet of British aristocracy, craving pity, and reaping a rich harvest of contempt, the slanderer of States and men re-appears in the Senate. We had hoped to be relieved from the outpourings of such vulgar malice. We had hoped that one who had felt, though ignominiously he failed to meet, the consequences of a former insolence, would have become wiser, if not better, by experience. . . .

"It has been left for this day, for this country, for the abolitionists of Massachusetts, *to deify the incarnation of malice,*

mendacity, and cowardice. Sir, we do not intend to be guilty of
aiding in the apotheosis of pusillanimity and meanness. We
do not intend to contribute, by any conduct on our part, to
increase the devotees at the shrine of this new idol. We know
what is expected, and what is desired. *We are not inclined again
to send forth the recipient of* PUNISHMENT *howling through the
world, yelping fresh cries of slander and malice. These are the
reasons,* which I feel it due to myself and others to give to the
Senate and the country, why we have quietly listened to what has
been said, and why we can take no other notice of the matter."

"Only one word," said Mr. Sumner, who with
difficulty gained the floor: "I exposed to-day the
barbarism of slavery. What the senator has said in
reply to me, I may well print in an appendix to my
speech as an additional illustration. That is all."

Mr. Sumner commenced his speech about twelve
o'clock, at noon, and continued till about four. The
galleries of the Senate were filled with gentlemen
and ladies from the North and South; and the most
ominous silence prevailed. Mr. Wilson, Mr. King,
Mr. Bingham, and Mr. Burlingame sat near the
speaker, and, had any attempt at personal violence
been made by Messrs. Keitt, Hammond, Toombs,
Wigfall, or others who were present, smarting under
the scourge of slavery, would doubtless have been
ready to repel it.

In commenting on this speech, the correspondent
of "The Chicago Press and Tribune" wrote, "The

speech of Charles Sumner yesterday was probably the most masterly argument against human bondage that has ever been made in this or any other country since man first commenced to oppress his fellow-man."

Frederic Douglass in his paper truly said, "The network of his argument, though wonderfully elaborate and various, is everywhere and in all parts strong as iron. The whole slave-holding *propaganda* of the Senate might dash themselves against it, a compact body, without breaking the smallest fibre of its various parts."

The London "Punch" said, "All the bludgeons in the hands of all the chivalry of the South cannot beat that demonstration of Mr. Sumner's case out of the heads of the public, in and out of the States."

The Democratic papers, however, took a different view; and their general opinion may be seen from this remark of "The Albany Atlas and Argus:" "No one can rise from a perusal of this speech without a contempt for the author, and a conviction of his unfitness for the place." Several of the Republican papers thought the speech too strong, and that it might retard the passage of the bill; but desperate cases require effective remedies.

Mr. Sumner received a large number of letters congratulating him for this splendid effort on behalf of human rights. "It will reach every corner of the land," wrote Salmon P. Chase: "'*cogens omnes ante thronum.*' 'C'est presqu'un discours antique,' said a French gentleman to me last Saturday. I say, 'C'est bien plus.'"

"It did me good," wrote Carl Schurz, "to hear again the true ring of the moral anti-slavery sentiment." "I do not know," wrote the Rev. Nathaniel Hall, "in our day a nobler instance of moral bravery." "It is the best arranged and by far the most complete exposure of the horrid rite of slavery," wrote John Bigelow from New York, "to be found within the same compass in any language, so far as known."

"I take pleasure in saying," said Horace White, in a letter written from Chicago, "that in my opinion your recent effort ranks with Demosthenes on the Crown, and with Burke on Warren Hastings." "Your speech," wrote A. A. Sargent (now senator from California) to Mr. Sumner, "stirred my heart with feelings of pride for the representative of my native State."

It was greatly feared by the friends of Mr. Sumner that personal violence would again be offered him; and, indeed, the attempt was made.

On the eighth day of June, a stranger called on him in the evening, stating that he had come to hold him responsible for his speech, when Mr. Sumner directed him to leave the room. He departed after some delay, with the menace that he and his three friends from Virginia would call again. Mr. Sumner sent immediately for Mr. Wilson; and in the course of the evening three men came to the door, desiring to see Mr. Sumner alone; but, as he was in company, they left word at the door, that, if they could not have a private interview, they would cut his throat before another night.

Messrs. Burlingame and Sherman remained as a guard until the next morning.

The friends of Mr. Sumner were much alarmed; and among others G. B. Weston thus wrote to him from Duxbury, Mass., "I am ready to shoulder my musket, and march to the Capitol, and there sacrifice my life in defence of free speech and the right." By the foresight of A. B. Johnson, Mr. Sumner's private secretary, a body-guard armed with revolvers was arranged, which attended him, without his knowledge, to and from the Senate-chamber.

Prompt to sustain him in his heroic defence of truth, the legislature of Massachusetts passed on the 20th of June these resolutions: —

"RESOLVED, That the thanks of the people of this Commonwealth are due, and are hereby tendered, to the Hon. CHARLES SUMNER for his recent manly and earnest assertion of the right of free discussion on the floor of the United-States Senate; and we repeat the well-considered words of our predecessors in these seats, in approval of 'Mr. Sumner's manliness and courage in his fearless declaration of free principles, and his defence of human rights and free institutions.'

"Resolved, That we approve the thorough, truthful, and comprehensive examination of the institution of slavery, embraced in Mr. Sumner's recent speech; that the stern morality of that speech, its logic, and its power, command our entire admiration; and that it expresses with fidelity the sentiments of Massachusetts upon the question therein discussed."

The Republican party in convention at Chicago in May, 1860, nominated Abraham Lincoln — who had manifested his ability and his devotion to the cause of freedom especially in his controversy with Stephen A. Douglas in Illinois, and who had said, " He who would *be* no slave, must consent to *have* no slave " — as its candidate for the Presidential chair.

John C. Breckenridge (nominated at Charleston, S. C.) was the Southern, Stephen A. Douglas the Northern Democratic, and John Bell (of Kentucky) the Union candidate. The grand question before the country was: Shall free or servile labor have the ascendency? Shall the vast territories of the Union come under the baleful domination of slavery, or be irradiated by the genial beams of freedom? The aim of the progressive party was the dethronement of the slave-power in the national

government, and the repression of that power to
within the limits of the sovereignty of the States.

Mr. Sumner clearly saw and felt the magnitude of
the question now at issue between the parties, and
with all the power of his commanding eloquence
threw himself into the exciting contest.   In a splendid speech before an immense audience at Cooper
Institute, on the eleventh day of July, he said that by
the election of Abraham Lincoln " we shall put the
national government right, at least in its executive
department; " " we shall save the Territories from
the five-headed barbarism of slavery ; " " we shall save
the country and the age from that crying infamy, the
slave-trade ; " " we shall save the constitution, at
least within the executive influence, from outrage
and perversion ; " " we shall help save the Declaration of Independence, now dishonored and disowned
in its essential, life-giving truth, — the *equality of
men;*" " and, finally, we shall help expel the slave
oligarchy from all its seats of national power, driving
it back within the States."   In conclusion he said,
" Others may dwell on the past as secure ; but, to my
mind, under the laws of a beneficent God *the future
also is secure,* on the single condition that we press
forward in the work with heart and soul, forgetting
self, turning from all temptations of the hour, and,
intent only on the cause,

' With mean complacence ne'er betray our trust,
Nor be so civil as to prove unjust.' "

In a strong speech at the State Convention of the
Republican party at Worcester, Aug. 29, he laid
open the fallacy of the double-headed doctrine of
popular sovereignty proposed by Mr. Douglas, " who
was ready to vote slavery up, or vote it down." So
in open-air meetings at Myrick's Station, Sept.
18, and at Framingham, Oct. 11, he made an admirable vindication of the policy of the Republican
party. At the latter place he said, —

" Freedom, which is the breath of God, is a great
leveller; but it raises where it levels. Slavery,
which is the breath of Satan, is also a great leveller;
but it degrades every thing, carrying with it master
as well as slave. Choose ye between them ; and remember that your first duty is to stand up straight,
and not bend before absurd threats, whether uttered
at the South or repeated here in Massachusetts. Let
people cry ' Disunion !' We know what the cry
means; and we answer back, ' The Union shall be
preserved, and made more precious by its consecra-
tion to freedom.' "

On the evening (Nov. 5), before the grand triumph of the Republican party in the election of
Mr. Lincoln, he said with rapturous emotion, in old

Faneuil Hall, " To-morrow we shall have not only a new president, but a new government. A new order of things will begin; and our history will proceed on a grander scale, in harmony with those sublime principles in which it commenced. Let the knell sound !

'Ring out the old, ring in the new !
Ring out the false, ring in the true !
　　Ring out a slowly-dying cause,
And ancient forms of party strife !
Ring in the nobler modes of life,
　　With sweeter manners, purer laws !'"

CHAPTER XV.

> " Ring in the valiant man and free,
> The larger heart, the kindlier hand.
> Ring out the darkness of the land!
> Ring in the Christ that is to be! "
>
> ALFRED TENNYSON.

> " Still as an unmoved rock
> Washed white, but not shaken by the shock;
> His heart conceived no sinister device:
> Fearless he played with flame, and trod on ice."

> "His was the celestial beauty
> Of a soul that does its duty."

THE Southern people possess magnanimous traits of character: they are brave, openhearted, courteous, and hospitable. But the brightness of these noble traits was somewhat

270

shaded by the baleful influence of slavery. They devote much time and attention to political studies; and the controlling power which they long exercised in the national government, even when a Webster led the North, is in attestation of their activity and skill in political management. But they misunderstood the spirit of this section of the Union, which was not that of domination or of violence, but of humanity and fraternity. They also underestimated the unity of sentiment and the valor of those they falsely deemed their enemies. For this their leaders were to a great extent responsible.

During the presidential canvass of 1860, the Southern States were secretly storing arms, and making other preparations for the dissolution of the Union; and, immediately after the triumph of the Republican party in the election of Abraham Lincoln to the presidential chair, in November, public meetings were held in South Carolina urging a secession from the Union. On the opening of Congress (Dec. 4), this determination at once became apparent; and a resolution was presented to the Senate on the following day, that a committee be appointed to inquire into the present agitated and distracted state of the country.

In speaking on this resolution, Mr. Sumner introduced with startling effect an unpublished autograph letter of Andrew Jackson, containing these remarkable words: "Haman's gallows ought to be the fate of all such ambitious men, who would involve their country in a civil war, and all the evils in its train, that they might reign and ride on its whirlwinds, and direct the storm. . . . The tariff was only the pretext (for nullification), and disunion and a Southern confederacy the real object. The next pretext will be the negro or slavery question."

To the Crittenden Compromise, introduced into the Senate Dec. 18, and recognizing slavery in the territory south of 36° 30′ north latitude, Mr. Sumner was unequivocally opposed. South Carolina passed the ordinance of secession on the twentieth day of December. Other States soon followed: stout hearts were trembling; yet through the tremendous agitation Mr. Sumner stood to principle firm as a rock. He saw the storm impending; he deprecated bloodshed; he felt that the best way to avert it was for the North to hold itself immovable. He exhorted every one to stand for the right with unwavering front. He wrote (Jan. 1) to William Claflin, President of the Massachusetts Senate, "Let the timid cry; but let Massachusetts stand stiff: God bless her!" To Count Gurowski, author of an admirable treatise on slavery, he wrote (Jan. 8), "These compromisers do not comprehend the glory of prin-

ciple. *Périssent les colonies plutôt qu'un principe !*"
In a letter to Gov. John A. Andrew, dated Jan.
17, he said, "Pray keep Massachusetts sound and
firm, FIRM, FIRM! against every word or step
of concession." In another letter to the same, dated
Jan. 28, he said, " *Timeo Danaos et dona ferentes:*
don't let these words be ever out of your mind when
you think of any proposition from the slave-masters. O God! Let Massachusetts keep true." So
again he wrote (Feb. 5), "More than the loss of forts,
arsenals, or the national capital, I fear the loss of our
principles;" and again (Feb. 10) he wrote to the
same, "I do not tremble for any thing from our
opponents, whoever they may be, but from our
friends."

On assuming the duties of his office (March 4), Mr.
Lincoln declared that he had "no purpose to interfere with the institution of slavery" where it existed,
and that in his opinion he had "no right to do so."

The course of the secession leaders had, however,
been elected; and the conciliatory inaugural of the
president served but to call forth their denunciation
and contempt. One after another the Southern
members withdrew from Congress, thus leaving the
Republicans in the ascendant; and Mr. Sumner was
on the 8th of April made chairman, in place of Mr.
Mason of Virginia, of the Committee on Foreign

Relations, for which, by his long residence abroad, and his profound knowledge of international law, he was admirably qualified.

He immediately made the acquaintance of Mr. Lincoln, of whom during the long and dreadful struggle which ensued he was a confidential adviser. He first presented to him emancipation as a war measure, the day after the battle of Bull Run, and steadily pressed it upon his attention until its proclamation. "There is no person," said the president to Mr. Sumner, near the close of his life, "with whom I have more advised throughout my administration than with yourself."

Mr. Sumner left Washington, then in a state of great excitement, on the 18th of April; and, while he was stopping at Barnum's Hotel in Baltimore, on the evening of that day, occurred the prelude to the bloody scenes which took place on the morrow. A noisy crowd surrounded the building, and demanded his person. He was fortunately absent from the house at the time, so that Mr. Barnum was able to satisfy the disorderly people, who retired. On Mr. Sumner's entering the hotel soon afterwards, by a private door, he was requested to leave at once, and not imperil the establishment; but he insisted on remaining, which he was finally allowed to do. Departing early in the morning of the 19th, he met, on his way to Philadelphia, the Sixth Regiment, which was called that day, while passing through the infuriated city of Baltimore, to sprinkle the altar of freedom with its blood. On arriving at New York, he visited the Third Battalion of the Massachusetts Rifles, to whom he made an encouraging address.

As the Southern States, one after another, swung away from allegiance to the government, and as the great drama of the war, opened by the Sumter guns, proceeded, an immense amount of hard and active service was demanded in the halls of Congress, as well as on the battle-field. True to his past record, Mr. Sumner brought himself up grandly to the new questions, and guarded with untiring vigilance the rights of the colored race. Through storm and through sunshine, he stood forth the learned, the eloquent, the indomitable defender of the slave. Had he been called to reconcile his peace principles with the musterings of the squadrons of the grand army, his reply would have been, —

"Slavery is a state of war. To secure peace, we must stand rock-like to the constitution, and under its broad folds remove the cause of war."

On the opening of the Thirty-seventh Congress, July 4, 1861, he was at his post; and the volumes of the Congressional Globe disclose the active part he took in almost every senatorial question through the war. In a speech at Worcester on the first day of October, 1861, he boldly affirmed that emancipation was the best weapon of the war. "Two objects are," said he, "before us, — union and peace, each for the sake of the other, and both for the sake of the country; but without emancipation how can we expect either?" This declaration startled the Republicans even, and drew forth severe animadversions from the Democratic press. But Mr. Sumner was at the front; and it was then truly said of him, —

> "Thou hast hurled
> Thy single pebble, plucked from truth's pure stream,
> Into the forehead of a giant wrong;
> And it doth reel and tremble. Men may doubt;
> But the keen sword of right shall finish well
> Thy brave beginning. Courage, then, true soul!"

Before a vast assembly at the Cooper Institute in New York, Nov. 27, Mr. Sumner made an eloquent speech, enriched by apt quotations and by cogent reasoning, in which he again intimated his desire that emancipation be proclaimed. "There has been," said he, "the cry, 'On to Richmond!' and still another worse cry, 'On to England!' Better than either is the cry, 'On to freedom!'"

Soon after the opening of Congress Dec. 4, Mr.

Sumner spoke earnestly on a resolution for the discharge of fugitive slaves from the Washington Jail, and characterized the Black Code, prevailing in the District of Columbia, as " a shame to the civilization of the age; " and on the 11th he delivered in the Senate, Abraham Lincoln being present, a very touching and appropriate eulogy on Senator E. D. Baker, killed at Ball's Bluff Oct. 21, while serving a piece of artillery. In the course of this fine tribute he said : —

" The nine balls that slew our departed brother came from slavery. Every gaping wound of his slashed bosom came from slavery. Every drop of his generous blood cries out from the ground against slavery. . . . The just avenger is at hand, with weapon of celestial temper. Let it be drawn! Until this is done, the patriot, discerning clearly the secret of our weakness, can only say sorrowfully, —

> 'Bleed, bleed, poor country!
> Great tyranny, lay thou thy basis sure;
> For goodness dares not check thee.' "

As the war went on, Mr. Sumner felt more and more convinced of the necessity of emancipation; and on the 27th of December he wrote a letter to Gov. Andrew, in which he said, —

" Let the doctrine of emancipation be proclaimed as an essential and happy agency in subduing a wicked rebellion. In this way you will help a majority of the cabinet, whose opinions on this subject are fixed, and precede the president himself by a few weeks. He tells me that I am ahead of him only a month or six weeks. God bless you!"

On the 9th of January, 1862, Mr. Sumner made in the Senate, then thronged with eager listeners, his exhaustive and noble speech on the "Trent" affair, which came near involving, as it afterwards appeared, this country in war with England. Messrs. Mason and Slidell, it will be remembered, who had been commissioned as rebel agents, the one to England and the other to France, were arrested on board the British mail-steamer "Trent," by Capt. Wilkes of the frigate "San Jacinto," and brought as prisoners to this country. England considered it a *casus belli;* and popular opinion here indorsed the course of Capt. Wilkes. Mr. Sumner, unmoved by public sentiment, discussed the question on the broad grounds of international law and maritime rights, and thus came to the conclusion that "the seizure of the rebel emissaries on board a neutral ship cannot be justified." "Let the rebels go," said he. "Two wicked men, ungrateful to their country, with two younger confederates, are set loose with the brand of Cain upon their foreheads; prison-doors are opened: but principles are established which will help to free other men, and to open the gates of the sea." Although many public journals criticized this calm and dispassionate review of the case, " The New-York Tribune " said, " It is already ranked in Washington as a State paper upon the question of seizure and search, worthy to be placed side by side with the despatches of Madison and Jefferson ; " and this is now the decision of the country.*

On the 11th of February following, Mr. Sumner brought into the Senate a series of resolutions which embodied the principles of emancipation, and pointed out a method of reconstruction of the rebel States. He held that slavery, having no constitutional origin or natural right, must cease with the lapsing of the State where it existed, and that Congress must then assume complete jurisdiction of the vacated territory. This was the first attempt made in the Senate for the settlement of two of the greatest questions of the war ; but, as usual, Congress was not ready for the advanced measures of this leading anti-slavery champion ; and the resolutions were laid upon the table. The speech which Mr. Sumner then pre-pared to make was published in the October number

---

* Messrs. J. M. Mason and John Slidell were released from Fort Warren, Boston Harbor, Jan. 2, 1862, and sailed for England. The former was the author of the Fugitive-Slave Bill, and died April 29, 1871: the latter died in London, July 29 of the same year.

of " The Atlantic Monthly " of the year following, and thus concludes : —

"Behold the rebel States in arms against that paternal government to which, as the supreme condition of their constitutional existence, they owe duty and love; and behold all legitimate powers, executive, legislative, and judicial, in these States abandoned and vacated. *It only remains that Congress should enter, and assume the proper jurisdiction.* If we are not ready to exclaim with Burke, speaking of revolutionary France, 'It is but an empty space on the political map!' we may at least adopt the response hurled back by Mirabeau, that this empty space is a volcano red with flames, and overflowing with lava-floods. But, whether we deal with it as 'empty space' or as 'volcano,' the jurisdiction, civil and military, centres in Congress, to be employed for the happiness, welfare, and renown of the American people, changing slavery into freedom, and present chaos into a cosmos of perpetual beauty and peace."

On Mr. Wilson's bill for the abolition of slavery in the District of Columbia, Mr. Sumner made (March 31) a very statesmanlike speech, advocating ransom rather than compensation, and clearly intimating what was soon to come.

"At the national capital," said he, "slavery will give way to freedom; but the good work will not stop here: it must proceed. What God and Nature decree, rebellion cannot arrest. And, as the whole wide-spread tyranny begins to tremble, then, above the din of battle, sounding from sea to sea and echoing along the land, above even the exultations of victory on well-fought fields, will ascend voices of gladness and benediction, swelling from generous hearts wherever civilization bears sway, to commemorate a sacred triumph, whose trophies, instead of tattered banners, will be ransomed slaves."

This bill became a law on the 16th of April. Just previous to its signature by the president, Mr. Sumner said to him, "Who is the largest slaveholder in the country?" "Who is he?" replied Mr. Lincoln. "You yourself, sir," returned the other, "holding, as you do, all in this District."

On the 23d of the month last named, he spoke eloquently on his bill for the' recognition of the independence of Hayti and Liberia, which was carried through the house mainly by the efforts of Mr. Gooch, and was signed by Mr. Lincoln June 6, 1862. "This law," Mr. Andrew wrote to Mr. Sumner, "will be a jewel in your crown." The Haytian people subsequently tendered an elegant medal to Mr. Sumner, which he, in accordance with views previously expressed, declined to receive. It was therefore, in 1871, deposited in the library of the State House of Massachusetts. On the 24th of April Mr. Sumner reported a bill, on which he made effective remarks, for the final suppression of the slave-trade, which, to the disgrace of humanity, was still protected by our flag. The bill was approved by Mr.

Lincoln July 11; and thus, by treaty with England, that inhuman traffic was at last prohibited.

In his anxiety for the suppression of the rebellion, and the uprising of the slave, Mr. Sumner spoke with great vigor in the Senate, May 19, urging the confiscation of rebel property, and emancipation, as in accordance with the rights of sovereignty and of war. He also again spoke with much force on the same subject, June 27, when he said in respect to liberation, " The language of Chatham is not misapplied when I call it the master-feather of the eagle's wing." His last speech (July 16) previous to the close of the session, was in accordance with his whole course from the opening of the war, — that the slaves must be set free, and employed for the suppression of the rebellion; and in a letter to the Republican State Committee, dated Boston, Sept. 9, he said, " Banks also symbolized the idea, when, overtaking the little slave-girl on her way to freedom, he lifted her upon the national cannon." In an admirable speech at Faneuil Hall, on the sixth day of October, which was received with great enthusiasm, he triumphantly refuted the objections to emancipation, and urged it with signal power, as the *military necessity.* " The last chapter of ' Rasselas,' " he felicitously said, " is entitled The Conclusion in which Nothing is Concluded; and this will be the proper title for the history of this war, if slavery is allowed to endure. If you would trample down the rebellion, you must trample down slavery ; and, believe me, it must be completely done."

On the first day of January, 1863, President Lincoln issued his grand proclamation, declaring " forever free the slaves in the States then in rebellion," excepting in certain parts occupied mainly by the Union army ; and he thus brought the nation up to its true position in the dreadful contest. By this glorious act, the gates to freedom were thrown open to three and a half million people, and the hearts of loyal soldiers strengthened for the combat : by it the doom of slavery, though slow to come, was sealed. Then the bell of time again pealed forth the rousing note of human progress ; and the world moved forward.

> " O dark, sad millions, patiently and dumb
>   Waiting for God ! Your hour at last has come ;
>   And freedom's song
>   Breaks the long silence of your night of wrong."

CHAPTER XVI.

> "Who is the HONEST MAN?
> He who doth still and strongly good pursue,
> To God, his neighbor, and himself most true."
>
> GEORGE HERBERT.

"In all things that have beauty, there is nothing to men more comely than
liberty. Give me the liberty to know, to utter, and to argue freely, above all
liberties." — JOHN MILTON.

> "Thy spirit, Independence, let me share,
> Lord of the lion heart and eagle eye:
> Thy steps I'll follow with my bosom bare,
> Nor heed the storm that howls along the sky."
>
> TOBIAS SMOLLETT.

ALTHOUGH Mr. Sumner had labored with
untiring assiduity for the advancement of the
Union cause, and in the discussion of international questions had shown himself a master, stren-

uous efforts were made to prevent his re-election to the Senate. A party opposed to emancipation held what was denominated the People's Convention, in Faneuil Hall, on the seventh day of October, and nominated State officers opposed to the policy of the Republicans. These nominations were adopted by the Democrats; and a bitter attack was made on Mr. Sumner. The old charge of fanaticism was reiterated; and it was asserted that next to Jefferson Davis he was worthy of the scaffold. To the strong good sense of the Commonwealth, however, it was clear that no man could so ably and so honestly as he represent her in the halls of Congress. On the fifteenth day of January, 1863, therefore, the Senate gave him thirty-three out of thirty-nine, and the house one hundred and ninety-four out of two hundred and thirty-five, votes for a third term of six years in the United-States Senate.

On the ninth day of February Mr. Sumner introduced into the Senate a bill for the employment of colored troops in the army, which in another form eventually prevailed; and, on the bill before the Senate for providing aid for emancipation in Missouri, he spoke earnestly in favor of immediate, instead of gradual liberation, as alone consistent with a sound war-policy. On the 16th of the same month, he advocated, in opposition to his colleague, the exemption of clergymen from military conscription; and on the 27th he moved, as an amendment to the house bill to extend the charter of the Washington and Alexandria Railroad Company, that " No person shall be excluded from the cars on account of color." The bill, thus amended, became a law on the 3d of March; and on the 16th of that month he proposed to amend the bill to incorporate the Metropolitan Railroad Company, by adding the words, " There shall be no regulation excluding persons from any car on account of color." He also proposed a similar amendment to the bill respecting the Georgetown Railroad Company. These amendments were stoutly opposed by Mr. Saulsbury of Delaware, and others, but were, through the energy of Mr. Sumner, finally carried and enacted. Mr. Hendricks of Indiana said, in respect to Mr. Sumner's persistency in following up his amendments, that it was folly to attempt to oppose him when he had a point to gain. There is no doubt his very earnestness appeared to some as arrogance, and raised an opposition to some of his measures, which otherwise would have been at once accepted. Although he manifested such untiring zeal in respect to the grand question of the country, he was by no means inattentive to other issues, and especially to those pertaining to our relations with foreign powers. His course was generally indorsed by thoughtful men in every section of the North. In a letter to Henry Wilson, dated Boston, March 4, 1863, the Rev. R. H. Neale, D.D., said, " I have followed your course with increasing admiration from the beginning of your public life, and think I see in you, and also in Mr. Sumner, unmixed and magnanimous regard for the right, and for the public good."

Mr. Sumner's earnest recommendation of E. M. Stanton to Mr. Lincoln as secretary of war, and his equally persistent opposition to Gen. G. B. McClellan as commander of the Army of the Potomac, appeared in the issue to have been alike founded on a just appreciation of the character of the men and the real situation of the country.

During the memorable days of July, in the early part of which occurred the tremendous struggles and Union victories at Gettysburg, Vicksburg, and Port Hudson, he was at Washington, encouraging the president and his cabinet, and making provisions for the sufferings of the wounded. Always confident of ultimate success, he threw his own deep convictions into the hearts of those around him, and inspired the faltering with hope and confidence. Immediately after the battle of Gettysburg, he issued a new edition of " The Barbarism of Slavery," dedicating it to the young men of the United States as a

" token of heartfelt gratitude to them for brave and patriotic service rendered in the present war for civilization."

Moved by various questionable motives, England and France assumed at the opening of the war, and persistently maintained, an unfriendly attitude towards the Union. They early acknowledged the Southern Confederacy as a belligerent power. Through her leading statesmen England sharply criticised the war-measures of Mr. Lincoln's administration, and, in disregard of international comity, permitted the piratical steamer "Alabama" and other vessels to be constructed in her ports, and to sail therefrom, to commit depredations on our commerce. This sympathy with States in rebellion, and the infringement of maritime rights, alarmed the public mind, and received the most profound consideration of our diplomats abroad. At a large meeting at Cooper Institute, New York, Sept. 10, 1863, Mr. Sumner, in a calm, dispassionate, and exhaustive speech, exhibiting profound historical research, as well as an exalted statesmanship, considered " Our Present Perils from England and France ; the Nature and Conditions of Intervention by Mediation, and also by Recognition ; the Impossibility of any Recognition of a New Power with Slavery as a Cornerstone ; and the Wrongful Concession of Ocean

Belligerency." "The New-York Tribune" characterized this speech as a "miracle of historical and
statesmanlike erudition." The questions at issue
were met on the high ground of fact and right; and,
while the tone of discussion was amicable, the aggra-
vating course of France and England towards our
government was most distinctly stated, and the false
position of these neutral powers condemned. Perhaps no other American could have so ably treated
this important subject; and it is justly esteemed as
one of Mr. Sumner's finest efforts. It was, of
course, criticised in England; but its effect was salu-
tary to that nation. At the close of his address, the
speaker tendered this advice, respecting our affairs at
home, to the assembly : —

"This is no time to stop. FORWARD! FORWARD! Thus do I,
who formerly pleaded so often for peace, now sound to arms;
but it is because, in this terrible moment, there is no other
way to that sincere and solid peace without which there will
be endless war. Even on economic grounds, it were better
that this war should proceed, rather than recognize any parti-
tion, which, beginning with humiliation, must involve the
perpetuation of armaments, and break out again in blood.
But there is something worse than waste of money : it is waste
of character. Give me any peace but a *liberticide* peace. In
other days the immense eloquence of Burke was stirred against
a *regicide* peace. But a peace founded on the killing of a
king is not so bad as a peace founded on the killing of lib-

13

erty; nor can the saddest scenes of such a peace be so sad as
the daily life which is legalized by slavery. A queen on the
scaffold is not so pitiful a sight as a woman on the auction·
block. Therefore I say again, FORWARD! FORWARD! . . .
Thus far we have been known chiefly through that vital force
which slavery could only degrade, but not subdue. Now at
last, by the death of slavery, will the Republic begin to live;
for what is life without liberty ?

"Stretching from ocean to ocean, teeming with population,
bountiful in resources of all kinds, and thrice happy in universal enfranchisement, it will be more than conqueror, —
nothing too vast for its power, nothing too minute for its care.
Triumphant over the foulest wrong ever inflicted, after the
bloodiest war ever waged, it will know the majesty of right
and the beauty of peace; prepared always to uphold the one,
and to cultivate the other. Strong in its own mighty stature,
filled with all the fulness of a new life, and covered with a
panoply of renown, it will confess that no dominion is of
value which does not contribute to human happiness. Born in
this latter day, and the child of its own struggles, without
ancestral claims, but heir of all the ages, it will stand forth
to assert the dignity of man; and, wherever any of the human
family is to be succored, there its voice will reach, as the voice
of Cromwell reached across France even to the persecuted
mountaineers of the Alps. Such will be this republic, —
upstart among the nations; ay, as the steam-engine, the telegraph, and chloroform are upstart. Comforter and helper like
these, it can know no bounds to its empire over a willing
world. But the first stage is the death of slavery."

The following tribute to Mr. Sumner for this
great effort appeared in " The National Era."

SUMNER'S GREAT SPEECH.

Immortal utterance of a noble mind,
   Tasked to a purpose worthy all its powers,
   By nature blest, and crowned by studious hours,
To brighten history's page, and bless mankind!
Lo! our dear country's basis, there defined,
   Rests on truth's rock, though bearing falsehood's weight.
   Her founders take the old heroic state,
While sweep the clouds of calumny behind.
The nation's heart exults; and all man's race
   Hail their proud beacon, rising still toward heaven.
Thus, from the sunshine of our Maker's grace,   .
   In these earth's latter days, while passion-driven,
We love upon her sinless prime to brood,
When her Creator's voice proclaimed *that all was good!*"

   CENTREVILLE, Ind., 1863.

Mr. Sumner was this autumn called to lament the death of his dearly-beloved brother George Sumner, who died in Boston, after a lingering illness, Oct. 6, 1863, in his forty-seventh year. He studied in Germany, travelled extensively in Europe, Asia, and Africa, and was an author and lecturer of marked ability. He resided long in Paris, and " had done more," said Baron Humboldt, " to raise the literary reputation of America abroad than any other American." Among other works he published " The Progress of Reform in France," 1853; and delivered an oration before the authorities of the city of Boston, July 4, 1859. He was never married.

Whether at Washington or at his home in Boston, Mr. Sumner never passed a day inactively. His portfolio was always open; and his friends almost always found him engaged in drafting bills, preparing speeches, carrying on his correspondence, or producing something for the public press. An elegant and learned article from his ready pen appeared in "The Atlantic Monthly" for November of this year, contrasting the diplomatic mission of Dr. Franklin with that of John Slidell at Paris, and ingeniously tracing the celebrated Latin epigram, " Eripuit cœlo fulmen, sceptrumque tyrannis," which was inscribed on the portrait of the great philosopher, to its origin. In this charming essay the writer's intimate acquaintance with the French literary and political history of that period appears to great advantage. The Latin verse, as Mr. Sumner clearly shows, was prepared by the celebrated statesman Turgot, who formed it from the line, " Eripuit fulmenque Jovi, Phœboque saggittas," of the " Anti-Lucretius," by Cardinal Melchior de Polignac. The cardinal derived his idea from the " Astronomicon," an ancient poem by Marcus Manilius, where the verse appears under the following form, " Eripuitque Jovi fulmen, viresque tonandi," which has been translated, " Unsceptred Jove, — the Thunderer disarmed."

From the critical acumen displayed in this article,

it might be supposed that Mr. Sumner had spent his life as a bibliophile, amusing himself with antiquarian researches, and the amenities of literature. He had, indeed, a taste for rare and curious books and autographs; and, in exhibiting his literary treasures to his friends, he would point with great delight to the Bible which John Bunyan had in Bedford Jail while writing his immortal " Pilgrim's Progress ; " to a copy of " Pindar," once the property of John Milton; to one of " Horace " which Philip Melancthon used; to a Testament of the dramatic poet Jean Racine; to some corrected proof-sheets of Pope's famous " Essay on Man ; " and especially to the original manuscript of Robert Burns's celebrated battle-song, " Scots wha hae wi' Wallace bled ! "

On the opening of Congress in December, Mr. Sumner was in his seat, and again ready for action as a faithful friend and guardian of the colored race. By the Act of Emancipation, and the successive victories of the Union arms, the chains of servitude were gradually breaking ; and the freedmen, until now denominated " contrabands," were in need of personal protection, and the acknowledgment of political rights. First and foremost in their defence, Mr. Sumner continued to press upon the attention of the Senate, not yet exempt from the leaven of secession, measure after measure for the security of the freedom of the colored people, of the slave-territory occupied or taken by our troops, from the bonds which still to some extent enfettered them. Early in January, 1864, he presented to the Senate a resolution for the appointment of a committee of seven, for the consideration of " all papers and propositions concerning slavery and the treatment of freedmen." The resolution was adopted, and he himself appointed one of the committee. This was the initiatory step in that body to his grand Freedmen's Bureau Bill, which he most appropriately styled the " Bridge from Slavery to Freedom," and which, after a long and arduous struggle, passed both houses, and received on the third day of March, 1865, the signature of the president. By this important measure the colored people were protected in their civil rights and privileges; and, for Mr. Sumner's efforts in carrying it through Congress, they will ever hold his name in grateful memory. On the 4th of February he spoke in favor of equal pay to colored soldiers, saying, " I wish to see our colored troops treated like white troops in every respect;" and on the 8th he introduced to the Senate a series of resolutions protesting against the restoration of any rebel States without guarantees in respect to freedmen. He thus early indicated a simple plan of reconstruction which after long debates and various modifications was adopted. He also on the same day proposed an amendment to the constitution, declaring " that all persons are equal before the law."

On the day following he presented to the Senate the petition of one hundred thousand men and women for universal emancipation by an act of Congress.

" Here they are," said he, referring to the roll of names, "a mighty army, one hundred thousand strong, without arms or banners, — the advance-guard of a larger army."

On the 29th he laid before the Senate two elaborate reports, the one against the fugitive-slave acts, and the other against excluding witnesses on account of color. On the 23d of March he reported a bill prohibiting commerce in slaves among the several States, which on the second day of July received the signature of the president, and thus broke up the traffic in human flesh between the States.

On the 4th of April he made a long and able report on claims on France for spoliations made on our commerce prior to July 31, 1801; and on the 8th he delivered his great speech, entitled " No Property in Man," on the Constitutional Amendment. In this speech he cites the following couplet from Voltaire as the origin of his favorite maxim, " *equality before the law :* " —

"La loi dans tout état doit être universelle :
Les mortels, quels qu'ils soient, sont égaux devant elle."

With touching truthfulness he refers to distinguished persons who were called in former times to drink the bitter tears of human servitude.

"How truly affecting are the words of Homer depicting the wife of Hector toiling as bondwoman at the looms of her Grecian master, or those other undying words which exhibit man in slavery as shorn of half his worth! The story of Joseph sold by his brothers has been repeated in every form, touching innumerable hearts. Borrowed from the Bible, it figured in the moralities of the middle ages, and in the later theatre of France. How genius triumphed over slavery is part of this testimony. Æsop the fabulist — one of the world's greatest teachers, if not lawgivers — was a slave; so also was Phædrus the Roman fabulist, whose lessons are commended by purity and elegance; and so, too, was Alcman the lyric, who shed upon Sparta the grace of poesy. To these add Epictetus, sublime in morals; and Terence, incomparable in comedy, who gave to the world that immortal verse, which excited the applause of the Roman theatre, 'I am a man; and nothing which concerns mankind is foreign to me.' Nor should it be forgotten that the life of Plato was checkered by slavery."

On the 27th he spoke in favor of a national currency; and on the 30th he opened the way to a great reform still needed, by the introduction of a bill "to provide for the greater efficiency of the civil service." In June following he took an active part in the debates on the Freedmen's Bureau Bill. In the course of his remarks he said: "The freedmen are not idlers. They desire work. But in their helpless condition they are not able to obtain it without assistance. They are alone, friendless, and uninformed. The curse of slavery is still upon them. Somebody must take them by the hand. . . . The intervention of the national government is necessary. Without such intervention, many of these poor people, freed by our acts in the exercise of a military necessity, will be left to perish. . . . Call it charity or duty, it is sacred as humanity."

Yet in carrying his favorite measure he was met at every point by those who clung with fatal persistency to the tottering institution of human servitude. But the hour was coming. Following up the president's proclamation by Congressional action, the friends of freedom, after many struggles, hard almost as those upon the battle-field, had the happiness to see the principles for which they so long and strenuously contended introduced into the organic law.

By Mr. Sumner's senatorial labors above cited, some idea may be had of his incessant assiduity, and of the debt of gratitude which a nation, now exulting in the deliverance from its most tremendous evil, owes to his memory.

The upright, honest heart of Mr. Lincoln could not but appreciate the straightforward and persistent course of Mr. Sumner; and hence, as above stated, the relations between them were most intimate and friendly. Though not himself a scholar, Mr. Lincoln held in great respect the learning of his friend, and heard attentively, though he did not always readily accept, his political suggestions. The president's reconstruction policy in respect to Louisiana, Mr. Sumner and his friends adroitly foiled, as not giving a sufficient guaranty to the freedmen. An estrangement naturally followed, which the public press proclaimed as very serious. But Mr. Lincoln knew the worth of Mr. Sumner; and, besides, vindictive feelings had no place in his great, loving heart. On the 6th of March, 1865, he sent the senator this card for the inauguration ball : —

DEAR MR. SUMNER, — Unless you send me word to the contrary, I shall this evening call with my carriage at your house, to take you with me to the inauguration ball.

Sincerely yours,

ABRAHAM LINCOLN.

Mr. Sumner accepted the invitation; the president called for him with his carriage, and on arriving at the ball-room desired him, greatly to the astonishment of those present, to take the arm of Mrs.

Lincoln, and the seat of honor. This was Mr. Lincoln's method of terminating personal animosities.

By the surrender of the rebel army, under Gen. Robert E. Lee, to Gen. Grant, April 9, Mr. Sumner saw with inexpressible delight the Union saved, and the chains of the bondmen rent asunder. But the hour of gladness often changes unexpectedly to the hour of sorrow. The joy attendant on the realization of his long-cherished hope of peace and freedom was on the evening of the 14th turned to the keenest agony, by the assassination of his noble and beloved friend the president of the United States.

Mr. Sumner attended the illustrious patriot in his dying hour; and none shed tears more freely at the sad announcement, "Abraham Lincoln is no more."

"This is the only time," said an intimate friend of the senator, "I ever saw him weep."

On the first day of June Mr. Sumner delivered in the Music Hall, before the citizens of Boston, a most touching and appropriate eulogy on the martyred president, portraying his sterling virtues, and his services to the colored people and to the nation, in words of pathos and of power. His constant and high regard for the race whose wrong the nation was so tardy to redress is seen in the following letter, which he wrote to Thomas Garfield in respect to the selection of clergymen for officiating on that occasion : —

WASHINGTON, May 6, 1865.

MY DEAR SIR, — Do as you please. The names you mention are excellent.

If I could choose one it would be Rev. Mr. Grimes, the colored preacher. It was for his race that President Lincoln died. If Boston adopted him as chaplain on the day when we mourn, it would be a truer homage to our departed president than music or speech. I can say nothing that could promise to be so effective on earth, or welcome in heaven. Think of this, and believe me, my dear sir,

Very faithfully yours,

CHARLES SUMNER.

His request was granted; and the Rev. Mr. Grimes assisted in the solemn services.

CHAPTER XVII.

> "The laws, the rights,
> The generous plan of power, delivered down
> From age to age by our renowned forefathers,
> So dearly bought, the price of so much blood, —
> Oh! let it never perish in our hands."
>
> *Cato, by* JOSEPH ADDISON.

"His public conduct was such as might have been expected from a spirit so high, and an intellect so powerful. He lived at one of the most memorable eras in the history of mankind, — at the very crisis of the great conflict between liberty and despotism, reason and prejudice. That great battle was fought for no single generation, for no single land." — THOMAS B. MACAULAY.

BY the surrender of the rebel army, which was soon followed by the capture of Jefferson Davis, May 10, 1865, the Southern States, exhausted and powerless, were ready to ac-

cept any terms of recognition which might have
been presented. This was a golden opportunity.
Mr. Sumner and other leading loyal statesmen entertained the idea that Congress had the right to prescribe
the conditions of re-admission to the Union; that the
freedmen should be endowed with the elective franchise, and be held in all respects "equal before the
law." "The just and honest method is," said he,
"the best." "A straight line is the shortest distance
between two points in statesmanship, as well as in
geometry." Had the vantage-ground been taken at
the outset, reconstruction and the establishment of
civil freedom, contemplated in the president's Act
of Emancipation, would have been soon effected.
But Andrew Johnson, having succeeded Mr. Lincoln
in the executive chair, early assumed the right of
deciding how the States recently in rebellion should
be governed, and on what terms they should be admitted to the Union. Adopting what he termed at
first an "experiment," and afterwards "my policy;"
forgetting, also, that his province was to execute, not
to frame, the laws,—he so encouraged the hopes of
the Southern States, that, on the opening of the
Thirty-ninth Congress, in December, 1865, a strong
demand was made by them for an immediate representation in that body. This arrogant attempt of the
seceding States to regain a seat in the national coun-

cils was sternly met by loyal Congressmen; and hence a disagreement soon arose between them and the president, which culminated in his impeachment, and did not terminate until his retirement from the executive chair.

By his re-actionary course, the partisans of slavery had time to gather strength; and thus, by involving simple measures of reconstruction in a variety of complications, several years were spent in acrimonious debates upon the terms of re-adjustment. Mr. Sumner watched intently every movement compromising in the least the freedom of the colored people, and never failed to raise his voice on their behalf. He entertained no feelings of hostility towards the South; he longed to see the States restored to permanent peace, to order and prosperity; he desired to have them once more represented in the halls of legislation: still he strenuously insisted that Congress, not the president, should prescribe the way, and that the rights of the freedmen should be faithfully guarded and protected. He urged with great persistency the passage of the constitutional amendments, and readily accepted any temporary measures that promised to afford security to the colored race until these additions to the organic law should be adopted by the people. He maintained, that, by the constitution itself, the very preamble

of which declares "that all men are born equal,"
slavery is abolished; yet, under the proclamation of
Mr. Lincoln and the Thirteenth Amendment (adopted,
after many earnest debates, Dec. 18, 1865), the South
still clung with strange tenacity to its long-cherished
institution: so deeply had its roots intwined themselves around the heart of social life. To render
the redemption of the captive perfect, Mr. Sumner
threw himself, with the full intensity of his deep
convictions, into every question which concerned the
welfare of the freedman. On the 20th of December,
1865, he made an earnest speech on the " Equality
Bill" of Mr. Wilson, which was to "maintain the
freedom of the inhabitants in the States declared in
insurrection and rebellion by the proclamation of
the president of July 1, 1862." He said, " When
I think of what occurred yesterday in this chamber;
when I call to mind the attempt to whitewash the
unhappy condition of the rebel States, and to throw
the mantle of official oblivion over sickening and
heart-rending outrages, where human rights are sacri-
ficed, and rebel barbarism receives a new letter of
license, — I feel that I ought to speak of nothing else."
This hard shot upon the policy of the president drew
forth sharp replies; and the word " whitewashing"
long rung through the halls of Congress. It was
the truth which it contained that drew the blood;
and this the president soon came to realize.

In the course of his remarks Mr. Sumner reviewed the condition of the freedmen in the several States, and in closing said, —

"I bring this plain story to a close. I regret that I have been constrained to present it. I wish it were otherwise. But I should have failed in duty had I failed to speak. Not in anger, not in vengeance, not in harshness, have I spoken; but solemnly, carefully, and for the sake of my country and humanity, that peace and reconciliation may again prevail. I have spoken especially for the loyal citizens who are now trodden down by rebel power, and who are without representation on this floor. Would that my voice could help them to security and justice! I can only state the case: it is for you to decide. It is for you to determine how long these things shall continue to shock mankind. You have before you the actual condition of the rebel region: you have heard the terrible testimony. The blood curdles at the thought of such enormities, and especially at the thought that the poor freedmen, to whom we owe protection, are left to the unrestrained will of such a people, smarting with defeat, and ready to wreak vengeance upon these representatives of a true loyalty. In the name of God, let us protect them! Insist upon guaranties. Pass the bill now under consideration; pass any bill: but do not let this crying injustice rage any longer. An avenging God cannot sleep while such things find countenance. If you are not ready to be the Moses of an oppressed people, do not become its Pharaoh."

To the urgent and eloquent utterances of Mr. Sumner is mainly due the passage of the Fourteenth Amendment without the obnoxious reference to a distinction in color, which the framers of the constitution took such pains to avoid. The joint resolution — with the clause, that, " whenever the elective franchise shall be denied or abridged in any State, on account of race or color, all persons therein of such race or color shall be excluded from the basis of representation "— had passed the House by a large majority, and was favorably entertained by the Senate, when Mr. Sumner, on the 6th and 7th of February, and on the 7th and 9th of March, 1866, in speeches characterized by cogent reasoning and historical illustration, unfolded the iniquity of the compromise, and emphatically denounced this effort to admit the idea of inequality and disfranchisement on account of color, into the constitution.

" After generations have passed, surrounded by the light of Christian truth, and in the very blaze of human freedom," said he, " it is proposed to admit into the constitution the twin idea of inequality in rights, and thus openly set at naught the first principles of the Declaration of Independence, and the guaranty of a republican government itself, while you blot out a whole race politically. . . .

" Who does not admire the English patriot who once said that he would give his life to *serve* his country, but he would not do a mean thing to *save* it? I hope we may act in this spirit. Above all, do not copy the example of Pontius Pilate, who surrendered the Saviour of the world, in whom he found no fault at all, to be scourged and crucified; while he set at

large Barabbas, of whom the gospel says in simple words,
' Now, Barabbas was a robber.' "

His opposition to all compromise he thus re-
asserts : —

"I have fought a long battle with slavery ; and I confess my
solicitude when I see any thing that looks like concession to it.
It is not enough to show me that a measure is expedient : you
must show me also that it is right. Ah, sir ! can any thing be
expedient which is not right ? From the beginning of our history the country has been afflicted with compromise. It is by
compromise that human rights have been abandoned. I insist
that this shall cease. The country needs repose after all its
trials : it deserves repose. And repose can only be found in
everlasting principles. It cannot be found by inserting in your
constitution the disfranchisement of a race."

For this and other noble pleas on behalf of the
elective franchise and the ballot-box for the freedmen, they will hold him, more than any other benefactor, in heartfelt and dear remembrance.

"The ballot is *protector*. Perhaps, at the present moment,
this is its highest function. Slavery has ceased in name ; but
this is all. The old masters still assert an inhuman power, and
now by positive statutes seek to bind the freedmen in new
chains. Let this conspiracy proceed unchecked, and the freedman will be more unhappy than the early Puritan, who, seeking liberty of conscience, escaped from the 'lords bishops'

only to fall under the 'lords elders.' The master will still be master under another name, as, according to Milton, —

'New presbyter is but old priest writ large.'

" Serfdom or apprenticeship is slavery in another guise. To save the freedmen from this tyranny, with all its accumulated outrage, is your solemn duty. For this we are now devising guaranties; but, believe me, the only sufficient guaranty is the ballot. Let the freedman vote, and he will have in himself under the law a constant, ever-present, self-protecting power. The armor of citizenship will be his best security. The ballot will be to him sword and buckler, — a sword with which to pierce his enemies, and a buckler on which to receive their assault. Its possession alone will be a terror and a defence. The law, which is the highest reason, boasts that every man's house is his castle; but the freedman can have no castle without the ballot. When the master knows that he may be voted down, he will know that he must be just; and everything is contained in justice. The ballot is like charity, which never faileth, and without which man is only as sounding brass, or a tinkling cymbal. The ballot is the one thing needful, without which rights of testimony and all other rights will be no better than cobwebs which the master will break through with impunity. To him who has the ballot all other things shall be given, — protection, opportunity, education, a homestead. The ballot is like the horn of abundance, out of which overflow rights of every kind, with corn, cotton, rice, and all the fruits of the earth; or, better still, it is like the hand of the body, without which man, who is now only a little lower than the angels, must have continued only a little above the brutes. We are fearfully and wonderfully made; but, as is the hand in the work of civilization, so is the ballot in the work of government. 'Give me the ballot, and I can move the world,' may be the exclamation of the race still despoiled of this right. There is nothing which it cannot open with almost fabulous power, like that golden mistletoe, offshoot of the sturdy oak, which, in the hands of the classical adventurer, unclosed the regions of another world; and, like that golden bough, it is renewed as it is used:—

> One plucked away, a second branch you see
> Shoot forth in gold, and glitter from the tree.'

"If I press these illustrations, it is only that I may bring home to your minds that supreme efficacy which cannot be exaggerated. Though simple in character, there is nothing the ballot cannot accomplish; like that homely household lamp in Arabian story, which, at the call of its possessor, evoked a spirit who did all things, from the building of a palace to the rocking of a cradle, and filled the air with an invisible presence. But it is as protector that it is of immeasurable power, like a fifteen-inch columbiad pointed from a monitor. Ay, sir, the ballot is the columbiad of our political life; and every citizen who has it is a full-armed monitor.

"Having pleaded for the freedman, I now plead for the Republic; for to each alike the ballot is a *necessity*. It is idle to expect any true peace while the freedman is robbed of this transcendent right, and left a prey to that vengeance which is ready to wreak upon him the disappointment of defeat. The country, sympathetic with him, will be in a condition of perpetual unrest. With him it will suffer; and with him alone can it cease to suffer. Only through him can you redress the balance of our political system, and assure the safety of patriot citizens. Only through him can you save the national debt from the inevitable repudiation which awaits it when recent rebels in conjunction with Northern allies once more bear sway. He is our best guaranty: use him. He was once your fellow-soldier: he has always been your fellow-man. If he was willing to die for the Republic, he is surely good enough to vote; and, now that he is ready to uphold the Republic, it will be madness to reject him. Had he voted originally, the acts of secession must have failed: treason would have been voted down. You owe this tragical war, and the debt now fastened upon the country, to the denial of this right. Vacant chairs in once happy homes, innumerable graves, saddened hearts, mothers, fathers, wives, sisters, brothers, all mourning lost ones, the poor now ground by a taxation they had never known before, all testify against that injustice by which the present freedman was not allowed to vote. Had he voted, there would have been peace. If he votes now there will be peace. Without this you must have a standing army, which is a sorry substitute for justice. Before you is the plain alternative of the ballot-box or the cartridge-box: choose ye between them. . . .

"The Roman Cato," said he, "after declaring his belief in the immortality of the soul, added, that, if this was an error, it was an error which he loved. And now, declaring my belief in liberty and equality as the God-given birthright of all men, let me say in the same spirit, if this be an error, it is an error which I love; if this be a fault, it is a fault which I shall be slow to renounce; if this be an illusion, it is an illusion which I pray may wrap the world in its angelic forms."

Thus would Mr. Sumner, on the principle that the State had ceased to be in practical relations with the Union, and that Congress had the power of reconstruction, press the advantage which the Union arms had won to the upraising of the colored people. He intended that "every drop of American blood that was shed should surely be consecrated to human freedom;" and he soon had the satisfaction to see his long and perilous efforts realized in the passage of the Fourteenth and Fifteenth Amendments to the Constitution, sweeping the baneful and degrading system of slavery away, and bringing a long and heavily oppressed people to enjoy the right of the elective franchise.

In June of this year (1866) Mr. Sumner came home to stand by the bedside and receive the parting benediction of his dying mother. She had attained the age of more than fourscore years, and had experienced many trials and afflictions, which she bore with womanly fortitude, and retained something of earlier grace and beauty to the last. "She was tall and stately," said one who knew her well, "with the old-school dignity of manner; and, if thought distant, you soon forgot, in her genial friendliness and evident superiority of mind, every thing except that she was one of the most admirable of women." When urged in her last illness to send for her son, she replied that his country had more need of his services than she, and that he had better remain at

Washington. He came, however, and stood beside her when she passed away. Returning from her grave, he bowed his head in the loneliness of sorrow, and exclaimed, "I have now no home!"

The summer was spent in revising his speeches for the press, and in making preparations for the coming conflict in the re-establishment of order in the Southern States.

On the twenty-seventh day of October he was united in marriage, by the Right Rev. Bishop Manton Eastburn, with Mrs. Alice (Mason) Hooper, the widow of Mr. William Sturgis Hooper, and daughter of Mr. Jonathan Mason of Boston. This alliance, owing to disparity of age and taste, was infelicitous; and a divorce was decreed May 10, 1873, by Judge Holt of the Supreme Court of Massachusetts. By this circumstance the friendly relations between Mr. Sumner and the Hon. Samuel Hooper, father-in-law of Mrs. Sumner, were in no respect disturbed.

In regard to naming children after great men, Mr. Sumner wrote this pleasant and sensible letter to a father in New York who proposed to call his son Charles Sumner : —

"MY DEAR ——, — Don't make a mistake. Never name a child after a living man. This is the counsel I give always, and most sincerely. Who knows that I may not fall? I, too, may grow faint, or may turn aside to false gods. I hope not; but this is one of the mysteries of the future. Therefore name your boy some good Christian name (it may be Charles, if you will; for that is general); but do not compel him to bear all his days a label which he may dislike. I once met a strong anti-slavery youth who bore the name of Martin Van Buren. He was born while New York sat in the presidential chair; and his father named him after the chief of the land. But the youth did not find the sentiments of the late Mr. Van Buren such as he wished to be associated with.

" Ever yours,
CHARLES SUMNER."

Steadily intent on the elevation of the African race, Mr. Sumner made in the Senate, July 12, 1867, a powerful plea for securing the elective franchise to the colored citizens of the North.

" How can you look the rebel States in the face," said he, " when you have required colored suffrage of them. and failed to require it in the other States? Be just: require it in the loyal States, as you have required it in the rebel States. . . . There is a clause in the constitution directing you to guarantee a republican form of government. It is a clause which is like a sleeping giant in the constitution, never until this recent war awakened; but now it comes forward with a giant's power. There is no clause in the constitution like it. There is no clause which gives to Congress such a supreme power over the States as that clause. Then, as I have already said, you have the two other clauses. Your power under the constitution is complete. It is not less beneficial than complete. . . . Regard it as the completion of these reconstruction measures : regard it as a constitutional enactment."

The rupture between Congress and the president, who had vainly endeavored to prevent the enactment of the second Freedmen's-Bureau Bill (passed, over his veto, July 16, 1866), and who had at every point opposed the reconstruction measures of the Republicans, continued to widen, until his suspension of E. M. Stanton, the indefatigable secretary of war, when measures were instituted for his impeachment. In these proceedings Mr. Sumner, always vigilant lest the rights of the Senate should be invaded, actively participated. He prepared several elaborate papers on the guilt or innocence of the president, and made the point that the chief-justice had no right to vote in the trial. Mr. Sumner voted on almost every count against the president. Mr. Stanton was re-instated by the Senate Jan. 14, 1868, under the Tenure-of-Office Bill (passed March 2, 1867, over Mr. Johnson's veto). The president, however, soon again removed him, appointing Gen. Lorenzo Thomas in his place *ad interim*, when Mr. Covode introduced into the house the resolution of impeachment. While Mr. Stanton was remaining in suspense concerning his own course of action, Mr. Sumner sent to him this epigrammatic letter, which in point of brevity surpasses even Cæsar's celebrated " *Veni, vidi, vici.*"

"SENATE CHAMBER, 21st February, 1868.

STICK.

Ever sincerely yours,

CHARLES SUMNER.

Hon. E. M. STANTON."

On the acquittal of the president in May following, Mr. Stanton resigned his office. On the 11th
of July Mr. Sumner spoke at length against the
president's scheme of repudiation, and in favor of
completing reconstruction through public faith and
specie payment. "The word of our nation," said
he, "must be as good as its bond." He strongly
urged economy; and, on the principle that State
affairs should be conducted on the line of uncompromising and eternal justice, said, —

"I call your attention to three things in which all others
centre. The first is the *public faith;* the second is the *public
faith;* the third is the *public faith.* Let these be sacredly
preserved, and there is nothing of power or fame which can be
wanting. All things will pay tribute to you, even from the
uttermost parts of the sea. All the sheaves will stand about,
as in the dream of Joseph, and make obeisance to your sheaf.
Good people, especially all concerned in business, whether
commerce, banking, or labor, — our own compatriots or the
people of other lands, — will honor and uphold the nation
which, against all temptations, keeps its word."

Although reconstruction, by the passage of bills
over the president's veto, for the admission of all

but three of the rebel States, had been virtually concluded at this session of Congress, Mr. Sumner said he should not consider the work completed until he saw a colored member in the Senate. During the presidential campaign of this year he favored the election of Gen. Grant, although he believed a better nomination might have been made.

On the 3d of February, 1869, he strongly advocated in the Senate the enactment of a law by Congress for equal suffrage in opposition to the constitutional amendment.

"Why amend," said he, "what is already sufficient? Why erect a supernumerary column? . . . Let this beneficent prohibition once find a place in our statute-book, and it will be as lasting as the national constitution itself, to which it will be only a legitimate corollary. . . . Once adopted, it will go into instant operation, without waiting for the uncertain concurrence of State legislatures, and without provoking local strife, so wearisome to the country. The States will not be turned into political caldrons; and the Democratic party will have no pudding-stick with which to stir the bubbling mass."

The bill for the amendment, however, prevailed; and the African race was thus constitutionally restored to the political privileges of American citizenship. To the achievement of this grand result, no one contributed more of eloquence, statesmanship, or personal effort than Charles Sumner; and by the liberated millions no name on earth is more revered. "If others forget thee," said Robert B. Elliott of South Carolina, "thy fame shall be guarded by the millions of that emancipated race whose gratitude shall be more enduring than the monumental marble." By Mr. Sumner's remarkable speech early in 1869, on "The Alabama" claims, which he undoubtedly over-estimated, and which led to the rejection by the Senate of the Clarendon-Johnson treaty, he somewhat endangered our friendly relations with England, and was severely criticised by the English press; yet his design was not so much to obtain heavy damages, as to exhibit the wrong done by England in furnishing that vessel to the rebels, and also the underlying principles of international law, by which sovereign states in their intercourse with each other ought always to be guided. He subsequently used his influence in securing the consent of the Senate to the treaty of Washington, by which an award of less consideration was secured.

In the following year Mr. Sumner pressed upon the attention of the Senate the importance of establishing colored schools at the South, of striking out the word "white" in the naturalization bill, of the odious income-tax from the tariff bill, and of reducing letter-postage. He also, June 23, reported a series of resolutions expressing warm and judicious sympathy with the Cubans, then suffering outrages from the collision between the insurgents and the Spanish government; but his most remarkable effort was in opposition to the president's Dominican treaty. Mr. Sumner no doubt honestly believed that the scheme of annexing the Republic of San Domingo to the United States was advocated by the administration and its supporters, not for the benefit of the people of that island, but for the enrichment of certain speculators; and he most frankly, perhaps too sharply, avowed his opinions on the subject. During the discussion of this measure, the severity of his criticism on the course of the president, whom he believed to act as an imperialist, bestowing undue favors on his special friends, led, in combination with other causes, to a rupture between him and the chief-executive. The tempers and habits of these distinguished men were totally unlike. There was no great love between them in the beginning; and, if I may change an expression of Shakspeare, it decreased on better acquaintance. The effects of the cruel blow received by Mr. Sumner in 1856 were still remaining; and, as they disturbed the functions of his physical frame, so they had, undoubtedly, some influence on his intellectual temper. On account of the opposition to his annexation scheme, and perhaps for some other reasons, Gen. Grant, against the advice of many of his supporters, removed in 1870, from his place as minister to England, Mr. J. L. Motley, the historian, and an intimate friend of Mr. Sumner. In a letter to the president, dated July 5, 1870, Mr. Wilson said in regard to the displacement of Mr. Motley, "I fear you will make a sad mistake if you remove him; and I beg you to consider the case carefully before acting. His removal is believed to be aimed at Mr. Sumner. Right or wrong, this will be the construction put upon it. Can you, my dear sir, afford to have such an imputation rest upon your administration? Mr. Motley is one of the best known and most renowned of our countrymen. . . . I need not say that they (the men of Massachusetts) are surprised at the rumor that he is to be removed. They are pained to have it said that his removal is on account of Mr. Sumner's opposition to the San-Domingo treaty. His removal will be regarded by the Republicans of Massachusetts as a blow not only at him, but at Mr. Sumner. . . . I want to see the President and Congress in harmony, and the Republican party united and victorious. To accomplish this, we must all be just, charitable, and forgiving.

"Very truly,

"HENRY WILSON."

In February, 1871, Mr. Sumner was supplanted as chairman of the Committee on Foreign Affairs by Simon Cameron. He had long fulfilled the duties attendant on this position with distinguished ability; and no man in this country was better acquainted with foreign affairs, or held in higher consideration by foreign courts. But he and the president were at variance.

On the 27th of March, 1871, he again spoke on the San-Domingo treaty.

"On evidence before the Senate," said he, "it is plain that the navy of the United States, acting under orders from Washington, has been engaged in measures of violence, and of belligerent intervention, being war without the authority of Congress. An act of war without the authority of Congress is no common event. This is the simplest statement of the case. The whole business is aggravated when it is considered that the declared object of this violence is the acquisition of foreign territory, being half an island in the Caribbean Sea; and, still further, that this violence has been employed, first, to prop and maintain a weak ruler, himself a usurper, upholding him in power that he might sell his country; and, secondly, it has been employed to menace the Black Republic of Hayti."

He denounced Baez as a usurper who would sell his country, and said that the treaty was a violation of the Constitution of the United States, as well as of that of San Domingo. On the ensuing day Mr.

Howe replied to Mr. Sumner, defending Baez; and he insinuated, in conclusion, that Mr. Sumner, Judas-like, was trying to stab the Republican party in the back.

Replying to Mr. Howe, Carl Schurz in a very brilliant speech said, "Mr. Sumner had plunged his dagger not into the Republican party, but into Cæsarism; and we cannot forget that the world has agreed to pronounce Brutus the noblest Roman of them all."

CHAPTER XVIII.

The Supplementary Civil-Rights Bill. — A Letter on the San-Domingo Affair. — The Tone of Mr. Sumner's Criticisms on the Administration. — His Illness. — His View of the Republican and Democratic Parties. — Letter to Colored Citizens. — Support of Mr. Greeley. — Reception in Boston. — Visit to Europe. — Nomination as Governor of Massachusetts. — Resolutions on the Battle-Flags. — Letters in Vindication of his Course. — Interviews with Friends. — His Desire to raise Money by Lecturing. — His last Visit to Boston. — Declining Health. — His Last Labors in Congress. — Recision of the Censure for his Resolution on the Battle-Flags.

"Let us have faith that right makes might; and in that faith let us to the end dare to do our duty as we understand it." — ABRAHAM LINCOLN.

> " La vérité, voilà mon offrande chérie.
>   Loin de toi pour jamais le vil encens des cours;
>   Flatter le souverain, c'est trahir la patrie,
>   C'est du bonheur public empoisonner le cours."
>
> P. D. E. LeBrun.

" A great man under the shadow of defeat is taught how precious are the uses of adversity; and, as an oak-tree's roots are strengthened by its shadow, so all defeats in a good cause are but resting-places on the road to victory at last." — CHARLES SUMNER.

N the twelfth day of May, 1870, Mr. Sumner, ever intent on the uplifting of the colored citizen, introduced his supplementary Civil-Rights Bill, declaring that all persons, without regard to race or color, are entitled to equal privileges afforded by railroads, steamboats, hotels, places of amusement, institutions of learning, religion, and courts of law. The same bill substantially was introduced by him again Jan. 20, 1871.

"Show me," said he, in speaking on this measure, "any thing created or regulated by law, and I show you what must be opened equally to all without distinction of color. Notoriously, the hotel is a legal institution, originally established by the common law, subject to minute provisions and regulations; notoriously, public conveyances are, in the nature of common carriers, subject to a law of their own; notoriously, schools are public institutions, created and maintained by law; and now I simply insist that in the enjoyment of those institutions there shall be no exclusion on account of color."

His maxim was, " Equality of rights is the first of rights; " and his whole life was but one glorious struggle to reduce the principle of the old *Magna Charta*, " *Nulli negabimus, nulli differemus justitiam*," into practical operation. His views in respect to the course of the administration in the San-Domingo affair may be seen in this letter: —

WASHINGTON, 9th July, 1871.

My DEAR REDPATH, — Your letter must have crossed mine. I send you this French translation of the Report. I cannot obtain the English.

The president's friends were afraid to propose the printing of extra copies, as that would have opened the whole question; so that only the ordinary number for the Senate was printed.

Meanwhile, I hear that the *dementia* continues. The flag of Samana still flies without authority; and money has been . obtained at New York to pay another year's lease. Here is usurpation. The treaty is dead: it died by lapse four months from date; yet under this dead treaty the flag flies, and the United States are asked to pay money. Nothing like this was in the articles against A. J.

Very truly yours,
CHARLES SUMNER.

If the tone of his criticisms, especially in his suppressed speech of March, 1871, on the administration, be considered too severe, it must be remembered that he was a mortal; that his system had been shattered by a tremendous blow; that the removal of himself, and his intimate friend Mr. Motley, from positions which they were so eminently qualified to fill, was another heavy blow; and that he honestly believed that favoritism and corruption had entered the very heart of that grand old Republican party of which he had been, to a great extent, the founder and the leader. After the delivery of his great speech, on the last day of February, 1872, in support of his resolution demanding an investigation of the sales of ordnance stores made during the war between France and Germany, the return of his old malady rendered it imperative that he should cease a while from mental labor. He returned, however, to the Senate in May, and made, on the last day of that month, a memorable speech, in which he declared his loss of confidence in the Republican party, and severely criticised the course of Gen. Grant.

"Both the old parties," said he, "are in a crisis, with this difference between the two, — the Democracy is dissolving, the Republican party is being absorbed. The Democracy is falling apart, thus losing its vital unity: the Republican party is submitting to a personal influence, thus visibly losing its vital character. The Democracy is ceasing to exist: the Republican party is losing its identity. Let the process be completed, and it will be no longer that Republican party which I helped to found, and always served, but only a personal party; while, instead of those ideas and principles which we have been so proud to uphold, will be presidential pretensions; and instead of Republicanism, there will be nothing but Grantism. Political parties are losing their sway. Higher than party are country, and the duty to save it from Cæsar."

This address was used as a campaign document. For several weeks subsequent to the presidential nominations, he remained reticent in regard to the two candidates; but on the 29th of July, in a letter to the colored citizens, he announced his intention of abandoning the Republican party, and of sup-

porting Mr. Greeley for the presidency. In this
letter he said, —

> "Never have I asked for punishment. Most anxiously
> I have looked for the time, which seems now at hand, when
> there shall be reconciliation, not only between North and
> South, but between the two races; so that the two races and
> the two sections may be lifted from the ruts and grooves in
> which they are now fastened, and, instead of irritating antag-
> onism without end, there shall be sympathetic co-operation.
> The existing differences ought to be ended."

His health did not allow him to take an active
part in the canvass; but returning to Boston, where
he was branded by some of his old political companions as an " apostate," and deserted by many of his
former anti-slavery coadjutors, — especially by Mr.
Garrison, who addressed to him a trenchant letter on
his defection from his party, — he spent some days
with H. W. Longfellow at Lynn, and on the 5th of
September left for Europe. On his arrival in Liv-
erpool, he received the news of his nomination by
the Liberals and Democrats as governor of Massachusetts. This honor he declined. He met with a
cordial reception both in England and in France,
and had interviews with Thiers and Gambetta; but
his health was so much impaired, that his time was
mostly occupied in looking over engravings and
other works of art. " I have not read an American

newspaper," said he, writing from London, "since I sailed out of Boston Harbor; nor have I concerned myself except with engravings, pictures, books, and society."

He reached home on the 26th of November, and was present in his seat at the opening of Congress, Dec. 18, when he introduced into the Senate a resolution declaring "that the names of battles with our fellow-citizens shall not be continued in the army-register, or placed upon the regimental colors of the United States."

A resolution of censure was immediately passed by the General Court of this State, declaring "that such legislation meets the unqualified condemnation of the people of this Commonwealth."

No man honored more than Mr. Sumner the bravery of the loyal troops; but, as soon as the contest ended, no man more than he desired a speedy restoration of harmony and peace: as early as May, 1862, he had introduced a similar resolution. He therefore was deeply aggrieved at the ill-advised censure of the State he represented. In this letter to his friend James Redpath, he declares his anxiety for strength to sustain his resolution: —

WASHINGTON, 25th Dec., 1872.

MY DEAR REDPATH, — I wish you a merry Christmas! I regret much that I cannot take advantage of your invitation; but I am under medical treatment, with the doctor at my house twice a day, the last time to inject under the skin morphine and strychnine. This vacation I give to the doctor reluctantly but necessarily. I long to be strong, that I may vindicate my resolution, which can be done against all assault. Twice before have I offered it with the applause of Gen. Scott and Gen. Robert Anderson.

Faithfully yours,

CHARLES SUMNER.

The following letter to Mr. T. A. Smith also exhibits his feelings on the battle-flag resolution: —

WASHINGTON, 27th Dec., 1872.

MY DEAR SIR, — I thank you sincerely for the kind, good letter you have written me. Never did I deserve better of Massachusetts than now; for never did I represent so completely that high civilization which is the pride of our beloved Commonwealth. Thrice before, once in 1862, I offered the same proposition. I received the applause of Gen. Scott and Gen. Robert Anderson. Accept my best wishes, and believe me, my dear sir,   Sincerely yours,

CHARLES SUMNER.

To his old college friend the Hon. G. W. Warren, who visited him in January, 1873, he said, "Since the assault upon me in 1856, I have never been entirely well; and just now I am feeling the painful effects more than usual." At that time Chief-Justice Chase, then quite ill, came in, and afterwards Mr. Agassiz. The conversation turning to Mr. Sumner's re-election, his friend the noble scientist, who passed away before another interview, said, " Of course you will be re-elected. Who is to be put against you? Your name is a weight; and there is no other which can outbalance it. . . . The people are not to throw away a great character for slight differences."

A senator, referring subsequently to some insignificant matter, said to him, " Mr. Sumner, how will this affect your re-election ?" " Affect what?" replied he. " Affect your election," said the other. " What election do you speak of? " said Mr. Sumner. " Why, next year, in 1875, the period of your re-election comes round." " Oh, yes ! " answered Mr. Sumner, as if suddenly taking his idea: " my re-election will come round in 1875; but I may die long before that; and as long as I live I can do my duty."

During a call made on him some time afterwards by Mr. Wilson, he said with great earnestness, " If my works were completed, and my Civil-Rights Bill passed, no visitor could enter that door that would be more welcome than death."

Having incurred losses by the great Boston fire, he found himself in arrearages at this time to the amount of about ten thousand dollars; but instead of receiving, as so many others, " back pay" from the public treasury, he determined, feeble as he was, to make up the deficit in the lecture-field. He therefore sent this letter to the Boston Lyceum Bureau: —

WASHINGTON, 13th May, 1873.

MY DEAR REDPATH, — Nobody is authorized to act as my agent; nor do I remember any communication with the New-York Bureau.

I should like to lecture next autumn, if consistent with my health; but this is still uncertain.

I congratulate you on your return home, which is a surprise. I supposed you would give a month to Vienna and the national honor. Sincerely yours,

CHARLES SUMNER.

On his last visit to Boston, in the autumn of 1873, his reception was almost an ovation, and in delightful contrast with that of the preceding year. He was greeted everywhere with enthusiasm, and pressed on every hand to honor literary and political re-unions with his presence. At a public dinner just before his last departure for Washington, he said in reference to Mr. Wilson the vice-president, sitting near him: "He is under the charge of his physician: he is also under my charge; for his life is too precious to be exposed. I watch over him at Washington, and endeavor to see that he does not undergo unnecessary exertion." "But who," some one exclaimed, "shall guard the custodian?" Although the

" custodian " was on that occasion in the very best of spirits, and made an admirable address, his health was rapidly declining; and he therefore sent with much reluctance this request to cancel his lyceum engagements.

COOLIDGE HOUSE, 3d Oct., '73.

DEAR MR. REDPATH, — In announcing me as a lecturer for the present season, and making engagements for me, you acted precisely according to understanding.   I felt at the time in condition to assume this heavy work, and am not conscious of any failure since.   But much-valued friends have represented to me, that, at this early period of convalescence after protracted disability, it would be imprudent for me not to allow myself further rest, and especially that I ought not to undertake a series of engagements so wearying as that proposed.

Had this representation proceeded from a few only, or had my friends been divided or less strenuous, I should not, perhaps, have felt constrained, as I do now, by their unanimous judgment in letter and conversation, leaving me no alternative.   It is with much reluctance, and in obedience to the sentiments of those whose kindness awakens my gratitude, that I now withdraw, and ask you to cancel any engagements made on my account.

Accept my thanks, and believe me, my dear sir,

Faithfully yours,

CHARLES SUMNER.

JAMES REDPATH, ESQ.

In November Mr. Sumner addressed a letter to a meeting held in New York, condemnatory of the outrages of "The Virginius," deprecating any menace of war, and advising the liberation of the enslaved in the West Indies.

During the last session of Congress, he opposed, as usual, any inflation of the currency, and advocated an early return to specie payments. His last speech in Congress, terminating a brilliant senatorial career of almost a quarter of a century, was made on Saturday, the 7th of March, in the discussion of his substitute for the Centennial Bill, which had passed the House.

He contended that the one hundredth anniversary of the Republic should be entirely national in its character; and, in accordance with his well-known patriotic and economical views, emphatically said, —

"I have three earnest desires in connection with our coming anniversary: first, to secure a proper commemoration of that great day, truly worthy of this Republic, and characteristic, so that Republican institutions shall thereby gain; secondly, to save the national character, which must suffer if the present scheme is pursued; and, thirdly, to save the national treasury.

Almost the last words he heard pronounced in the Senate-chamber were those read by his colleague of the resolution of the Massachusetts legislature, rescinding and annulling the act of undeserved censure of Dec. 18, 1872. On being asked if he should address the Senate when it was presented, his reply was, " The dear old Commonwealth has spoken for me ; and that is enough."

CHAPTER XIX.

"In the long roll of martyrs in the cause of liberty, the name of Charles Sumner shall stand conspicuous, as worthy of the applause and reverence of manhood." — WILLIAM L. GARRISON.

"The dear and noble Sumner! My heart is too full for words; and in deepest sympathy of sorrow I reach out my hands to thee, who loved him so well. He has died as he wished to, at his post of duty, and when the heart of his beloved Massachusetts was turned toward him with more than the old-time love and reverence. God's peace be with him!" — JOHN G. WHITTIER.

"He had intense sympathy for moral principles. He was raised up to do the work preceding and following the war. His eulogy will be, a lover of his country, an advocate of universal liberty, and the most eloquent and high-minded of all the statesmen of that period in which America made the transition from slavery to liberty." — HENRY WARD BEECHER.

MR. SUMNER'S house at Washington, a handsome structure with a façade of brown free-stone, was built on an eligible site subsequent to 1867, and overlooks Lafayette Square. It adjoins

334

The late Residence of CHARLES SUMNER, Washington, D. C.

the Arlington Hotel; and the entrance is near the centre of the broad front. The sitting-room is on the right of the hall, which contains an old Dutch clock with a beautiful chime. The parlor, upholstered with yellow satin, is on the left, and above this Mr. Sumner's sleeping-room, which commands a fine view of Lafayette Square and the White House. Contiguous to this room is the library, or what the senator called his "workshop."

Of refined taste and high culture, Mr. Sumner had surrounded himself with rare and exquisite specimens of the fine arts, in the study of which he found a solace for his senatorial cares. His rooms were crowded with the works of genius, — rare and costly books, beautiful paintings, engravings, illuminated pictures, medallions, statues in bronze and marble, — so that they had almost the appearance of a museum of art. Among other paintings in his bedroom was a landscape representing " Ellen's Isle," painted by a colored artist. In the dining-room was a bas-relief of Christ as the " Good Shepherd," taken from the Catacombs of Rome. Among countless curiosities in his study, there was a photograph of John Bright, plainly framed, which was once owned by Mr. Lincoln. Among his other treasures of art were an " Ecce Homo," after Guido Reni ; " The Miracle of the Slave," by Tintoretto (bequeathed to his friend J. B. Smith); a portrait by Sir Peter Lely; and pictures of the Giotto of Florence, the grand staircase of Versailles, and the façade of the Louvre. "These last three things," said Mr. Sumner to a friend, "are perfect. When I come home from the senate tired and cross, I like to look at them: it comforts me to think there is something perfect and above criticism." Of his rarest literary treasures was an illuminated prayer-book of Margaret of Anjou, which cost three hundred dollars. The desk in which he was struck in the Senate was not the least interesting of his curiosities.

On Tuesday, the 10th of March, Mr. Sumner in his seat in the Senate complained to Mr. Ferry of painful shocks in his left side: they soon subsided; and in the evening he had as guests at his table two of his intimate friends, — Henry L. Pierce and B. Perley Poore. After the retirement of these gentlemen, he was again attacked with terrible pains in the heart. He was soon, however, somewhat relieved by his physician, Dr. J. T. Johnson, and passed a comparatively comfortable night; but in the morning he was cold and almost insensible. At ten o'clock he recognized Judge Hoar, and said, "Don't forget my Civil-Rights Bill." Observing Mr. Hooper near him, he exclaimed, "My book! my book is not finished." Later in the day he moaned, "I am so tired!

I am so tired!" and, when Judge Hoar brought him
a message from Mr. Emerson, he said, "Tell Emerson I love him and revere him." "Yes, I will tell
him," replied the judge; "for he says you have the
largest heart of any man alive." The judge soon
afterward took his hand; and at ten minutes before
three o'clock, P.M., March 11, 1874, Charles Sumner
ceased to breathe.

The news spread instantaneously over the nation;
and millions were in tears. No death since that of
Abraham Lincoln had so touched the hearts of the
American people. Congress had already adjourned.
On Friday, March 13, it assembled to pay tribute of
profound respect to the departed senator. The
obsequies were simple but impressive. The body
of Mr. Sumner, embalmed and enclosed in a massive
casket, on which had been placed a wreath of white
azaleas and lilies, and a branch of palm-leaves, was
lying in the south parlor of his house; and the features presented an appearance of dignity and repose.
It was borne thence, in a hearse drawn by four
white horses, followed by a body of about three
hundred colored men and a long line of carriages,
to the Capitol, where, in the rotunda beneath the
dome of that magnificent building, thousands gathered to view the silent face, and shed the parting
tear.

15

At half-past twelve the casket was removed to the Senate-chamber, which, with Mr. Sumner's chair, was draped in mourning. A cross of flowers, sent by Miss Nellie Grant, was placed upon the casket; but a more noticeable offering was a broken column of violets and white azaleas, placed there by the hands of a colored girl. She had been rendered lame by being thrust from the cars of a railroad, whose charter Mr. Sumner, after hearing the girl's story, by a resolution in the Senate caused to be revoked. In the presence of the president and his cabinet, the members of Congress, the Judiciary, foreign legations, and a large concourse of reverent citizens, the Congressional chaplains — the Rev. Drs. Butler and Sunderland — appropriately performed the solemn services.

At the close of the benediction, the president of the Senate, rising, said, " The funeral services having ended, the Senate of the United States intrusts the remains of Charles Sumner to the sergeant-at-arms and the committee * appointed to convey them

* The Congressional Committee consisted of Messrs. Henry A. Anthony of Rhode Island, Carl Schurz of Missouri, Aaron A. Sargent of California, John P. Stockton of New Jersey, Richard J. Oglesby of Illinois, and Thomas C. McCreery of Kentucky, on the part of the Senate ; and Messrs. Stephen A. Hurlbut of Illinois, Eugene Hale of Maine, Charles Foster of Ohio, Joseph H. Rainey of South Carolina, Charles Clayton of California, Henry J. Scudder of New York, Samuel J. Randall of Pennsylvania, Joseph B. Beck of Kentucky, and John Hancock of Texas, on the part of the House.

to his home, there to commit them, earth to earth, ashes to ashes, dust to dust, in the soil of the old Commonwealth of Massachusetts. Peace to his ashes ! "

The remains, attended by a delegation from Congress, arrived by special train in Boston, late on Saturday evening, and were borne to the Doric Hall at the Capitol, when Senator H. A. Anthony, chairman of the delegation, committed the casket to Gov. W. B. Washburn in this felicitous address : —

"May it please your excellency: We are commanded by the Senate of the United States to render back to you your illustrious dead. Nearly a quarter of a century ago, you dedicated to the public service a man who was even then greatly distinguished. He remained in it, quickening its patriotism, informing its councils, and leading in its deliberations, until, having survived in continuous service all his original associates, he has closed his earthly career. With reverent hands we bring to you his mortal part, that it may be committed to the soil of the Commonwealth, already renowned, that gave him birth. Take it: it is yours. The part which we do not return to you is not wholly yours to receive, nor altogether ours to give. It belongs to the country, to mankind, to freedom, to civilization, to humanity. We come to you with emblems of mourning which faintly typify the sorrow that dwells in the breasts upon which they lie. So much is due to the infirmity of human nature. But, in the view of reason and philosophy, is it not rather a matter of exultation, that a life so pure in its personal qualities, so high in its public aims, so fortunate in the fruition of noble effort, has closed safely before age had marred its intellectual vigor, before time had dimmed the lustre of its genius?

"May it please your excellency: Our mission is completed. We commit to you the body of Charles Sumner. His undying fame the Muse of History has already taken in her keeping." .

The body lay in state, attended by a guard of colored soldiers under Major Lewis Gaul, and was visited by throngs of sad and tearful people. On Friday afternoon, by a proclamation from the governor, both branches of the legislature assembled; and eloquent tributes were bestowed upon the departed statesman by Pres. George B. Loring, and Gen. N. P. Banks, of the Senate, and also by Messrs. Phillips, Codman, and Sanger, of the House. While the funeral train was on its way, the sorrow of the citizens of Boston found an expression in a crowded meeting, held in Faneuil Hall (draped for the occasion) at noon on Saturday, when very eloquent and eulogistic speeches were made by Mayor S. C. Cobb, Richard H. Dana, jun., A. H. Rice, N. P. Banks, William Gaston, Rev. E. E. Hale, and J. B. Smith, a noble, warm-hearted, and intimate friend of Mr. Sumner. In the course of his address, he with moving pathos said, —

"I can go back to the time when I sat under the eagle in this hall, and when I saw some one stand on the platform; and I did wish, when I heard certain expressions, that I could sink. I can go back to my boyhood, when I have seen other boys in their sports and plays, and I would walk off in the woods, and say, 'O God! why was I born?'

"I can remember forty-five years ago on a Christmas Day passing through the orchard, and saw a silk-worm hanging to the leaf of a tree, when my eyes turned up to my God, and I said, 'Why am I here?' There hangs something out in the cold; but it will be a butterfly. I took it home, hung it in the room, put it where it was warm; and it hatched out before the atmosphere was prepared to receive it. I lifted the window; and it flew off, but had to return, as it could not stand the atmosphere. And just so I was brought forth by the eloquence of Charles Sumner; and I have been turned loose on the public atmosphere; for really I had to suffer intensely; and I could only feel at home and feel well when I turned back into his presence; and his arms were always open to receive me. (Applause.)

"And now, Mr. Mayor, our ship in which he has commanded is still adrift: we are standing out now in the open sea, with a great storm; and, in behalf of those five millions of people of the United States, I beg of you to give us a good man to take hold where he left off. (Applause.)

"We are not educated up to that point. We cannot speak for ourselves: we must depend upon others. We stand to-day like so many little children whose parents have passed away. We can weep; but we don't understand it. We can weep; but we must beg of you to give us a man who will still lead us forward until we shall have accompanied all those thousands for which he offered his life."

The public press throughout the country paid generous tributes to the departed statesman; and many
clergymen on the sabbath spoke impressively of the
national bereavement. The discourses of the Revs.
Edward E. Hale, Dr. C. A. Bartol, James Freeman
Clarke, George L. Chaney, T. W. Higginson, C. D.
Pradlee, J. W. Hamilton, Samuel Johnson, James B.
Dunn, Dr. S. K. Lothrop, Henry Ward Beecher,
Dr. E. B. Foster, were particularly eloquent and
appropriate. It is estimated that as many as forty
thousand people visited Doric Hall to view the remains of the beloved senator. The room was elaborately draped in mourning; and the catafalque and
casket resting in the centre were covered with most
exquisite floral decorations. At the head of the
coffin stood a beautiful cross formed of callas,
violets, japonicas, and other flowers; and at the foot
a broken shaft of roses, covered with a pall of violets.
On the top of the casket the colored citizens placed
a large floral heart, with this inscription: "From
the colored citizens of Boston. Charles Sumner,
you gave us your life; we give you our hearts."
Above the casket was suspended a crown, beneath
which floated a white dove holding an olive-branch.
At about half-past two o'clock on Monday afternoon,
the remains were borne to King's Chapel, which was
tastefully hung in black and decorated with costly

The body of Charles Sumner lying in state, in Doric Hall, State House, Boston.

flowers, when appropriate funeral services were performed by the Rev. Henry W. Foote, the pastor.
At the close of the services, the funeral *cortége*, in
which there was a body of more than one thousand colored citizens, proceeded, through a dense
crowd of reverent people, to Mount-Auburn Ceme-
tery. It arrived, just as the sun was setting, at
the open grave in the Sumner lot, on Arethusa
Path, which winds along the declivity, a little to
the westward of the tower. The avenues, the
knolls, and hills were crowded with hushed and
pensive people. Near the grave stood the Congressional delegation, the surviving members of the
class of 1830, H. W. Longfellow, R. W. Emerson,
O. W. Holmes, and other intimate friends of the
deceased. The Horatian ode, "*Integer vitæ sceleris-
que purus*," was then sung by fifty male voices, accompanied by trombones; and, at the close, the
clergyman pronounced the solemn words, "I heard
a voice saying unto me, Write, Blessed are the dead
which die in the Lord from henceforth: yea, saith
the Spirit, that they rest from their labors; and their
works do follow them." As the body, in the last
beam of fading day, was lowered into the grave, the
grand old song of Luther, "*Ein feste Burg ist unser
Gott*," arose; and a cross and wreath of rarest flowers,
prepared by the request of Mrs. Julia Hastings, sister

of the deceased in California, was dropped by Miss Maud Howe upon the casket, amidst the statuesque silence of the surrounding multitude, broken only by the reverberation of the tolling of the distant bells.

> 'God rest his gallant spirit! give him peace,
> And crown his brows with amaranth, and set
> The saintly palm-branch in his strong right hand.
> Amid the conquering armies of the skies
> Give him high place forever! let him walk
> O'er meads of better asphodel; and be
> Where dwell the single-hearted and the wise,—
> Men like himself, severely, simply good,
> Who scorned to be ambitious; scorned the snares
> Of office, station, rank; but stood sublime
> In natural greatness . . . O Eternal King,
> O Father, Son, and Spirit! give him peace."

In person Mr. Sumner was tall, dignified, and commanding. His countenance generally wore a serious aspect; and his deportment was that of a well-bred and courteous gentleman. The whitened locks and furrowed cheek bespoke in later years the care and suffering to which his iron frame had been subjected. His friends are pleased to fancy that in respect to face and form, as well as character, he somewhat resembled Edmund Burke. Had he been more sensible to the charms of this visible creation, to the harmonies of nature, and to the tones of music; had he more fondly cherished the affections of domestic life, — his heart would have known more consolation, his character would have been more completely rounded out. But, as the ancients often said, " It is not meet that every good should be conferred on one alone." He held in most profound respect the principles of Christianity, and based thereon his strongest arguments for the freedom of the slave, and his expectations for the future elevation of the human race. To a friend, referring to his religion, he once said, " I take religion differently from other people; nor have I much to boast of, any way." Just before leaving Boston for the last time, he made an address at the Church of the Disciples, " in which," says one then present, " with profound and even tearful emotion, he spoke of the love of Christ as no man could speak who had not long and intimately known that love."

Mr. Sumner's works, published in elegant style by Messrs. Lee and Shepard, received his critical revision, and will constitute his most enduring monument. Well could he say of them, —

" Exegi monumentum ære perennius."

His last book, now in press, is entitled " Prophetic

Voices concerning America," and displays to great
advantage the extent of his historical researches, and
his anticipations of a glorious future for this continent.

The style of Mr. Sumner is clear as sunlight. As
the course of some majestic river it flows on, smooth,
full, free, and harmonious. It is always elevated,
always earnest, often nervous, strong, and impassioned. Every sentence indicates the man of culture: every word is well selected, well wrought in
to the solid structure. Though insensible to the
charms of music, he had still a fine rhythmical
perception, and the art of bringing his periods to a
harmonious close. His language teems with classical quotations, drawn from the whole range of
ancient and of modern literature; yet they are so
aptly chosen, as not only to illuminate his theme,
but also to make some compensation for his want
of wit and humor. Though he had not the massive strength of Webster, the sententious point of
Wirt, or the matchless grace of Everett, he still
excelled them all in learning, in earnestness, and
in the grandeur of his aspirations. If, as Mr. Webster has remarked, true eloquence must exist in the
man and the occasion, then will Mr. Sumner ever
stand forth as the great orator of emancipation in
America.

As a statesman he was incorruptible. Intrenched in his integrity, no money, gift, nor bribe could move him. Deep in his heart he held that "honesty is the best policy:" he proclaimed this doctrine, and he practised it. Amidst the strategic arts for power, the venality, the duplicity, the gloat and greed for greenbacks, which characterize political life at Washington, he bore a clean, unsullied palm. No Credit-Mobilier scheme, no annexation plot, no "back-pay" subterfuge, could tempt him from his stronghold. "Is it right?" not "Will it pay?" was with him the first, the central, and the last question. "People speak of Washington," he once *naïvely* said, "as being corrupt. I have lived there many years; and I have seen no corruption." His condemnation and exposure of the corruption, and the connivance at corruption, of the government, demand the gratitude of the people; and his great name will ever plead, as the names of Lincoln and of Washington, for integrity in the head of the nation.

No man was ever more consistent in his political career. While so many others trimmed the sail, and veered with every shifting wind or current to the popular course, he pressed onward by an undeviating line, though lightnings flashed around his head, to the attainment of his end. His defection from the Republican party was but the logical result of his adherence to his principles, or, in other words, of his consistency. True as steel to duty, he expected every other man to do his duty; and hence sometimes he seemed imperious in his exactions; but his desire was never to repress, but to bring others up to his own position. He raised his head above the murky atmosphere of the demagogues at the Capitol; and hence they hated him. But the world will some day reach his level. "No man," says Mr. Whittier in a recent letter to me, " had ever warmer friends; and no man was ever truer in his friendships ; " but those friends breathed with him the upper atmosphere. Congress has had men of originality and wit more brilliant, but none of industry more persistent, or scholarship more profound. His rank will be, not among the politicians, but among the unspotted and prophetic statesmen of the country. He spoke, even on subordinate questions, as if the whole world, and not the members of the Senate only, were his audience. Before the march of modern ideas, slavery, perhaps, without his aid, would soon have fallen ; but it became his province to bring the liberal thoughts of the Old World and the New to illumine the question, to strike, with weapons which no other Congressman possessed, and with the force of a God-sustained combatant, the brutal system through and through, up to its final overthrow. His affluence of learn-

ing, outflowing in allusions and quotations which
his opponents, while denouncing, did not hesitate
to borrow, was consecrated to the high and ultimate
purpose of his life, — the liberation and the civiliza
tion of the captive; and it was no dishonor to the
nation that it had one man, at least, in its highest
council-chamber, who could speak, and who did
speak, Greek. " He consecrated himself," wrote Mr.
Garrison to me the other day, "to the cause of im-
partial liberty and equal rights with a vigilance, an
ability, a thoroughness, and a devotion, that cannot
be too highly extolled by the historian." On the
record of the grandest movement of the age, cul-
minating in the dominion of right over wrong, in
the liberation of millions from thraldom, and in the
establishment of freedom over this broad continent,
his name will ever stand conspicuous. It will be
enshrined in the breast of the freedman as the word
of God in the ark of Moses; and, on the banner that
waves above the incorruptible, it will be surrounded
by an aureole of glory. Wherever in this wide
world a human heart quivers beneath the rod of
the oppressor, it will derive hope and inspiration
from the fearless utterances of this illustrious
champion in defence of civil rights, equality, and
fraternity.

Passing by the stately mausoleum of titled grandeur, the sons and daughters of freedom will come with reverent step from every clime to cast a chaplet of white lilies, and to shed the tear of gratitude over the grave of CHARLES SUMNER.

APPENDIX.

APPENDIX.

MR. SUMNER'S WILL.

THE necessary petition for the probate of the will of Mr. Sumner was filed in the Probate Court by Francis V. Balch, and was acted on at the regular session of that court, on Monday, April 6, 1874. The will is written wholly by himself, in a handwriting at once bold, clear, and distinct. Each page bears his signature, the name being written in the lower right-hand corner, after the manner of the old-style books, and evidently written as each page was finished. The sheets are bound together at the top by a delicate purple ribbon. Not a blot or erasure is discernible on the pages of the will; but the outside is much soiled, as if it had been used when partially folded to brush ink-stains from his desk. It is in full as follows, says "The Advertiser:" —

THE LAST WILL AND TESTAMENT OF CHARLES SUMNER OF BOSTON, MASSACHUSETTS.

1. I bequeath to Henry W. Longfellow, Francis V. Balch, and Edward L. Pierce, as trustees, all my papers, manuscripts, and letter-books, to do with them what they think best, with power to destroy them, to distribute them in some public library, or to make extracts from them for publication.

2. I bequeath to the trustees above mentioned $3000, or so much as may be needed to complete the edition of my speeches and papers, should the same be unfinished at my death. It is hoped that no part of this sum will be needed.

3. I bequeath to the library of Harvard College my books and autographs, whether in Washington or Boston, with the understanding that duplicates of works already belonging to the college library may be sold or exchanged for its benefit.

4. I bequeath to the city of Boston, for the Art Museum, my pictures and engravings, except the picture known as "The Miracle of the Slave," with the injunction that the trustees shall do with them what they think best, disposing of all for the benefit of the Museum.

5. I bequeath to my friends of many years, Henry W. Longfellow and Samuel G. Howe, my bronzes, to be divided between them; also to Henry W. Longfellow the Psyche and that bust of the young Augustus, in marble; to my friend Joshua B. Smith the picture known as "The Miracle of the Slave;" and to the city of Boston, for the Art Museum, the bust of myself by Crawford, taken during my visit to Rome in 1839.

6. I bequeath to the daughters of Henry W. Longfellow $2000; also to the daughters of Samuel G. Howe $2000; and to the daughters of James T. Furness of Philadelphia $2000; which I ask them to accept in token of my gratitude for the friendship their parents have shown me.

7. I bequeath to Hannah Richmond Jacobs, only surviving sister of my mother, an annuity of $500, to be paid by my executor for the remainder of her life.

8. I direct my executor to make all provision for perpetual care of my mother's lot at Mount Auburn.

9. I bequeath to the president and fellows of Harvard College $1000, in trust, for an annual prize for the best dissertation by any student of the college or any of its schools, undergraduate or graduate, on universal peace, and the methods by which war may be permanently suspended. I do this in the hope of drawing the attention of students to the practicability of organizing peace among nations, which I sincerely believe may be done. I cannot doubt that the same modes of decision which now prevail between individuals, between towns, and between smaller communities, may be extended to nations.

10. All the residue of my estate, real and personal, I bequeath

and devise to my executor, in trust, to be sold at such time and in such way as he shall think best, the proceeds to be distributed in two equal moieties, as follows: One moiety to be paid my sister Julia Hastings, wife of John Hastings of San Francisco, Cal., for her sole and exclusive use, or, should she die before me, then in equal portions to her three daughters or the survivor, each portion to be for the sole and exclusive use of such daughter. The other moiety to be paid to the president and fellows of Harvard College, in trust, for the benefit of the college library, my desire being that the income should be applied to the purchasing of books relating to politics and fine arts. This bequest is made in filial regard for the college. In selecting especially the library, I am governed by the consideration that all my life I have been a user of books, and, having few of my own, I have relied on the libraries of friends and on public libraries; so that what I now do is only a return for what I have freely received.

11. I appoint Francis V. Balch executor of this will, and desire that the trustees of my papers may be exempt from giving bonds.

In testimony whereof I hereunto set my hand this second day of September, 1873, at Boston.

CHARLES SUMNER.

Signed and published by the administrator as his last will and testament, before us, who, in his presence and in the presence of each other, have at his request set our names as witnesses.

H. J. EDWARDS.
GEORGE A. BULLEN.
JOHN E. HECKTER.
F. V. BALCH.

EPITAPH.

HUMANITAS JUSTITIAQUE
MAERENT ET MAEREBUNT
TE,
SUMNER JUSTITIAE CULTOR EXIMIUS,
JUSTITIA OB VITAM PURISSIMA
INTER SORDIORES
HUMANITAS UT TIBI NUSQUAM
ALIENA
TU FINE LABORUM
IMMORTALIS INITIO
GAUDEAS
TALI MORTE
TALE SUPERSTITE NULLO.
FELIX FAUSTUS FORTUNATUS
GLORIA RESURGENS
AVE.

The following may be given as nearly a literal translation:

HUMANITY AND JUSTICE
MOURN AND WILL MOURN
THEE,
O SUMNER, MOST RENOWNED FOSTERER
OF JUSTICE!
JUSTICE ON ACCOUNT OF THY MOST PURE LIFE
AMONG THE BASE;
HUMANITY IN THAT SHE NEVER WAS A STRANGER TO THEE.
THOU REJOICEST IN THE END OF LABORS AND THE
BEGINNING OF IMMORTALITY.
O HAPPY, BLESSED AND FORTUNATE ONE,
IN SUCH A DEATH THAT NONE LIKE THEE REMAINS,
RISING TO GLORY,
HAIL!

www.ingramcontent.com/pod-product-compliance
Lightning Source LLC
Chambersburg PA
CBHW051118120726
47905CB00005B/1335